A Certain Malice

Felicity Young

CREME DE LA CRIME

First published in Great Britain in 2005
by Crème de la Crime Books
Crème de la Crime Ltd, PO Box 523, Chesterfield,
Derbys S40 9AT

Typesetting by Yvette Warren
Cover design by Yvette Warren
Front cover photography by Acestock.com
www.acestock.com
Printed and bound in England by Biddles Ltd,
www.biddles.co.uk

ISBN 0-9547634-4-0

A CIP catalogue reference for this book is available from
the British Library

www.cremedelacrime.com

For Mick, with love

About the Author

Former nursing sister Felicity Young has no problem ensuring the accuracy of procedural details in her crime writing – her brother-in-law is a retired police superintendent. These days, when she's not busy penning novels, rearing orphan kangaroos or satisfying her thirst for action and adventure as an active member of the local volunteer bushfire brigade, Felicity manages her own Suffolk sheep stud in a small West Australian country town.

Acknowledgements

The author would like to thank Tania Hudson, Margaret Johnson, Christine Nagel, Trish O'Neill, Iain Pattison, Lynne Patrick, Susannah Rickards, Carole Sutton, Larry Votava, Michael Young, Ben Young, Peter Young and Superintendent Simon Young (NT Police, retired). Also Tom and Pip, for putting up with wrong turns, blank stares and general withdrawal into the 'zone' while the book was being written.

Extract from lyric of *Women in Uniform* by G Macainsh reproduced by kind permission of Mushroom Music Publishing.

Author's note:

For the benefit of readers who don't speak Australian –
A lamington is a small chocolate and coconut cake; a lamington drive raises funds for charity by selling them.
CWA stands for Country Womens' Association.
WAFL is Western Australian Football League.

1

MONDAY

"First I heard the thumping feet, then I caught a flash of the kangaroo bounding through the burned bushland. I started running after her, hoping to capture her on film. She hopped over the log and I followed, nearly tripping over the body, although of course I didn't realise what it was then. The kangaroo disappeared into the parrot bush and when I turned around I saw the body lying next to the log."

The woman's tone lost some of its animation. She ran a hand through her tousled dark hair. "I had a closer look. It was awful."

Twenty years in the Police Service hadn't made Senior Sergeant Cam Fraser blasé about human misfortune or caused him to develop an overly black sense of humour. But it was, he rationalised, still possible to enjoy the way Cecelia Bowman chose to tell her story if not the story itself. She was an English teacher; that accounted for a lot. Her sweeping gestures and clear diction made him wonder if she also taught drama.

He hoped she wasn't embellishing the facts for dramatic effect. "And about what time was this?" he asked.

"Six and a half minutes past ten."

He was unable to hold back his smile. "Six and a half minutes past ten?"

"Roughly," she said, smiling back. This was the first time she'd smiled during the interview and the ease with which she did so told him he was speaking to a woman well used to laughing at herself.

She smelled of wood-smoke and eucalyptus and reminded him of a picture of a wood nymph he'd seen once in an old-fashioned fairytale book.

Cam looked at the burly Senior Constable standing next to him. Vince Petrowski seemed unaffected by Cecelia's humour and continued to stare at some fixed point in the distant hills, eyes slitted against the abrasive wind. The lines on his face were encrusted with red dust, giving him the powdered appearance of an old woman.

"I'd only just looked at my watch. I didn't want to be late for the staff meeting," Cecelia added.

Cam followed her gaze to the small collection of teachers standing well away from the crime scene tape that whipped about in the relentless easterly. They'd been in the staff room attending a pre-term meeting when Cecelia had discovered the body in the school grounds.

"Why did you decide to visit the scene of yesterday's fire only minutes before the staff meeting?" Cam asked.

Cecelia's fair skin blossomed into pink. "I suppose it does seem a bit suspicious, doesn't it?"

"Not suspicious, Ms Bowman, just strange; you're hardly dressed for a bushwalk." Cam tried to keep his eyes away from the knee poking through a hole in her stocking.

"I'm an impulsive person, Sergeant. I was out for a walk, thinking about the upcoming meeting, and I had my camera." She held it up by its carry strap for him to see. "There're some exciting projects going on at the school right now, including the establishment of a small media department. I've been busy all holidays buying equipment and setting it up. I wanted to try out the new camera. While I was walking I saw the kangaroo." She indicated to the blackened area behind them. "It looked like one I'd hand-reared a couple of years ago then put back in the wild. I'd recognise Pinky anywhere. Her jaw was crooked from being fed with an artificial teat."

Cam cleared his throat.

"Sorry, Sergeant, I'm afraid I tend to go off on a tangent."

"Before, you said you nearly tripped. I take it that means you didn't actually tread on the body?"

"No, but I was kind of aware of it as I leapt over the log. I could have easily stepped on it though, it was the same colour as the burned wood."

"Yeah, just like it," Vince agreed, worrying at a husk of sheep turd with the toe of his boot. His khaki shirt billowed in the wind, creating the image of an inflating hot air balloon.

Cam looked at him for a moment, fantasising the lift-off. When it became clear that Vince would remain firmly rooted to the ground, he turned back to Cecelia.

"So you didn't touch the body at all?"

"Absolutely not, it was revolting. I was almost sick."

"Can you remember how it was lying?" Cam asked.

She swallowed as if to contain rising nausea. "On its side."

Cam looked over to Vince. The Senior Constable put his hands on his hips and bunched up the muscles of his jaw. "It was on its back when I got here," he said, fixing his eyes upon Ms Bowman's.

She held his pointed stare. "I don't like your tone, Constable."

Vince turned back to the sheep turd and shrugged. "You could easily have tripped over it," he muttered.

"Then I would mention it. It's no skin off my nose – why should I lie?" Though she only came up to Vince's shoulder, Cam could see his Senior Constable didn't intimidate her. And she was right. She had nothing to lose by admitting she touched the body. Vince, on the other hand, had everything.

Cam stopped Vince's retort with an outstretched hand and a frown. He reached into his top pocket for his notepad and began to write, conscious of her eyes upon his scarred hand. The awkwardness of his penmanship would not be overlooked; she was a teacher after all.

He'd just finished noting down her account of the body's position when a gust tore into his notebook, riffling the pages and forcing him to dig his heels into the ground. He'd forgotten how unforgiving these desiccating Wheatbelt winds could be, an indication of just how long he'd been away from home.

Vince held on to his peaked cap and said something indecipherable.

"Thank you for your help, Ms Bowman." Cam had to raise his voice to stop it from being swept away. "I'd like you to return to the school now with the other teachers. We might still need to ask you some more questions. It's pretty unpleasant here and you've all been standing around long enough."

She nodded and walked over to the group of teachers. A tall woman with blonde curly hair reached for her hand and pulled her into a hug.

Cam wiped his arm across his dripping forehead, surprised there was any moisture left in his body at all. He reached for the small bottle of water he'd earlier jammed in his pocket, and drained its tepid contents. His mouth still felt as if he'd been licking out the floor of a sheep truck. Resisting the urge to spit, he spoke to Vince instead.

"Do you know her?"

"In Glenroyd most people know each other," Vince said,

barely opening his mouth. "Rumour has it she's a dyke. That's her girlfriend," he added with a nod towards the tall blonde.

"Turn you down, did she?" Cam said, really needing to spit now. Vince said nothing. The corners of his thick moustache drooped to follow the contours of his mouth downwards.

Cam said, "Go back to the school with the staff and get started on the other interviews. Find out about yesterday's bushfire. Ask if anyone saw anything then check it out with the local bushfire brigade. I'll join you later after I've called SOCO."

"Scene of Crime Officers? Out here?"

"Why the surprise?"

"With all due respect, Sarge, you don't call SOCO out to cases like this; this isn't Sydney." He shrugged. "It's obvious what happened here anyway."

"It is?"

"Yeah." Vince folded his arms, satisfied that he'd put Cam back in his place.

Within hours of their first meeting Cam realised that people skills were not among the Senior Constable's strengths, if he had any strengths at all. Cam's predecessor had left behind a pile of complaints against Vince he either would not or could not deal with. Cam had spent days trying to untangle the mess of paperwork and still hadn't got it all sorted.

He'd chosen to delay action until he'd settled into the new police subdistrict and Vince, sensing Cam was on his case, had thrown every obstacle imaginable at him to make the settling in process as difficult as possible. He'd given him the wrong directions to one of the outlying farms, forcing him to stop at the BP to ask for help. He'd forgotten to tell him that the petrol gauge on the ute was faulty, which meant he'd rolled to an embarrassing stand-still on his way to an emergency call. He'd hindered Cam's paperwork by giving him the wrong forms. Now here he was, taking advantage of the fact that Cam had spent many years out of the state to deliberately misinform him on police procedure.

But Cam had been the sole parent of a difficult teenage girl for several years. He'd learned that verbal battles inevitably led to outright war, with victory to the side best prepared. In Vince's case, he knew he needed to dig in for a winter campaign.

"How do you see it, then?" Cam asked, rubbing his chin.

Vince puffed himself up. "Some lush was in the bush having a drink, fell asleep, dropped his smoke and whoosh, instant crispy critter with fries. You don't call SOCO out over the accidental death of one pisspot. I've been here eight years, Sarge; you've been here eight days. Toorrup has enough on its hands with the bikie gangs right now; they'll have your balls if you bother them with this."

Cam shrugged.

"See you back at the school, then, Vince. I'll keep Leanne here with me." He looked around for the young probationer. "Where's she gone?"

"Last I saw, she was spewing her guts up behind that tree over there." He pointed to a large jarrah looming above the ragged scrub.

"That's right. You were having a good laugh about it, weren't you? Get on back to the school. I'll see you there."

Cam turned his back on Vince, reached for his phone and called SOCO. They said they'd be there in about two hours.

Behind him, there was a hiss of escaping air.

2

Cam shaded his eyes to follow the convoy of cars making its way along the gentle gradient of the dirt road back to the school. It was a clear straight view, unhindered by hills or trees of any substance. Apparently the science teacher, Ruth Tilly, had spotted the smoke from yesterday's fire when she was working in the science lab.

Hands on hips, Cam regarded the distant school buildings. Glenroyd Ladies' College had been built nearly one hundred years ago to cater for the needs of enlightened farming families who wished their daughters to have the same advantages as their sons. Only the state's wealthy could afford to give their daughters such an education, but despite few early enrolments, the school's reputation in excellence grew and it was soon attracting pupils from interstate and overseas.

It was twenty-five years since Cam had last stood in the grounds of his wife's old school. The countryside hadn't changed much. The winter creek beyond the burned patch was maybe wider and rockier than he remembered, and the hill beyond, once sparse of decent trees, was now covered in healthy regrowth.

And the prickling parrot bush was as thick as ever.

For a moment he could see Elizabeth and himself on horseback, stuck smack in the middle of it. She hadn't known whether to laugh or scream at their predicament and he'd had to dismount to lead her protesting pony into the clearing. She'd slid her feet from the stirrups and jumped to the ground, turning her back on him to pick the holly-shaped leaves from her saddle blanket. He'd reached to circle her in his arms from behind, nuzzling the back of her neck so she would turn for that first kiss.

They'd been standing at the future site of yesterday's fire.

"What now, Sarge?"

Her voice made him start; he shut the door on his memories.

"Sorry, am I interrupting?" Leanne said.

"No, I was just thinking."

He turned to the young constable. She had to be at least twenty-one but her round face made her look no older than his fifteen-year-old, Ruby. Her thin hair had fallen from her cap and the wind was lashing it against her cheeks, red and shiny as store-bought apples.

"I want to have another look at the body," he said.

"Oh jeez, Sarge."

"I'm sure you've seen worse things on the road."

"MVAs don't smell like Mum's Sunday roast, but." She grimaced, bringing her hand to her mouth.

Cam stepped over the tape. "Stay in my footprints and don't touch anything."

With their eyes on the blackened ground, they walked towards the body. The scorched earth was snaked with tyre tracks and stamped with the print of heavy work boots. He hoped SOCO would attempt plaster casting, despite the surface ash. Cam pointed out the vague indentations of their own police boots to Leanne and compared them to the heavier prints of the firemen.

The fallen log lay at an angle across the path, the body next to it, so well camouflaged he could see how it could have been mistaken for an extra branch. Blackened bottles and broken glass gleamed on the ground near their feet.

Cam hitched his uniform pants at the knee and squatted

down, beckoning Leanne to his level.

"OK, Leanne, what can you tell me about this body?" The girl made a gagging sound and turned her head away.

"Turn back and look at it carefully. Don't let yourself think this was once human. Hell, we don't even know who it is yet. Look at it as evidence, that's all. Build up a picture in your mind and tell me what you see. It's speaking to you, Leanne – what's it saying?"

Won over by the patience of his tone, Leanne sniffed and straightened up. After scanning the surrounding bush for a moment she lowered her gaze to a blackened bottle, still unable to focus on the charred body.

Into her hand she said, "He was drinking and fell asleep. The bush caught fire."

Here we go, Cam thought, manipulating the evidence to fit her theory. "Is that the evidence talking or is that Vince, Leanne?"

She said nothing for a moment as she tried to collect her thoughts. Then, with a sudden squeal she sprang back and broke into a vigorous jig, smacking at the bottoms of her pants as if beating out flames.

"Christ, Sarge, there's ants everywhere. Shit..."

Cam brushed some ants off his own legs then pointed to a pile of fine stones about two metres from the body. There were so many ants on it the rocks themselves seemed alive.

"I've never known someone so drunk they would take a kip next to an ant heap – what do you reckon?"

She squatted down again, forcing herself to look at the body with some of the detachment Cam had encouraged. Finally she said, "Cecelia Bowman was right when she said the body was the same colour as the burned log. And it's a bloke, what do you reckon, Sarge?"

Cam nodded; judging by the size, the body was most

probably a man's. He pointed to the bent arms.

"Looks like he's about to go a round in the ring with Mike Tyson. Heat caused the muscles in the arms to contract, making it look like he's boxing. The posh word for this is pugilist. Remember that. It's always important to use the correct terms if you can, it impresses the jury."

Cam leaned towards the head. Although the mouth was clamped shut, the lips were peeled back like the skin of a baked apple, revealing two missing front teeth. "ID through dental records shouldn't be too hard with this one," he said.

The fire would not have been long or intense enough to destroy the internal organs, and though badly charred, Cam was sure the autopsy would confirm his feeling that the body was burned post-mortem.

He made a circular motion with a finger over the victim's chest.

"See that hard yellow patch there? That means the victim was probably dead when he was burned. If he were burned alive, given the lack of heat intensity, the skin would probably be blistered and still seeping clear cellular fluid. Hopefully the fire won't have destroyed the internal organs so we should learn more from the post-mortem."

"Maybe he died of natural causes first?"

Good. She was finally beginning to think.

"It's a possibility. Could have OD'd on booze and pills first or had a heart attack. We have to explore every option." He took in the anthill again, saying almost to himself, "Or maybe he was murdered."

Leanne looked up in surprise.

"We'll know more when the pathologist gets here. Until we know otherwise, I'm treating this as a suspicious death." He paused and stared hard at the body for a moment. "One thing I do know, though: this body has been moved."

His knees cracked as he rose to his feet and walked to the other side of the body. He reached for his reading glasses and resumed his examination.

"The victim's lying on his back now, but have a look along his left side." He pointed. "See there? The skin's more pink than black."

"Hey, yeah," exclaimed Leanne. "It's got small pieces of twigs and grass on it, too." She seemed pleased with her observation and gave him a tentative smile.

"The fire never had the chance to get roaring hot before it was put out. When the body's removed, I'll bet SOCO finds a strip of ground that's hardly been touched. That's where he'd have been lying, on his side, as if he were asleep. Someone moved or tripped over this body and it ended up on its back."

"But who? Cecelia said she never touched it."

Cam thought for a moment. "Were you with Vince when he made the initial examination?"

"No, he was walking back when I arrived. He told me to go and look. When I saw it, it was already like this."

There was little doubt in Cam's mind that Vince had tripped over the body, a mistake he'd never admit. It wouldn't have taken much of a kick; it had already halved its original weight through fluid loss. Scuffle marks beyond the body added credence to this tripping theory.

Leanne pushed a strand of hair from her eyes and squinted up at him. She opened her mouth to speak, then stopped. He looked at her, raising his eyebrows.

"If you don't mind me asking, Sarge…" she said.

"What?"

"You seem to know a lot about fires. I thought you were

with the National Crime Authority, not the arson squad."

"NCA, that's right."

Without thinking he touched the rough skin of his misshapen right ear lobe then traced the quilted pattern of scars running up his right arm. They fanned the underside of his jaw before ending at the hairline behind his ear.

He turned his face to the wind, narrowing his eyes against the flying dust and ash.

In his peripheral vision, Leanne appeared to be swaying on her feet. The dried leaves of the parrot bush rattled like tiny bones.

Cam thought: You're a cop; it's been over three years, you should damn well be able to block it out by now.

Leanne's voice sounded far away, like she was speaking down a faulty telephone line. A familiar, distracting buzz began in his head and he had to suck in a deep breath for it to fade. He forced his gaze back to the body, to the head, to the face, to the ants eddying through the empty eye sockets. A fly emerged from one nostril. He watched the breeze carry it into a nearby bush.

And then something caught his eye: something pressed flat against the quivering parrot bush.

Cam pulled an evidence envelope from his pocket and used a stick to drop the strip of rag into it. After taking a sniff he placed the envelope under Leanne's nose.

"Petrol?" she said, screwing up her face.

Cam nodded. "Under normal conditions, we leave the evidence for SOCO to gather, but I don't want to lose this in the wind." He handed her the envelope. "So remember to give them this and tell them exactly where we found it."

"Me?" her eyes widened. "Where will you be?"

"I want to see how Vince is going with the interviews at the school."

At that moment there was a rustling in the bushes. Leanne gave a small start, clamping her pudgy fingers on to Cam's arm as a skinny merino bounded into the clearing. It stopped and stared at the intruders, a piece of dry grass hanging from its mouth like a bent cigarette.

Cam made a move towards the sheep, waving his arms. His farmer's whoop sent it crashing back through the bushes to rejoin its hidden flock.

He turned back to Leanne. "And for God's sake keep them away."

"I think they belong to the farmer next door," she blurted, her eyes darting around like panicked beetles. "I think he agists some of his sheep on the school property. How 'bout I call him and get him to drive them away?"

Not waiting for his answer, she turned in the direction of the police ute.

"Hey!" Cam beckoned her back and pointed to the ground. "You stay right here. You're more than capable of keeping a few sheep away. It'll give you something to do while you wait for SOCO and the pathologist."

She folded her arms. The white lines around her mouth were a stark contrast to the rest of her cherry red face. Funny, he seemed to have that irritating effect on young girls. Still, he couldn't resist just one more stir of the pot. He reached into his pocket and handed her a tube of sunscreen. She took it with a roll of her eyes, letting out a long sigh, just as his daughter would do.

By the time he'd left she was gleaming with grease like a blob of melted ice cream.

3

The atmosphere in the staff room loomed like a headache. Cam realized it was caused by more than the chemical smell of the surrounding newness, and silently berated himself for allowing Vince to tackle the first round of interviews on his own.

Vince introduced Cam to Anne Smithson, the principal, and her husband Jeffrey, explaining that he'd allowed the other staff members to leave.

Cam remembered reading about the couple in his wife's Old Glenroydians' Magazine. They'd been recruited from the eastern states by the School Board in a last ditch effort to prevent the school from closing down. Assisted by the generous endowment of an old girl, they had, according to the magazine, been performing restorative miracles, including an ambitious building renovation programme.

Smithson rose from the table and offered Cam a firm, moist hand but no smile, in keeping with the sobriety of the occasion.

"As I was explaining to the constable here," he said, "we were not even on the school grounds the day of the fire. We'd been to the city for the day -"

"They have an apartment in the city – all right for some eh, Sarge?" Vince exaggerated a wink. Cam felt the temperature in the room drop several degrees.

Mr Smithson shot Vince a look that suggested he'd just picked him off the sole of his shoe. His wife frowned when Cam shook her hand, telling him with her deep grey eyes that she'd had about as much of the Senior Constable as she could endure.

Mr Smithson continued in a tone of restrained calm. "The first we knew about the body was when Cecelia arrived at Monday's staff meeting, late as always." He caught his wife's eye in a way that suggested this topic had been discussed before. "And broke the news."

Anne Smithson nodded her agreement. "We've given our statements. May we go home now, Sergeant?"

"I won't keep you much longer, Mrs Smithson. Please bear with me for just five more minutes."

Anne Smithson pursed her lips, the only sign of impatience she gave. Her ash blonde hair, stretched tight against her skull, was fastened at the back with a tortoise-shell clip. She sat in her straight-backed chair, hands clasped in her lap, her eyes half-closed. Cam wondered if she was reciting her getting-through-appointments-with-ranting-parents mantra. He knew the signs; he'd used the technique often enough himself on tedious witnesses.

Jeffrey smoothed down his thin moustache and beat a soft tattoo on the table's surface, waiting for Cam to finish skimming through the witness statement forms. When Cam met his eye over the top of his reading glasses, the drumming abruptly stopped. Then, as if deciding the ordeal had lasted long enough, Jeffrey pushed his chair back and climbed to his feet. A small round belly peeped through a gap in his blazer when he indicated the door to his wife with a tilt of his head.

Cam held out his hand for her to stay where she was. "Mrs Smithson," he said. "At the moment the body is unidentifiable, but sometimes people have vague ideas about who a victim could be. Can you make a guess? Have you been aware of any itinerants hanging around the school grounds? Did any of your groundsmen not turn up for work this morning? Have you given anyone permission to camp on the grounds during the school holidays?"

Mrs Smithson's thin fingers reached for the double string of pearls resting on the bosom of her silk blouse. The nervous mannerism did not escape Cam. He had a fleeting glimpse of the kind of vulnerability the head-mistress of an elite school would be forced to hide.

"No, Sergeant, although there have been plenty of people coming and going all holidays to work on the renovations," she said. "I suppose one of the builders might have decided to go for a walk and accidentally started the bush fire."

Cam turned to Vince. "Check with the builders. See if there was anyone away from work this morning."

The big man gave a nod.

Mrs Smithson rose from the table with a waft of Chanel.

Cam said, "Thank you for your co-operation, I don't think we'll be needing to ask you any more questions for the moment." He smiled. Number 5 had always been his wife's favourite. When she moved to stand by her husband, he noticed she was the taller by about three inches.

Mrs Smithson gave Cam a tight smile back. "Please turn the lights off when you go."

Vince grunted out a reply. When the Smithsons turned to leave, he caught Cam's eye and flicked the end of his nose with his finger. Cam ignored him and glanced back to one of the forms on the table. He addressed the departing couple.

"Before you go, I'd like to have a bit more of a chat with Ms Tilly, the science teacher." He tapped at the form in front of him with his pen. "It says here she lives in a flat at the school. Can you please point me in the right direction?"

"I hope it won't take long. We need to get home, it's been a long day," Mr Smithson said.

"I quite understand. I don't need you to accompany me, just tell me where I can find her."

"This way," Mr Smithson said, leading Cam away from his wife into the vestibule. He glanced back at the staffroom and gripped Cam's arm. No longer within earshot of his wife, he dropped his previous tone of forced politeness and spoke through clenched teeth.

"My wife and I have done everything in our power to co-operate with the police over this unfortunate incident. I want you to know that we found Constable Petrowski's blunt questioning very disturbing. The details he gave us about the condition of the body were totally unnecessary. It was as if he was deliberately trying to upset us, to bully us into taking some kind of responsibility for this tragic accident."

Cam worked hard not to show his irritation with Vince over his tactless handling of Smithson. One of the first rules of a preliminary interview is to keep the witnesses on side, talk to them in a relaxed manner, steer the questions in a way that would put them at ease and encourage them to do the talking. It seemed the only thing Vince had encouraged was aggravation. It was going to take a lot of smoothing over to get the Smithsons back on track.

"I apologise on his behalf. I'll have a word with him and I'll be happy to assist if you wish to make a formal complaint," Cam said.

Mr Smithson thought for a moment. "I might just do that. I'll discuss the matter with my wife. In the meantime, if you wish to re-address this topic, Sergeant, please ring in advance for an appointment and speak to me. It is not necessary for my wife to hear all the gruesome details. I'm sure I can answer any further questions you might have. She doesn't have to be included."

Irritated himself by the man's arrogant tone, Cam could imagine how he and Vince had goaded each other. He shrugged off the hand that gripped his arm.

"I quite understand, Mr Smithson, but I'm afraid I probably will have to speak to both you and your wife again. Until then, good day, sir."

Ruth Tilly's flat was on the third floor of the classroom block, directly above the science lab. Access was by way of curling stone steps rounded with wear, the banister cruelly knobbed to prevent impetuous schoolgirls from taking the easy way down.

Cam was about to mount the final set of stairs when the sound of clinking glasses and female laughter caught his attention. He turned, moving towards the noise until he was standing outside a half-open door marked Science Laboratory.

The laughter grew louder.

He raised his hand to knock, glancing into the room as he did so. One of the occupants was Cecelia Bowman. He hesitated when he noticed she'd taken off her shoes and stockings and was sitting on one of the science bench tops with her legs dangling. The other woman had her back to him. She was leaning against the bench, looking out of the window. Cecelia said something and the woman erupted with laughter. She turned her head and Cam saw she was the blonde science teacher, Ruth Tilly.

Without further hesitation, he knocked and pushed the door open.

Cecelia sprang from the bench top and slid something behind her back. If guilty looks were just cause for arrest, Cam would have called for the paddy wagon right away. Ruth's jaw fell, but when her eyes met Cecelia's, an unspoken message triggered more helpless laughter.

Cecelia wasn't laughing, though her face beamed with an impish grin. All her energy seemed to be directed to the task of remaining upright.

The two women were as drunk as skunks.

"Ye Gads! It's the big bad policeman come to arrest us. Quick, Cecelia, we must make haste with our escape!" Ruth said, doing no such thing. The shining material of her fashionable summer dress clung to her generous curves like a dusting of fine sugar as she lent back against bench.

"Your private drinking is no concern of mine, Ms Tilly," Cam said, "but I'd like to ask you some -"

"Oh, you've met, have you?" Cecelia said, slurring her words.

"Well, not officially," said Cam. "I have some questions for Ms Tilly about the fire."

"Let me introduce you then. Senior Sergeant Fraser, meet Ruth Tilly, MS, Dip Ed and —"

"Moonshine brewer extraordinaire?" Cam said.

"Curses, betrayed by our own carelessness!" Ruth glanced at the beaker on the bench and snapped her fingers. Then she moved with fluid motion towards a large chest freezer. "But how rude of me. You will join us I hope, Sergeant," she said, hefting up the freezer lid. Cam's attempted refusal became a gawk of surprise as the clouds of cold air settled to reveal rows of neatly piled yellow lab rats. In the middle of one row, flanked on each side by a bagged frozen rat, rested a chemical flask of clear liquid.

"It's eighty percent proof, never freezes," Ruth said.

Cecelia let out a snort, then a giggle. "And that's not the only thing she brews up here." Her hand flew to her mouth as she looked at her friend.

"It's OK, Cecelia, this is a good opportunity to come clean." Ruth placed her hand over her heart and bowed her head. "The Sergeant needs to know the lengths we girls have to go to protect ourselves. Go on, show him."

Cecelia bent down to rummage in one of the newly painted cupboards.

Cam looked at his watch and frowned. "I haven't much time, ladies. I need to get back to the scene."

"Here it is," Cecelia exclaimed as she heaved herself up from her stooped position, holding a tiny glass vial. "Ruth made it. One whiff guaranteed to keep away even the likes of Vince Petrowski. *Voila!*" She lifted the small glass tube above her head.

Ruth's laugh sounded like a machine gun. At any moment, Cam expected to hear the shattering of glass.

Cecelia pulled out the stopper and tried to shove the vial under Cam's nose. He turned his head away, but not before he caught the scent. He had to put his hand over his nose to stop himself from gagging.

Ruth puffed up with the pride of genius. "I call it *Eau De CaaCaa.*"

Cecelia laughed. "She says it works better than Mace."

Cam fought to retain his professional composure, comforting himself with the thought of their embarrassment when they discovered he was to be a new school parent. He hoped to be present when they found out.

He shook his head when Ruth tried to thrust a beaker of moonshine into his hand.

"I'll have a coffee though, if there's some going. I need to ask you some questions." He looked around the science lab, searching for a kettle. It would be a waste of time trying to get answers from the women in their present state of intoxication.

"I'll have a coffee too please, Ruth," Cecelia said.

Ruth sighed. "Pikers, the both of you." She vanished through a small side door into a kitchenette and soon they heard the clattering of cups. Cecelia made a move towards the sound then stopped as if she thought her disappearance might seem suspicious. She changed direction and walked back to the bench.

Cam put his hands in his pockets and ambled around the lab, whistling something tuneless between his teeth. Benches lined the walls topped with strategically placed Bunsen burners and sunken sinks. Equipment, bottles of chemicals and jars of dead animals adorned the shelves. He tapped at a jar holding some kind of embryo; pieces of dead tissue spun around like snow in a snow globe.

He saw a brown rat in a wire-covered aquarium nibbling on a chunk of dried corn held between its tiny, needled paws. It stopped nibbling, twitched its nose and gave him a furtive glance. In another glass tank a snake followed Cam's every move with shiny black eyes and darting tongue. Cam shivered and turned to Cecelia who was now sitting on a tall stool by the window.

"I don't like snakes," he said for conversation's sake.

"Neither do I." She laughed, smoothing the skirt over her legs. Her hand crept to the collar of her blouse, rolling it between her thumb and forefinger. Some of the drunken glow had faded from her soft brown eyes, leaving in its wake the smart of self-conscious awareness. He pulled up the stool next to hers and sat down.

"I'm sorry about this," Cecelia said. "I'm afraid we've made fools of ourselves. We're not usually this bad. I've had a terrible day and Ruth was trying to cheer me up. I hope we haven't made you feel too uncomfortable."

"I've had to deal with a lot worse, Ms Bowman," Cam

reassured her, wrapping his long legs around the stool.

"Please, call me Cecelia," she said.

Ruth returned from the kitchenette with a tray and put mugs of coffee on the bench in front of them. "Oh no, Cecelia," Ruth said, "our little spectacle won't have concerned Cam in the least. He always was a cool customer. I remember him as a man of few words." She smiled. "And he obviously still is."

The familiarity in her voice startled him. He swivelled on his stool and stared at her, searching back through time for a memory he felt he should have been able to grasp.

"You've no idea who I am, have you? You've changed a lot, but I suppose that's to be expected after twenty-five years." Ruth turned to Cecelia. "Cam was always tall, but very skinny. He's filled out, must have been all that football. Oh yes, and he wore his hair in dreadlocks then."

"They weren't dreadlocks," he said to Cecelia, for some reason feeling the need to explain. "It just gets like that when it's long." He ran his hands through the waves of his short greying hair, suddenly feeling hot. He caught sight of a frog hanging suspended in a jar of formaldehyde. Its long flippered legs hung motionless in its watery crypt, its skinny arms raised in supplication.

Ruth laughed. "OK, I'll put you out of your misery. I used to go to school here. I was a couple of years younger than Elizabeth. We both kept ponies at the school stables. You used to groom for us at the weekends."

Many of the girls had kept ponies at the school in those days. Cam still had no recollection of this woman, but it was easier to nod knowingly than continue as the clown in this circus of embarrassment. He cleared his throat and reached for the witness statement forms.

"We'll have to get together sometime and chew over our

old memories. For now I need to ask you some questions."

"Fire away then," Ruth said, resting her head on her hand.

"It says here that you were working in the lab when you first noticed the fire."

She yawned, gave him a nod.

"Do you often work at the lab during the school holidays?"

Ruth lifted her head up and looked at him with eyes the colour of butane flames. "Is this an interrogation? Am I under suspicion?"

"Not at all."

"You're making it sound as if I am."

"Please, Ruth, just answer the questions." He eased the tension in his jaw with a sip of coffee.

"OK, I'll tell you." She glanced at Cecelia, drew a deep breath then turned back to Cam. "I was humping Jeffrey Smithson on this bench here. In the height of my passion I turned to face the window and saw the smoke. Funny, I always thought one was supposed to see fireworks."

Cecelia almost choked on her coffee. Cam didn't smile.

"For God's sake, Ruth, be serious for a change," Cecelia said, hiding her smile behind her hand. She said to Cam, "Like me, Ruth has been putting in extra work because of the renovations. The whole lab's been rebuilt and she's spent a lot of time cleaning, unpacking and re-stocking. That's what she was doing when she saw the smoke."

"Cecelia, you're a killjoy sometimes," Ruth said.

Cam looked out of the large front window. Ruth Tilly was trying to provoke him and he was careful not to show any sign of annoyance.

The view of the crime scene was unimpeded from here. He noticed that the coroner's van and another vehicle had arrived. It was time to wind up this meeting and get back to Leanne.

He glanced back at the form in his hand. "It says here the smoke you saw was dirty grey. I'd like you to think hard about this."

"I can only say what I saw, Cam."

"Did you see any flames?"

"Not at first, just the smoke."

"When you did finally see some flames, what colour were they?"

"Just your normal common garden variety of flame, kind of orange yellow."

Cam considered this for a moment, nodded. "Do you think it'd been burning long when you first noticed it?"

"No, I don't think so; there wasn't even much smoke. I called Cliff Donovan from the bushfire brigade as soon as I saw it. You know how quickly fires get out of control at this time of year."

Cam agreed. "How long did the bushfire guys take to respond?"

Ruth folded her arms. "Is all this necessary? I've already been through it with Vince."

Cam felt the muscles in his jaw tighten again. She sighed, fluttering her eyes to the ceiling. "Oh, all right. I'd say about twenty minutes."

"Did you notice any people or cars in the vicinity before you saw the smoke?"

"No."

Cam made a note then slid off the stool, collecting his papers. He still had more questions but felt he'd do better speaking to Cecelia alone. He was heading for the door when Ruth's voice made him turn.

"I'm sorry about Elizabeth and your son. I read about it in the Old Glenroydians' Magazine."

She sounded as sincere as her intoxication would allow, but Cam still reeled from the unexpected blow. He looked at Cecelia to gauge her reaction and saw his own shock mirrored in her eyes.

"I sent you a sympathy card and a long letter but you obviously never got it," Ruth continued.

"I – we – got lots of sympathy cards. I lost track." He let out a ragged breath and ran a hand across his face, before pinching his right ear lobe between his thumb and fore-finger. It did nothing to allay the jolting shiver that ran up his body.

Cecelia looked at Ruth, knitting her brows with a silent rebuke.

He gave Cecelia a faltering smile and left the lab with the roar of flames in his ears.

4

Cam scowled when the door yielded to the first nudge of his key, sighing at the blatant disregard of his instructions. He took in the sight before him: the unpacked cartons, the precarious stacks of furniture, the piles of books, and everything else that contributed to the warehouse appearance of his new home.

"Hey, looks like you've been busy," he said to his daughter as their small white poodle, Fleur, jumped at his legs.

Ruby didn't look up. It seemed she had barely moved since he'd left her earlier that morning, though she had managed to summon up the energy to unpack the TV. She now lay on the floor with her head on a pillow, apparently too engrossed in the midday movie to acknowledge his presence.

Cam patted the dog, then walked to the TV and punched the off button, plunging the room into sudden silence.

"Where's Cindy?" he asked. Cindy was a university student he'd employed to help around the house until he could find a suitable, permanent housekeeper. He'd hoped, being reasonably close in age, Ruby might have found something in common with her.

"Cindy's gone," Ruby said.

"What? For good?"

"Yeah, I think so."

Cam's voice rose. "But she never rang me to say she was quitting. I was told she was very reliable."

"It was some kind of emergency, I think. Half the youth

26

choir down with flu or something." Ruby turned and looked her father in the eye. "That or maybe her calculator broke."

Cam plunged his clenched fists into his pockets, counting to ten in his head. Exactly what his daughter had done to drive away the congenial Cindy he did not wish to contemplate.

"Well, I'll have to see about finding someone else. I can't have you roaming about town on your own for the rest of the school holidays."

Ruby groaned and said something unintelligible. Cam clapped his hands and rubbed them together. "Come on then, let's make some headway here. I've got a few free hours, we should be able to get quite a bit of this stuff stowed away."

Ruby pushed herself up from the ground and leaned towards the TV controls. Cam beat her to it, pulling the plug from the socket.

"This stays off until these boxes are unpacked," he said, deflecting her acidic look with his well-used neutral expression. "This is a bonus, we're lucky to get this stuff so early, cartons from Sydney can take weeks. The place will start to look much more homey with our things in it."

"This place sucks." Ruby reached for Fleur and buried her face in the soft white curls of her hair.

"Let's not go into that again."

Ruby said, "I want to go back to Sydney. I miss my friends." She lifted one of Fleur's tiny paws and spread the toes wide, searching too carefully for grass seeds.

"As soon as you're settled you can start looking for a part-time job, save up to fly back for a visit," Cam said.

He hoped that by the time she'd raised the money, she'd have settled in so well she'd have forgotten her loser friends in Sydney.

"Gramma said all I had to do was ask and she'd send me the money."

Yes, Gramma had always been very accommodating.

He picked up one of the cartons and plonked it down beside her. "This looks like your junk. How about we start arranging your room?"

Ruby released the dog and rolled on to her stomach, sticking her bum in the air and burying her head in the pillow. She used to sleep like that as a toddler and it had always made them laugh.

He didn't feel like laughing now.

Her voice was muffled through the pillow. "I hate my room. I hate the bed. The mattress is stained, it's lumpy and there's lino on the floor. I want a carpet."

"I'll look into the cost of carpet. I can't promise anything straight away but we can start looking. How about we drive up to Toorrup next Thursday and do some late night shopping? We can grab a bite to eat and look at the prices of carpet then. I think they have a cinema in Toorrup now. Never did when I was a kid; we might be able to catch a movie."

"Whoopy-doo."

He tried for another angle of positive reinforcement, if that was what it was called. He had a feeling it was just plain, unadulterated bribery.

"I've been keeping my eyes out in the local paper for a pony but haven't had any luck so far. I'll check at the stock feeder's on my way back to the station."

Ruby slapped her hand down hard on the burnt-orange shagpile, shooting him a death stare.

"Dad, how many times do I have to tell you? Read my lips." She pointed to her mouth and mimed, "I don't want a fucking pony."

He ignored her and dragged a box into the kitchen. Of course she still wanted a pony. She'd wanted a pony ever since she'd been old enough to write a Christmas list. He opened one of the kitchen drawers and wiped out the mouse droppings with a dishcloth, then started clattering the knives and forks into their compartments.

Ruby moaned and picked herself off the floor. She started to scrabble at a carton with her fingernails in a futile attempt to break the seal. When she realized she was getting nowhere, she swore and sloped from the lounge into the kitchen. One of her dragging feet caught in a patch of torn vinyl and propelled her into her father's arms.

"Enjoy your trip?" he said, laughing. She pushed away from him. Her face was pink and streaked with sweaty strands of hair. "You're supposed to say, See you next fall," he said, willing her to smile with a silly grin of his own.

She reached for a knife and held it upright in her fist, looking at him with eyes of chipped sapphire. For a moment he thought she was going to stab him; maybe she thought so too. He hadn't needed the police psychologist to tell him his daughter had poor impulse control and anger management issues.

But then she relaxed. Her hand dropped to her side and she returned to the carton in the lounge. Cam went to the fridge and gulped some iced water from the bottle.

Through the open kitchen door he watched her unpack a carton. Some things she flung to the lounge floor, others – stuffed toys and animal posters – she carried to her bedroom. He was about to suggest she drag the whole box to her room when she reached for something wrapped in tissue paper. In a moment her expression changed from sullen belligerence to a look of sadness that made his throat constrict.

He tossed the remaining cutlery into the drawer and walked through, desperate to engulf her in a bear hug, to tell her how everything would work out, that he was doing it all for her. But he stopped, remembering how she'd stiffened in his arms and turned to face him with eyes so full of hatred, they'd seared him with a pain almost physical.

He gently took the picture from her hands. After wiping the dust off the glass on the leg of his pants, he placed it on the mantelpiece above the gas fire.

"There we go. They can keep a good eye on us from up here," he said, trying to smile.

His wife and son had been dead for over three years but there were still times when he felt Elizabeth's presence in bed next to him and smelt her perfume, or heard the excited peals of Joey's laughter. Moving from one side of the continent to the other had done nothing to diminish these sensations. Now, looking at the picture again, he felt the same bittersweet ache, sensing them even here in this drab police cottage.

The phone rang. Cam could see the immediate relief on his daughter's face; another tense moment with Dad had been avoided. Earlier he'd had to show her how to work the heavy old-fashioned dial phone and now she held it to her ear as if it were a black brick.

She listened for a moment then shoved the receiver at him. "It's PC Pork, for you."

Cam hissed and put his finger to his mouth.

"Well, you've called him a lot worse, Dad," Ruby said in a loud voice, though by now Cam's hand was clamped over the receiver.

He turned his back on her and listened to the voice on the other end. After a few succinct words, he hung up. "I've got to go back to the station. It looks like they've ID'd that body," he said.

She had returned to the packing carton. She shrugged her thin shoulders then gave a start, remembering something.

"Uncle Rod called this morning. He wants to meet you at the Glenny Arms tonight, at six."

Superintendent Rod Cummings was Cam's immediate superior in Toorrup and his friend from their Police Academy days. He was largely responsible for the string-pulling necessary to get Cam back to WA and secure his posting to Glenroyd.

"Right, I'll come home after work to change, then head out again." Cam said. "I don't imagine the meeting with Rod will take long." He walked back to the kitchen and checked the fridge. It was empty except for a can of beer and a bottle of mayonnaise. "Looks like fish and chips again; I'll bring some home after I've seen Rod," he said.

Ruby made no response. There was a time when she would have done anything for fish and chips.

"Try and get some more unpacking done, OK, love? Oh, and I put the wheels on your bike last night, so if you like you can cycle down to the shops and pick us up some groceries from the general store."

"They don't call it a general store any more, Dad, it's called a supermarket." She stretched the word, emphasising the syllables.

"It was always the general store when I lived here."

"Yeah, like a hundred years ago."

He reached into his pocket and put some money on the breakfast bar. "Until we find a replacement for Cindy, I want you to ring and tell me where you're going."

"I'd ring if I had a mobile phone," she said with a sly smile.

"Mobile phones don't even work half the time around here. You will ring, young lady, and keep the door locked – until I can find someone else to keep you company."

Ruby responded with a sigh and a roll of her eyes. But as soon as the door closed behind him, she jumped to her feet and moved to the front window. She prised open the venetians and watched the tall figure of her father walk through the jelly haze of the footpath towards the police station. With a small jump of excitement, she hurried over to Fleur who stood gazing at the front door with troubled eyes.

"Come on, Fleur," she said to the dog, her voice high and breathless. "We're going to the park."

5

The general store might have revamped into a supermarket, but little else had changed in Glenroyd over the last twenty-five years. Cam walked down Main Street, past the same tin-roofed fibro cottages he remembered from his youth, the same small shops decorated with the same archaic advertising logos, faded by the sun and meaningless to anyone under forty.

The stock feeder's and the farm machinery were the largest retail establishments, but the town also boasted a small newsagency, a post office, a bank, two pubs and two petrol stations. There were enough amenities in Glenroyd to provide basic goods and services, but anyone with a need for anything out of the ordinary would be forced to make the hour and a half trip to Toorrup, the closest town of any size.

The rusting wrought-iron lacework of the pubs and the sloughing paint on the historic post office were visual evidence of the recent agricultural slump. Fifteen-year-old cars dotted the streets or filled up with fuel from the domed shaped bowsers of flat-fronted garages. On market day wobbly-armed women in sleeveless cotton frocks and men in gut-stretched work shirts stood in segregated groups, as they always had, discussing wool prices and CWA, horse racing and lamington drives.

Cam peered through the grimy window of one of the town's two boutiques where post war dummies with large busts and wasp waists modelled last summer's sun-bleached clothes.

No wonder Ruby hated it here.

But given time, she'd learn to love it. The town might be small, grotty and old, but this was home: this was where they were meant to be.

The sun was heavy on his head as he scooted between the shady shop awnings, but a wave of cool air rolled over him when he reached the open door of the Glenroyd Arms. He stopped for a moment to savour the sour tang of beer and listen to the contented murmuring from within. For those citizens of Glenroyd with the money and the time, this was the only place to be on a stifling day such as this. Even the adjacent TAB had lost all but its hardcore gamblers to the cool allure of the pub.

He paused again at the window of the stock feeder's to peruse the For Sale section. The sun-faded pictures of quaint weatherboard houses surrounded by bucolic farmland were photographed in spring before the summer sun and wind had dried the countryside to a dustbowl. He skipped past these, spending longer on the lists of second-hand tractors, posthole drillers and harvesters, his breath whistling through his teeth when he noticed the prices.

When he came to the equestrian section, he rubbed his chin, reading through the descriptions of over a dozen horses and ponies. The ponies were too small, the horses too young and flighty for an inexperienced rider. At five foot six, Ruby would have to have something between fifteen-two and sixteen-two hands, an old bombproof schoolmaster who had done it all. But the right horse would come along, if they bided their time.

A gentle tapping on the window drew his attention from the notices to the smiling face of an elderly woman on the other side of the glass.

"Mrs Wilmot?" he mouthed. Her face lit up. Her hair, like a white powder puff, bobbed from side to side as she nodded her head.

"Cameron Fraser, crikey Moses – aren't you a sight for sore eyes!" she said as he entered the store. It took a moment for his eyes to adjust from the baked whiteness of the street. The store was cool and dark and smelt of grain and dried dog food.

"They said you'd come back. I nearly dropped in at the station the other day, but held back knowing how busy you've been since you arrived."

He laughed. "You know you're always welcome, Mrs Wilmot."

She frowned, tapping at her cheek. "Well, come on then, what are you waiting for? Don't I deserve a kiss?"

He gave her an extended kiss on the cheek and moaned with mock passion.

She laughed. "OK, you don't have to eat me alive. Stand back so I can have a look at you."

He stepped back and braced himself for her reaction. When she tilted her head to one side, he focused on the dust motes dancing in a beam of filtered light.

She clasped his hand. Hers were fibrous and knotted like pieces of root ginger. "I'm so sorry, Cam, sorry about everything."

"The worst is over."

She nodded. "There's always the future to look forward to."

"And what about you? You still have the teashop?" he asked, keen to change the subject.

"Crikey, no. I gave that up not long after you left, went to work at St Luke's Retirement Home. I'm retired from that too now." She chuckled. "I suppose you could call me a lady of leisure."

Cam doubted that. She laughed again and smoothed the imagined wrinkles in her faded cotton frock.

"I still dream about your vanilla slices."

"You and half the boys from St Bart's, I'm sure. I'm hoping them that used to steal 'em are still getting nightmares."

"I'll bet they are. You had the fastest wooden spoon in the west. How are Greg and Mark?"

"They run this place now. Doing a grand job at it. I'm just minding the store for the moment 'til Greg gets back from lunch," she said. "Mark's at the hospital in Toorrup with his Kate, having their first."

"So you're about to be a grandmother?"

"Heavens, no – Greg has four already."

"Wow, and you not a day over forty-five. I'd never have guessed."

"Tease," she said, pushing him with her palm. "Speaking of kids, was that your Ruby I saw in the park the other day? I had to do a double take; for a moment I thought I was looking at a fair-headed Elizabeth. How strange that you and Elizabeth would produce a girl with such blonde hair, you two so dark and all."

Cam looked around the store for eavesdroppers and put his fingers to his lips. "Actually, Mrs W, I think it's from a bottle."

She shook her head. "Kids today, what they do to themselves, I don't know. Still, there's a lot worse than a bit of hair dye. That boy she was with, well, I wouldn't want to meet him at night down a dark alley."

Cam felt as if he'd just received a body blow. He had to jerk in a breath to get the words out. "Boy? What boy?"

"Goodness, Cam, have I said something I shouldn't?"

He forced out a smile. "She never told me, that's all. Do you know who he is?"

"What's-his-name's apprentice, you know, runs the mechanic shop."

"Cliff Donovan?"

"That's him, and the boy's Angelo, Angelo Arnoldi. He helps out with the bushfire brigade too. He can't be too bad if he does that I suppose. I've always said young people these days don't have enough community spirit, so it makes a change to have one who's willing to help out."

A man in work clothes walked into the shop and started to look around. "Can I help you with anything, love?" Mrs Wilmot asked him.

An idea came to Cam while he waited for her to finish serving her customer. When he asked, she said she'd be happy to have Ruby help out in the shop every now and then. But even with the arrangements made, he continued to the station with heavy steps, eyes to the ground, concentrating on the cracks in the pavement.

6

The police sub-district of Glenroyd covered an area of over two thousand kilometres, so it was rare to find all five officers at the station at any one time. Theirs was an integrated system meaning that no one specialised in any particular duty, all spending equal time on traffic, crime and community duties. Vince and Leanne were where Cam had left them earlier, and the other two officers, Derek and Pete, were still out on traffic patrol.

Vince was hunched over the computer keyboard, struggling with Monday's interviews. Leanne was manning the front counter and communications. She started at Cam's entrance, shoving a meat pie on to her lap and betraying herself with a guilty look that did nothing but draw his attention to the blob of sauce on her chin. She flashed him a self-conscious grin; perhaps she hoped to encourage some good-natured banter. But his frown wiped the smile from her face as quickly as her hand could dash away the sauce and she hunched further into the counter.

Cam pulled up a chair next to Vince. "Tell me all," he said to the sweating Senior Constable. Vince seemed more than happy to have a break from the computer. After pecking out one last word, he rocked back in his chair until it creaked.

"You said the body had been ID'd," Cam said.

Vince picked up a fax from his desk. "Victim identified from dental records as fifty-six year old Herbert Bell, no fixed address."

"Background check?"

"Yup, it's all here," he said waving the fax. "Next of kin listed as a Mr Toby Bell, brother. He's a real estate agent in Toorrup."

Cam looked at his watch. He should have plenty of time to get to Toorrup, break the bad news and be back home before dark.

Vince continued. "Criminal record, numerous court appearances, fines, community service, but no time spent inside. His offences ranged from petty theft to…" Vince gave a snort and narrowed his eyes as if he were reading this for the first time "…indecent exposure." He guffawed with ugly laughter and turned to Leanne with a loose, wet smile. "You know what that means, don't you, Leanne?"

Leanne gritted her teeth but said nothing. Vince had obviously been savouring the revelation of this titbit until Cam's return. He seemed to take special delight in embarrassing Leanne in front of her new sergeant.

"It means he liked flopping his doodle out at…"

Cam slammed his fist on the desk as the blood rushed to his face. "Vince! Shut the hell up. Leanne knows exactly what that means!"

"OK, OK, I was only joshing her. I've known Leanne since she was a nipper. We're always joshing, aren't we, Leanne?"

"Doesn't mean I like it," Leanne said.

Cam snatched the fax from Vince's desk and took it to his own glass-walled cubicle. As he sank into his grey metal chair he caught sight of the telephone and made a move towards it. He stopped himself and reached for his palm exerciser instead, kneading the spongy ball in his scarred hand until he felt the tension ease.

He was halfway through the fax when he gave a start.

The palm exerciser fell from his hand and rolled on to the floor.

"Last known place of employment: Glenroyd Ladies' College." His voice bounced loudly off the steel furniture of the stark office.

With mounting excitement Cam flicked the pages of the fax until he came to the coronial section: Autopsy yet to be completed. Then the SOCO report: Yet to be completed. Shit, the frustration of small town policing.

Then he reminded himself why he was here and his eyes were drawn again to the phone.

He forced his attention back to the fax in front of him. There was a PS from SOCO. It seemed he was correct in identifying the smell on the rag as petrol (premium unleaded, said the lab) and what's more, they'd identified the rag as part of the waistband of a pair of King Gee work shorts. He wondered if the waistband could be matched up to any clothing the victim was wearing. There'd been no visible trace of clothing on the burned body but there was always the chance of fibre or chemical residue.

He tapped his pen against his teeth for a moment, then phoned the pathologist in Toorrup. He'd met Doctor McManus at the crime scene the other day and had been struck by his pleasant, approachable manner.

"Can't you tell me anything yet, Doc? Fibres? Chemicals?"

"Sorry, no, Sergeant. He's on tomorrow's list though."

"You checked out his teeth, so you must have had a look at him."

"Just a cursory glance when I made the dental impression I'm afraid."

"How about a time of death then?"

"Oh, going by the crusting of the skin and the hydration levels, I can pretty well make an estimate that this person was dead approximately twelve hours before he was burned. I can't give you anything more accurate until I've opened him up."

Twelve hours before he'd been burned.

Cam thanked the pathologist and hung up, then started to scribble a time line on the pad in front of him. Ruth Tilly reported the fire at eleven on Sunday morning. The fire brigade arrived at 11.20 and extinguished the fire. They hadn't noticed the body, situated as it was away from the perimeter of the fire and camouflaged among the burned debris.

Cecelia Bowman found the charred body at approximately ten o'clock the following morning, Monday.

Herbert Bell must have died sometime late Saturday night or early Sunday morning.

He doodled some curly question marks on the pad, then wrote the name Cliff Donovan. Cliff was captain of the Bush Fire Brigade and town mechanic. Underneath Cliff's name he wrote Angelo Arnoldi, fire assistant, apprentice mechanic.

Ruby's boyfriend?

His chin dropped on to his hand and he drew some large circles around Angelo's name.

There was a tap at the door.

"Hey, Sarge. You looked like you needed a cuppa." Leanne peered into the office as if there might be a man-eating lion sitting at his desk.

"Thanks, put it here." Cam cleared a space on his messy desk. The girl put the cup down and turned to leave.

"Wait a minute," he said. "Shut the door and come in, take a seat."

Leanne glanced back at Vince's hunched form in the front office.

"We need to talk about the Bell case," Cam said in a voice loud enough for the Senior Constable to hear.

He unlocked the filing cabinet, riffled through the bulging dividers then thumped a pile of files on his desk. "I've been going through some old case files, trying to get a feel of the place, pinpointing the trouble spots. There's not much I wouldn't expect to find in a country town of this size: stock theft, burglary, property damage, shoplifting – some cases solved, others unsolved." He stopped reading and looked at her over the top of his glasses. "I've also been going through the personnel files, and frankly, I'm not liking everything I read."

She shifted in her chair and began to bite at her lower lip.

"Relax. I'm talking about Vince." Cam shuffled through the stack of files before him.

She blew the fringe out of her eyes and leaned towards the desk, her eyes straining to look at the extracted file. He tapped at it with his pen. "This is the hoo-hah over the liquor licence for the footy club."

Lanne jumped to her feet. "But Sarge, I tried to explain that to Sergeant Baker."

Sergeant Baker was Cam's predecessor and was married to Vince's sister. Upon his retirement he had taken off on a world cruise and was now conveniently incommunicado.

"I've no idea how that happened," she continued with a wail in her voice. "It's gone into my file, hasn't it?

"The paper trail led to you."

"But shit, Sarge—" Her hand flew to her mouth. "Sorry, excuse me. *Gosh,* Sarge, I wouldn't do anything like that. I don't even like beer and neither does mum. Why would I put a dodgy liquor licence through for a lousy carton of beer?"

"Sit down, will you?"

She sat with a heavy thump and crossed her arms.

"Don't worry, I know you didn't and if Sergeant Baker thought you did, he'd have taken more action. Someone else compromised you to save their own arse, someone who's been milking the system for too long. You're just one of many who've been affected."

Cam shot Vince a look through the glass partition before delving into another file, producing a wad of complaints. "I've spent the last couple of days going through these," he said. "Do you know anything about the dangerous driving ticket issued to Ms Cecelia Bowman last month?"

Leanne shook her head.

"It was issued by Vince. Later Ms Bowman lodged a complaint against him for sexual harassment – though the complaint's now been withdrawn. I'm going to have a word with her. I want to know why she suddenly withdrew it." He thought back to the scene in the science lab and the concoction in the vial. "She and her friend gave me the impression that Vince had been giving them a hard time."

"I don't know anything about that," Leanne said. She was obviously uncomfortable with his line of questioning; a bullying senior officer could make life hell for a probationer.

"There are scores of other complaints against Vince. I'm compiling the facts for an Internal Affairs investigation. You'll have to do some serious thinking and get your liquor licence story straight. You might even be called to testify against him."

Leanne swallowed. "You mean become a whistleblower?"

"Any instances of sexual harassment need to be thought about, too. That was a fine example in the front office just now. He gave her an encouraging smile. "Don't worry, I'll be behind you all the way."

The look on her face told him his reassurances didn't count for much.

"You won't be the only one. I'll be speaking to the others." Cam took a sip of coffee. Leanne took it to be a sign of dismissal and stood to leave.

"Hang on," Cam said. "We have Bell's approximate time of death as late Saturday night to early Sunday morning. I want you to trace his movements over that weekend. Find out who was last to see him alive. Get his picture off the computer and start with the pubs."

Leanne glanced nervously in Vince's direction.

"I can't spare Vince. You'll have to go alone."

Leanne sighed with relief.

"Off you go now," Cam, said, reaching for the phone.

7

Leanne looked again at the mug shot of Herbert Bell. It was surprising she didn't recognise his face considering she'd spent almost her whole life in this town. A copy of a copy, the picture quality softened the harsh lines and angles of a face shaped by misfortune and alcohol. His thin grey hair hung down in a way that would have been irritating and made Leanne suspect he usually tied it back. Shit, she'd forgotten to mention this to the guys at the Shearer's Rest. Maybe if she pointed it out to the patrons at the Glenny Arms she'd be able to jog a few more memories.

She'd not been looking forward to her visit to the Glenny. It was the pub her dad used to drink at and was full of his old cronies. None of them ever seemed to take her seriously. She would always be little Leanne Henry to them no matter how large she became, whatever uniform she wore. And the fact that she had replaced the supermarket uniform with a police uniform seemed to make no difference; they'd give her a hard time, regardless.

As she slid out of the police Commodore she expected the worst and wondered about the wisdom of, if not the reasons for, her special request to be posted back to her hometown.

Catcalls and whistles greeted her as she pushed against the heavy hinged door to make her way through the lunchtime crowd to the counter. Out of the corner of her eye she caught movement at the jukebox, heard the tinkle of coins.

There was a snigger then a snort, then the buzz of the

crowd was drowned by Skyhooks' *Women In Uniform*, so loud she could hardly hear herself think, let alone shout above it.

She walked over to the offending machine with her gut squirming. There was a curved rib of vinyl forty-fives, song lists and numbered buttons, but nothing that said Stop. A man in Stubbies and a blue singlet delved into the small pocket next to his straining belly, about to slot another coin and select another track.

Leanne reached for his wrist and stopped the action, shouting to be heard. "Hold on a sec, sir. Please don't play any more music. I need to make a public announcement."

He feigned a look of surprise and gave her a reluctant nod.

She continued towards the bar until a rough hand grabbed hers. She looked down to find Ham Martin kneeling at her side. He was lip-synching the song's chorus and gazing up at her with an expression of mocking love.

Women in uniform sometimes they look so cold
Women in uniform but ooh they feel so warm

She tried to yank her arm away without making a scene but he reached out with his other hand and caught her tight. What should she do now? She might have won the marksmanship trophy at the academy, but she could hardly shoot him for this; it wasn't even just cause for pepper spray. At the Academy they had been drilled on how to handle almost every situation, but shit if she could remember the correct terminology for this kind of harassment. Her nervousness had made her mind go blank. Even if she'd remembered the by-the-book response, he'd never be able to hear her above the racket of the jukebox.

She couldn't think, and all she could feel was the flush of her own humiliation scratching against the collar of her uniform shirt.

The song finally finished and the laughter died to an acceptable hum.

"I see you left your brain in the cup by your bed again, Ham," Leanne said.

Ham's grin faded, and he let go of her hand. Several of the patrons chuckled. She tried to ignore the crude remarks as she moved over to the bar, conscious of fifty pairs of eyes boring into her back. She leaned against the bar and slid the picture of Bell across to Kylie the barmaid. But as Kylie opened her mouth to speak she was interrupted by a voice from behind. It was Terry Carmichael, one of her dad's best mates.

"Have you heard from Bob recently, Leanne?"

Jesus Christ, just let me get my job done.

"This isn't a social visit, Terry." She looked into his weathered face seeing only concern in his sun faded eyes. At least he wasn't making fun of her.

"He's in Broome now," she amended, feeling the stiffness of her breast pocket where the dog-eared postcard lay next to her heart.

"Lucky bugger," he sighed then added in a softer voice. "How's Mavis taking it? Still bad?"

She wanted to say, why don't you go and see for yourself, but held herself in check. Most of the townspeople seemed unnerved by her mother, never knowing how she would be from one day to the next. It was understandable; even Leanne found herself walking on eggshells around her most of the time. If there was something good on the box, blackberry nip in the fridge and plenty of anti-depressants in the bathroom cupboard, she was fine. But if any of these ran low, watch out.

"Hey, Leanne, I know that guy." Kylie thumped a finger

on to the printout. Leanne was grateful to Kylie for steering everyone back on topic. They'd been to Toorrup High School together and knew each other pretty well, as you'd have to when you sat on a bus together over four hours every day. Leanne considered Kylie to be one of her few good friends.

"That's that old sod, Herb Bell. You sometimes drink with him, don't you, Sid?"

The barmaid turned to a wizened monkey of a man sitting at the bar, quietly dribbling into his beer.

"Yup." Sid belched.

"Can you remember when you last saw him, Sid?" Leanne asked.

"Nope." Sid belched louder. Someone started to laugh.

Leanne grabbed a teaspoon from the bar and tapped it against a glass. She turned around to face the crowd, drew a deep breath and said, "As you all probably know, a burned body was discovered in the Glenroyd School grounds on Monday. The victim has been identified as Herbert Bell."

There was a low murmur from those whom the town grapevine had not yet reached.

"I'm circulating a picture of Herb, hoping to jog some memories. The picture has him with his hair dangling down, but I think he usually had it tied back in a ponytail. I want you all to think about when you last saw him, and come and tell me. We are especially interested in talking to anyone who saw him last Saturday."

Kylie helped Leanne distribute the pictures. The last few in the pile were wet from resting on the bar. When Leanne tried to separate them they fell apart in her hands. She screwed them up and shoved them in her pocket and glanced around, hoping no one had noticed. Her gut lurched.

"A face only a mother could love," she heard someone say.

Someone else tacked the picture to the dartboard. Leanne shoved her way through the crowd and managed to pull it down before the first dart could be thrown. She backed the offender against the wall away from his mates, and spoke to him low and mean, like Sarge did when he'd caught Tim Robinson letting down little Ian Knox's bicycle tyres.

"You knew Herb well enough to want to throw darts at him, did you?"

"Err, not really, Leanne. I hardly even spoke to him."

The guy was younger than she was and seemed nervous of her. Now, that was a first.

"I think someone who wants to throw darts at someone else's picture could hate him enough to want to kill him. What do you reckon, Shorty?"

Shorty swallowed and took a breath. "I was only joking, honest, Leanne, ask anyone here," he said nodding to the rabble over her shoulder.

"He's right Leanne. He never knows nothing. He's a dumb little shit."

Beery gusts of laughter interrupted Shorty's character reference. Leanne gave the kid a final glare and returned him to his mates with a push.

"Oh, there is one thing, I don't know if it helps," the kid said just before he scuttled off.

"I'm listening."

The boy turned to his mates for encouragement and was met by blank stares. He took a gulp of beer. "He was always bragging about how rich he was going to be." He smacked his lips, failing to get rid of the beer froth. He looked like the Milky Bar Kid.

"He was talking about winning Lotto, you moron," one

of his friends interjected.

"When was this?" Leanne asked the boy.

"Last few weeks I guess," he said, shrugging. "Is that any help?"

"Probably not, but thanks anyway."

Leanne left the pub knowing as little about Herb Bell's last movements as she did when entering it. Her stomach gave an empty growl. She decided she needed a therapeutic slice of mud cake. She could question Flo at the diner while she ate.

8

"I hate him, I hate his guts."

Angelo looked at Ruby with astonishment. "That sounds a bit harsh," he said before taking a bite from a sandwich as big as the lunch-box it had come from. A blob of mayonnaise dripped from the sandwich and collected in the cleft of his chin.

His hands and nails were filthy, his overalls were covered in grease and his hair was gelled into short spikes. A gold ring pierced the bruising of his swollen left eyebrow. Ruby thought he was the most beautiful young man she had ever seen.

But his neutrality on the issue of her father annoyed her and made her more determined to milk her miserable life story for all it was worth.

"I've been asking for a pony all my life and now I've finally grown out of the idea, he offers to get me one. It was his way of making me want to come here. Can you imagine that? At my age, he tried to bribe me with a pony."

"It would have been a bit hard to keep a pony in Sydney," Angelo said.

He spoke as slowly as he chewed, thinking long and hard over every word, savouring them just as he savoured every bite of his lunch. He wasn't looking at her, but somewhere off into the distance, maybe at Fleur who was sniffing around the swings or maybe at the stagnant pools of the drying river.

Why was he always so fair and reasonable? She tried to get a hold of the emotions that blew like tangled ribbons through her mind. Sometimes even she didn't know what she really felt.

"I think what I hate the most about him is what he did to Mum and Joey."

"It's not like he killed them, Ruby," Angelo said as he inched closer, his arm snaking her waist. He took another bite of his sandwich. She listened to his chewing, the occasional drawing in of his breath. He smelt of grease, cigarettes and mayonnaise.

"No, but it's his fault they're dead." She allowed a quaver to escape into her voice. "If he hadn't been a cop, they wouldn't have died. The bomb was supposed to be for him. The bikies planted it so he wouldn't testify against them in court. He's guilty about it but taking it out on me. He thinks of this..." she almost said dump, then remembered Angelo had always lived here "...place as home. He said he had the happiest days of his life here and he wants me to share in the fuzzy warm glow of his memories."

She looked up the sky trying not to let the tears spill. A tangle of tree branches blocked some of the blue, lacing above their heads like a net. Her father had told her how he and his mates would sit in this Moreton Bay fig and pelt innocent passers by with the rotten fruit. They'd steal fruit from the trees in people's gardens and play chicken on the railway track. If the monks from the Boys' Home caught them, they were put in the boxing ring with the school champion or else they were caned until they bled. Mum had told her that part; he never spoke about the bad things. He always pretended that everything was just wonderful.

God, how she hated all this nostalgic crap.

"He's changed so much since we got here. He's over-protective. He smothers me and his jokes are worse than ever."

Even his accent is different, she thought. He calls everyone mate, dinner has become tea and a bottom is now a bum. Mum always used to tell him off for that kind of language, but now he used it all the time. Before long he'd be blowing his nose on to the pavement. She looked at the boy beside her. And what would Mum have thought of you, she asked herself?

She decided to put that thought to the back of her mind.

Angelo took her hand and gave it a squeeze, looking at her through earnest brown eyes. "Are you glad you're here now?" he asked. He leaned towards her and brushed her lips with a soft kiss before reaching to cup her breast. She deepened the kiss, enjoying the unfamiliar sensation that tingled from her centre to her toes. Finally she drew back, blinking away the tears.

"Yes, but I'm not going to tell him that."

"Did you manage to get rid of that geek, Cindy?"

"Yup," she said, smiling now. "I annoyed her so much she ended up wanting to bash me even more than that bible she was always carrying on about."

Angelo laughed. "Do you think he'd ever let you come to Toorrup with me? I have a mate who lives there and a key to his house. He's hardly ever at home." Angelo grinned and continued to massage her breast through her thin T-shirt.

"Not likely, he hardly even lets me out of the house. He's not going to let me go to Toorrup with someone who's still on P-plates."

In her mind she could hear him. "I'm not letting you out with someone who has spiked hair and a ring through his eyebrow!" The imagined scene made her smile. She wondered if Angelo had any tatts under those overalls. The shock value of tatts would be even better than the eyebrow ring.

"Hey, Angelo, have you ever tried drugs?"

His hand dropped from her breast. "Is this truth or dare or something?"

She shrugged. "I'm just curious. I figure that when people have a relationship, start to go out and everything, they should tell each other stuff like that. I used to smoke cones in Sydney," she said, hoping to impress him, to seem older than she was. "I was wondering if you knew how to go about getting them over here?"

He shook his head. "Nah, that's not how I operate, Rubes. I never buy them. Besides…" He waggled his eyebrows. "There's better things than drugs, I reckon."

"But you've had mull, right?"

"Sure, hasn't everyone?"

"And if you were given some, you'd like it, right?"

"Well yeah, but I wouldn't waste my money buying it." He gave her a puzzled look, then smiled and tapped on the side of her head. "What's going on in that pretty little head of yours?"

Ruby smiled.

Cam left the station when his phone calls home remained unanswered. Ruby wasn't in the house and the dog was gone. He guessed the park, but why hadn't she rung? Was it because she was meeting that boy?

She could still have rung. Something must have happened to her.

From his house he jogged down the rough path to the park and by the time he got there he'd roused himself into a panic; paperwork and Vince were forgotten, the Bell case might never have existed. He came to a halt alongside the wobbly Lion's Club sign that dedicated the park to the citizens of Glenroyd. As he leaned against its wooden post to catch his breath he gasped in the muddy river smells that wafted up the embankment.

The park sloped down to the drying riverbed, connected to the stunted scrubland on the other side by a metal bridge he always used to think looked like a dinosaur's backbone. Now it was just an ugly metal bridge. Knotted ropes and swings with tyre seats hung like limp spaghetti in the afternoon air, and squiggles of heat slithered up from the tarmac wicket, making the ground quiver. He squinted through the heat haze. The park was deserted. Except for Ruby and a boy sitting on a bench overlooking the river.

Fleur raced over to jump at his legs. He picked her up and headed towards the bench. Ruby's hair shone in the sun like corn silk, but the head of her male companion was no more than a spiky silhouette.

Cam clutched the poodle tightly to his chest as he got closer. He stopped a few feet away and cleared his throat. The sound was drowned by Ruby's raised voice.

"Gramma always said he put his job before us. She said things might be different now, but she's wrong, his job still comes first. He doesn't give a shit about me."

Cam willed himself to take a step forward. "Ruby?" No response; surely she'd heard him?

He stood and watched the kid reach into his pocket for a greasy rag to wipe her cheek. When she moved her head her eyes met Cam's and with a look of calculated defiance, she turned back to the boy and planted a firm kiss on his lips.

Cam pushed himself into taking another step.

"Hey, Ruby," he said, "I found Fleur on the road. You'd better keep her on the lead next time."

The kid jumped to his feet and turned around. His hair was gelled into short dark spikes with bleached tips. It looked like he had a wet echidna on his head.

"Um, Dad, this is Angelo," Ruby said.

Angelo thrust out a dirty hand. The wrist that disappeared into the overall sleeve was skinny as a girl's.

"Good to meet you, er, Mr…"

"Sergeant. Sergeant Fraser," Cam said, tapping at his nametag.

After shaking hands, Angelo wiped his nose on the sleeve of his overalls. Cam could only imagine what those long sleeves might be hiding.

"Watch you don't hook yourself on that eyebrow ring, son," he said.

Angelo's mouth opened like a fish's.

Ruby clenched her face. "Dad, don't be so rude!"

"It looks like he's hooked himself up on it once already." Cam leaned forward to have a good look at the boy's eye. It was eggplant purple and swollen to a slit, the holes on each side of the ring a livid pink. "You should have taken that thing out."

Angelo spoke to Cam's shoes. "I guess I'd better be getting back to work now." His gaze travelled up Cam's leg to the holstered Smith and Wesson. He swallowed so hard his Adam's apple almost bounced into his mouth.

"Yeah, guess you'd better," said Cam. But he changed his mind when the boy turned to leave, realising that this would be a good opportunity to find out what kind of a kid his daughter was hanging about with. "Say, I may as well come back to the workshop with you, I've been meaning on having a chat with your boss."

"Wait for me then, I just need to put my shoes on," Ruby said, scrabbling with her sandals.

"This is police business, love. I'll see you back at the house."

Ruby folded her arms and turned down her mouth, but

Cam knew he was safe; she wouldn't risk scaring off a new boyfriend with a temper tantrum now.

They separated at the edge of the park; Ruby headed for home, Cam and Angelo on to the mechanic's near the centre of town. While they walked Cam attempted to make conversation with the kid. The grunts of response became so irritating he gave up trying.

The double front doors of the mechanic's were locked. A grimy piece of paper that read BACK IN THIRTY MINUTES had been taped above the handle.

"Cliff's still at lunch." Angelo stated the obvious. "You'll have to drop by again later."

"Oh, that's OK. You'll do just as well." Cam gave him a pleasant smile. "Where's the other entrance then? Round the side?"

Before Angelo could offer up any form of protest, Cam disappeared down the side alley towards the back of the workshop. He opened the gate and found himself in a high-walled yard that looked to be the final resting-place of anything in Glenroyd ever loosely termed mechanical. Part of an old-fashioned push-mower, a large copper kettle and a set of sheep shears shared space with piles of tyres and mounds of rusting car and truck parts. The four-wheel drive fire unit and a tow truck were parked within easy access of some locked double gates at the end of the yard.

But it was what was standing alongside the tin wall of the workshop that interested Cam the most: a custom-made Harley with studded leather saddlebags and more chrome than a Mack truck.

"Umm, er, Sergeant Fraser. Cliff's not going to like it that you're down here in his yard. Shouldn't you have a search warrant or something?"

"Why? I'm not searching for anything. I'm merely talking to you." Cam bent over the bike. He ran his hand over the chrome mudguard and made appropriate sounds of appreciation.

"Do you know something about bikes then?" Angelo asked with a glimmer of interest.

"Not really. I used to ride one, that's all."

"A bike copper then?"

"No. I just rode for fun."

"What, a rice burner?" Angelo said with the lip curl of a serious bike enthusiast.

"A Fat Boy."

Angelo's good eye lit up a pleasant face that glowed with an intelligence Cam hadn't noticed earlier. "Cool," he said.

It always amazed Cam how teenagers could elongate that one word into two or three syllables. He looked back at the bike, caressing the silky paintwork of the fuel tank, then stopped. He glanced at Angelo then back at the blemish under his fingertips. It was a sticker: a triangle with two dots for eyes making it look like a hood. Around the border of the triangle were the words *Made For Whites By Whites*. He had seen stickers like this often enough and they never failed to make his neck prickle. This white supremacist sticker was a clear indication that the machine did not belong to any weekend biker.

Cam straightened up. "Who owns this bike, then?"

"A mate of Cliff's."

"In a club?"

Angelo took a breath. "Maybe."

"Is Cliff in it?"

"No. He says bikes are death machines. He just works on them sometimes."

"And you?"

Angelo shrugged. "I like bikes. But I don't have anything to do with the bikies, they're a mob of animals."

"Sensible man, stay right away from them," he said, jotting the bike's numberplate in his notebook.

Angelo wiped his forehead with the back of his hand. "Is this all you wanted to talk to me about, bikes?"

"No. I wanted to talk about Sunday's fire."

"Yeah. What about it?"

"You got there at about 11.20?"

Angelo nodded and licked his dry lips.

"When you first arrived, what colour was the smoke?"

"Um, the other cop asked Cliff that. Just ask him."

"But I'm asking you," Cam said.

Angelo shifted his weight from one foot to the other. Cam moved to one side so the sun shone into Angelo's face like a spotlight.

"Greyish white I guess," he said. A bead of sweat trickled down the side of his face.

"Like an ordinary bush fire?"

Angelo shrugged. "I dunno."

"Of course you know. You're a fireman, for Christ's sake. You know full well different fuels make different coloured smoke."

Angelo took a step back.

Cam softened his voice. "How'd you get the black eye, son?"

"I slipped in the shower."

Cam folded his arms and stepped forward, his eyes fixed on Angelo's face. The kid swallowed but this time stood his ground.

The sound of footsteps broke the silence; the boy glanced at the side entrance. The gate creaked and the sun was eclipsed by the shadow of one of the biggest men Cam had ever seen. Angelo seemed a midget beside him. He introduced Cliff Donovan to Cam before scuttling off into the workshop.

The mechanic watched Angelo's retreat. The thick beard around his mouth moved, suggesting a smile, though there was no evidence of one in his eyes.

"He's a good kid," he said, paternally. "It's hard to find decent apprentices these days, he's one of the best I've had." He paused. The heat radiated off the tin of the workshop walls, shooting stars of light off the chrome of the Harley.

Cliff saw Cam looking at the bike. "How about coming into the workshop for a coffee? It's a lot cooler in there."

Cam declined. "I won't keep you long, sir. I just wanted to clarify the time you got to the fire."

"Let me see now," the big man said. He scratched his bearded chin, making a sound like wire wool on a cooking-pot. "I had a real early start that morning. I like to work on a Sunday, it's more peaceful, you know?" Cam nodded his agreement and Cliff continued, "I was working on old man Ronnin's truck from about seven am. He came to check up on it at about 7.30. Angelo turned up for work soon after. His folks need the extra money so I often let him come in on Sunday. Then I had a long phone call from John Campbell, the shire president, about a fishing trip he's planning."

Cam had not asked for an alibi, but he seemed to be getting one.

"After that I went to Flo's diner for smoko, chatted with Flo there for a while and got back here about eleven when I got the fire call. Would have got to the school at about 11.20, like I told Vince."

Cam wrote in his notebook and they made some small

talk. Cam didn't ask him about the smoke. It was in Vince's report.

He'd said the smoke was oily black.

"You were spying on me weren't you?" Ruby said the minute Cam walked through the front door.

She'd opened another of the cartons and was surrounded by books. His mechanical manuals and law books were piled incongruously next to Elizabeth's leather bound classics, Joe's *Where's Wally* stash and her own animal books. Ruby sat in the middle of the piles as if inside a walled fortress.

"No, of course I wasn't spying on you – you damn well knew I was there. I'd forgotten something. I came home to get it, you weren't home and as you didn't ring to say you were going out, I got worried. I don't care that you have a boyfriend," he lied. "It's just that after what happened to Mum and Joe we have to look after each other, keep each other safe and above all tell each other what's going on."

She sprang to her feet and twisted her face. "Lock me in prison, you mean! Embarrass me in front of my friends!"

"He seems nice. How long have you known him?"

Ruby stared at him for a moment, trying to read his neutral mask.

"Since we first arrived." She seemed to be expecting some kind of outburst. When none came, hope brightened her face and sped up her voice. "He has a good job. He's an apprentice mechanic, but he wants to become a chromer. They're the guys who put the silver stuff on old-fashioned cars and motorbikes. "

Cam arched his eyebrows. "Really? I'm impressed."

"Can I see him again, then?"

Cam frowned. "How did he get the black eye?"

"He walked into a door," Ruby said, innocently. "So?" she added.

"So what?"

"Can I see him again? I'm only asking to be polite, I don't have to." She stopped as if she knew that an argument at this stage of the negotiations would do nothing to help her cause.

"I'll think about it," Cam said, picking up one of Elizabeth's books. He sniffed at the leather cover and ran his thumb over the edges of the gold leaf: *Wuthering Heights*, one of her favourites. She must have read it a dozen times and it never failed to make her cry. He could never understand why she kept reading it.

"I ran into an old lady I used to know at the stock feeder's." When Ruby didn't answer he continued. "She needs someone to help out in the shop and was wondering if you could give her a hand this afternoon."

"Paid?"

"Yes." He'd already arranged to give Mrs Wilmot the money.

Ruby shrugged. "Maybe."

That was good enough. "Good. Let's go do some more unpacking, then I'll take you over there and introduce you."

"What about your work?"

Cam paused for a moment, thinking about the conversation he'd overheard in the park. "It'll keep," he said.

9

Cam was running late. He'd hoped to catch Toby Bell in his real estate office but was informed by the secretary that after waiting in as long as he could, Bell had left for a Home Open down the road.

The real estate agent didn't notice Cam pulling up in the police ute. His head was in the boot of his mustard coloured BMW where he was trying to untangle a bunch of Home Open signs. With a start, he jerked himself out of the boot and stuck his hand between his knees, bellowing a blue string of expletives into the quiet suburban street. Cam hurried over to assist, receiving some murmured words of thanks. It was only when they'd finished unpacking the signs that Bell gave him the benefit of a glance. One look at the uniform and he paled, dropped the sign he was holding, missing Cam's foot by inches.

"Sorry to startle you, sir," Cam said.

"Jesus Christ, Officer. Tracking me over here is really too bloody much. Don't you have anything better to do with your time? I thought my lawyer had sorted it all out with those wankers, they have no right to..." He looked at Cam for a moment. A glimmer of an idea crossed his doughy features. "Ah, I know what your game is." He reached into his back pocket. "Maybe we could come to a mutual understanding - will a fifty keep that annoying little piece of paper in your pocket?"

He flashed Cam a smile as sweet as glass toffee and just as brittle.

"This isn't about any kind of summons, sir," Cam said,

"if that's what you mean. Please put your wallet away."
He paused for a moment, trying to make his voice gentle.
"I'm afraid I have some bad news. Can we go into the
house?" He nodded in the direction of the Home Open.
"You might need to sit down."

Toby Bell ran his fingers through his bleached curls.
"I think I've made a bit of a faux pas haven't I?"

"Given the circumstances, I'll forget it."

"OK, OK." Bell's hand went to the gold chain at his
throat. "Bad news?" His voice faltered. He leaned back
against the car. "Is it my, er, niece, Tiffany?"

"Please come with me, sir."

Cam led the way into the house and sat Bell in the dingy
living room. This was the hard part; he never got used to
this side of the job. Despite his years of experience, he
knew he was clumsy and inadequate when dealing with
the emotional pain of others.

Cam took a step back. The man would need space.
"I regret to inform you that the remains of your brother,
Herbert, were found in bushland on Monday. The cause of
death has not yet been ascertained."

"Herbert? You're talking about Herb?"

He drew his breath in and stared at Cam for a moment.
From his briefcase he removed a silver hip flask. After a
large gulp he let out his breath, closed his eyes and leaned
back against the headrest of the sofa.

Everyone reacted differently to grief; Cam decided to
give the man time to collect his thoughts.

The room in which they sat was claustrophobic and
dark and smelled of old people. A faded portrait of a very
young queen stared down at them next to a Highland
landscape print. Souvenir mugs from English seaside
resorts lined the wooden mantelpiece. Cam could just

imagine the flying ducks on the wall in the kitchen and the Kookaburra stove in the corner. Though not to his taste, he liked the generic familiarity of this home; at least there were no surprises here.

Bell started at the sound of a car door slamming and voices coming closer. He sprang to his feet. "Quick, quick, you have to hide. You can't be seen here. You'll put them off."

"But I still need to ask you some questions," Cam said. He'd expected the man to at least cancel the Home Open.

"Oh, Jesus, they're coming in." Bell's eyes darted around the room. "OK then. You just stand behind the door here." He tried to manhandle Cam behind the open door of the lounge room, and said in an urgent whisper, "I'll leave off showing them this room 'til last. When you hear us coming back into the passageway, you slip into the bedroom opposite, got me?"

Clearly a master of avoidance: court officials, ex-wives, debt-collectors, police. Cam knew the type. He removed Bell's hands from his shoulders. "That won't be necessary, sir."

"Knock knock, anyone home?" said a woman in a singsong lilt.

Bell turned to Cam in a panic.

Cam said, "Just let them in. I'll slip out by the back lane and return when they're gone. I'll start bringing the signs in. It's not a good idea to continue with this Home Open thing. You might find you have a delayed reaction to the shock."

Bell opened his mouth in protest but closed it when he caught the look on Cam's face. He shrugged his shoulders. "Whatever." He shot the cuffs of his black silk shirt, pasted the smile back on his face and moved towards the front door.

*

Toby Bell took another slug from his hip flask then offered it to Cam who shook his head.

"Of course my brother had a drinking problem you know," Bell said.

Cam wished he hadn't chosen to sit next to him on the three-seater. He shifted closer to its overstuffed arm. "When did you last see your brother?" he asked.

Bell stuck his feet out in front of him and leaned back. "Mum's funeral."

"And when was that?"

"Oh, five years ago at least. We had a bit of a falling out. I was Mum's favourite you see. What little she had she left all to me."

It was hard to imagine this man being anyone's favourite. Cam wrote himself a note to ask the Toorrup money guys to check into Bell's financial affairs.

"To be honest, Sergeant…"

Cam straightened in his seat. That phrase always activated his radar.

"He was a black sheep, an embarrassment. I didn't even know he was still in the state. Thought he would have gone to Queensland by now," Bell said.

"He was living in Glenroyd. He had part-time job at the school there."

"Well, good for him," said Bell.

"We are regarding his death as suspicious."

"You think someone might have knocked him off, then?" With a sound like an emptying water-cooler, Bell took another slug from the hip flask. "That doesn't surprise me," he said. "It was probably that old bitch he lived with, unless he did her in first, which wouldn't have surprised me either. They were about as bad as each other."

"Do you know the name of this woman?" Cam asked.

Bell looked to the ceiling and tapped on the flask with his manicured fingernails. "Um, it was a while ago. Began with G." He sounded the letter like a kindergarten teacher. His eyes rolled around the room for a moment then he snapped his fingers, "Gay, that's it. I remember thinking how inappropriate it was. Unless it was the other kind of gay. Now *that* I could imagine."

"Surname?"

"No idea." He made a humming noise and touched his hair. His fingers bounced off his head as if the tight curls were springs. "Unless they married; but probably not. He was a professional social securities con; they got more money by staying single. They were a couple but as far as the government was concerned, they just shared a house."

"Interesting," Cam said, writing in his notebook.

"Oh, it gets better."

Cam raised his eyebrows. Bell gave him a calculating look in return. "It seems to me that I'm providing you with quite a lot of useful info here," he said. "It's been bloody inconvenient for me to close up the house. God knows how many potential buyers could have been through by now. I might have sold the place twice over. I don't suppose…"

"No. You don't suppose, sir. Withholding information during a murder investigation is an offence."

"OK, OK, don't fart sparks over it. I'll co-operate. What else do you need to know?"

Cam took a deep breath. "How old was your brother?"

"Well." Bell paused and did some mental calculations. "Fifty-six or sixty-six, it depends."

"On what?"

Bell slapped his hands on his knees and laughed. "On

which birth certificate you're looking at! He told me this scheme of his years ago, and to be honest," – there it was again – "I thought of dobbing him in over it often enough. He'd a fake certificate you see, saying he was ten years younger than he actually was."

Cam could see where this was going. "Had he been claiming an invalid pension?"

"Yeah, he'd been on one for years. Sore back or some such crap."

"So he could go on receiving the invalid pension instead of the aged pension, which pays out a lot less."

"Spot on."

"You've mentioned this Gay woman. Do you know the names of any other friends or associates of your brother?"

"Never have and never want to."

"Any other family members?"

"No, just him and me."

"For the record sir, where were you last Saturday night?"

Bell did not seem surprised or offended by the question. "That depends," he smiled, giving Cam the feeling that he was in fact quite keen to divulge his whereabouts.

Jesus, here we go again. "Depends on what?" Cam asked.

"On who you ask."

"Your niece?"

Bell drew an hourglass shape in the air with his hands and winked. "You're a quick one, Sarge, I'll give you that. OK, I'll cough up. Tiffany and I went out to dinner, then I went back to her place. I didn't get home till late Sunday afternoon. My wife thinks I was in Albany. Now I hope I can count on your discretion here." He tapped the side of his nose. "You really don't need to write it down in your little book." He shifted a buttock and reached for his wallet, freezing when he saw the look on Cam's face. His voice smarted with hurt. "My card, Sergeant, I want to give you my card." He extracted a crumpled card and held it out. Cam took it as if it was smeared with something foul.

"I don't suppose you're in the market for a house, are you?" Toby Bell said.

10

The sun stabbed at Cecelia's eyes as she stepped away from the school's cool front entrance. She stopped for a moment, thinking that what she saw had to be an illusion caused by the glare. She put down her heavy book basket and rummaged in her bag for her sunglasses. But this was no trick of light. Her car door was clearly open and someone was leaning into it from the driver's side.

Some bastard was trying to steal her car!

She looked around. The school was deserted. Hers was the only car in the car park. There was no one she could call for help.

Without a second thought she ran down the path and vaulted the small wrought iron fence that bordered the ornamental front garden. She wouldn't warn him with a shout, she wanted to catch the creep red-handed.

But the thief must have heard her footsteps. He pulled his head from the car, looked at her and swore. It was then Cecelia realised he was a girl.

There was a pushbike leaning against the side of the car. The girl sprang on to it and took off. But in her panic to get away she skidded and the bike slid from under her.

Cecelia watched with a strange mixture of delight and horror as the girl shot several feet across the gravel before coming to a whimpering halt.

Cecelia wasted no time. "Serves you right," she said, as she clamped her hand around the girl's wrist and pulled her to her feet.

"Get off me." The girl tried feebly to yank herself free.

"Child abuse, child abuse!" she screamed to the deserted car park.

Cecelia gripped her wrist harder, ignoring the blood dripping from the girl's elbow on to the ground.

"There's no one to hear you; scream all you like. I'll let go when you've told me what you were doing in my car."

"That's none of your fucking business you cock-sucking – ouch!"

Cecelia took a deep breath to calm herself. "I suppose I'd better just call the police and get this over with." She moved to extract her phone from her pocket.

But the word police was like water to flame. "No police, please." The girl's aggressive tone vanished, replaced by one of rising panic. Her free hand began to twist at the hem of her top.

Cecelia regarded her coolly. The girl seemed intelligent enough to realise that aggression and bad language would get her nowhere. "Please let go of my arm, it hurts," she said.

Strange, the accent was more polished than Cecelia had expected. The girl's long tanned legs disappeared into a pair of skimpy designer shorts; her top was white and lacy with spaghetti straps. She turned her head away from Cecelia's scrutinising stare.

"I'll let go of your arm when you tell me what you were doing," Cecelia said. "You wanted the car for joy riding, I suppose?"

The girl looked over her thin shoulder to the flower power 1978 VW. Its surface topography of hills and valleys could have kept a mapmaker busy for a month. Baling twine kept the front bumper attached to the body, and the upholstery on the back seat was ripped down to the springs. Even the dreamcatcher dangling from the rear view mirror looked more like a piece of dead bird than any kind of esoteric charm. It was interesting, Cecelia reflected, to view one's own precious possessions through a stranger's eyes.

A ghost of a smile raised the side of the girl's painted lips, as if she too could see the absurdity of the accusation. As some of the tension eased, Cecelia loosened her grip, keeping her hand close, ready to clamp down again should there be a sudden bolt for freedom.

"I was just looking for… stuff," the girl said, now with more embarrassment than bravado.

"It's hardly a rich person's car. Oh, I see. You saw an old bomb covered in psychedelic flowers, and you put two and two together. Well, young lady, you've failed your maths but I hope you have learned a good lesson in life. Appearances are often deceiving. Am I making myself clear?"

The girl looked down at her feet.

"I've never seen you before. Do you live around here?"

The girl nodded, watching the blood from her grazed knee trickle down her leg and ooze between her toes.

"I'll give you a lift home. You'd better get those cuts attended to." Cecelia moved to the damaged bike, wondering how she was going to fit it into her car. When she pulled the battered bike upright there was a distinct tinkling of glass. Her disappointment escaped with a sigh when she saw what had caused it: the photo of an eagle she'd had framed for her mother's birthday, smashed on the ground. She took a breath, stooped to pick it up and prised at the broken glass to assess the damage.

"I'm sorry about the picture," the girl said.

Puzzled by the sudden sincerity, Cecelia noted the care the girl used to take the broken picture from her hand. She chewed at her bottom lip as she looked at it. "It really just needs framing again," she said.

There was something almost wistful about the way she looked at the photograph, Cecelia thought, as if the image of the wedge-tailed eagle had transposed her to another place, another time.

"What's your name?" Cecelia asked softly.

The girl traced the outline of the eagle with her finger and shook her head, as if trying to shake away the fog of a dream. She raised her eyes to Cecelia. They were electric, like the blue of spring wildflowers. "Ruby."

"Why did you want to take the picture, Ruby?" Cecelia was careful to keep an accusatory tone from her voice.

After a moment the girl said, "I don't know really, I just liked it. The way the light shines on its feathers, the arrogant look in its eye – it's beautiful. It's free. Did you take it?"

"Yes."

"How?" she whispered, as if trying not to startle the bird to flight.

"It's not as clever as it looks, I'm afraid," Cecelia said. "The bird was in a cage at the wildlife sanctuary. I scanned the original photo into my computer and erased the bars of the cage." She gave a small laugh. "See? Things are not always as they seem."

Ruby handed back the picture and hung her head. "I'll work to pay for the cost of a new frame." Cecelia saw the sincerity shining through the watery glaze of her eyes.

"We'll talk about that on the way back to your place. Are your parents home?" Cecelia asked.

"There's only Dad and he's at work." Ruby hesitated. "Are you going to tell him about this?"

"Maybe, maybe not."

Ruby swallowed. "What do you mean?"

"That depends on you. I won't tell if you repay your debt to me and stay out of any more trouble." Cecelia rubbed her chin and thought about her plans for tomorrow. "I'll collect you at nine tomorrow morning for a three hour cleaning session. That should be enough to pay for a new picture frame."

Ruby agreed to the arrangement, and they managed to get the bike on to the roof of Cecelia's car. She had no roof rack, so by the time they had finished tying it on her car looked like something Leonardo Da Vinci had dreamed up.

They stood back to survey their handiwork. Cecelia reached up and spun the wheel. "I'll have to drive really slowly – let's hope the cops don't pull us over for this." She was only a whisker away from getting a yellow sticker from Vince.

Ruby stared hard at the wheel ticking around. "They'd better not," she said with a puzzling degree of vehemence.

11

Cam spotted his old friend through the smoke haze of the pub, sitting at a small table in the furthermost corner of the room. Superintendent Rod Cummings appeared relaxed though the cigarette in his hand was testimony to the stress of the job, the Royal Commission and the bikie problems that plagued the state.

The bar room was filling up. When Cam went to the bar he noticed Ruth Tilly and Cliff Donovan sitting at a table next to Rod's. They seemed an unlikely couple, the huge working man and the voluptuous academic. Attraction of opposites, Cam supposed. Ruth must have noticed his pensive look and flashed him a smile so sweet it made his teeth ache. Cliff acknowledged Cam's presence with a nod, then turned back to Ruth who was leaning towards him across the table, enticing him with the soft valley of her cleavage. She took a cherry from her drink and impaled it on a blood red fingernail. As she put it between her teeth, she turned to Cam. The faint smile on her moistened lips, the way her eyes turned from Cliff's to his, told him the performance was for him.

Cam slid his gaze away and tried to visualise her witness statement form. In the marital status box he was sure she'd ticked the box for widow. Merry Widow, he thought, his discomfort turning to wry amusement.

Rod scooped up the beer Cam slid across the table to him. "So, is it good to be home?" he asked in his soft baritone.

"I wish we'd never left in the first place," Cam said. He sat down and took several long pulls from the glass before putting it back on the table.

"You weren't to know how things would turn out," Rod said. "How's Ruby taken the move?"

"About as bad as I expected."

"Kids are resilient, she'll adapt."

"Sure she will," Cam said, without conviction.

Their afternoon's unpacking had gone well until he'd dropped Ruby at the stockfeed shop for 'work.' She didn't seem to mind the idea of spending the afternoon there until she'd overheard him talking to Mrs Wilmot about her starting as a permanent housekeeper next week. He hadn't forbidden her to see Angelo, but he had now made it very difficult. His cowardice over the issue left him with a feeling of self-disgust which he tried to wash away with another gulp of beer. According to Mrs Wilmot, Ruby had not stayed long after he'd left; she said she had to do some emergency grocery shopping. He'd come home to a still empty fridge, a busted bike and a daughter covered in cuts and bruises and no satisfactory explanation.

"We're meeting with the principal of Glenroyd Ladies' College on Friday," Cam said, "She starts next week. She doesn't want to go, says it's all high walls and lesbians."

Rod laugh lifted ten years from his face. "Wasn't that Elizabeth's school?"

"Yes, that's where we met. Elizabeth would have loved Ruby to go to GLC and it's about the only thing me and my in-laws have ever agreed on. It's also closer to me. She'll be safer there."

"You know Saint Bart's was turned into an Ag college?" Rod asked.

Cam glanced towards Ruth and Cliff. The action now seemed to be taking place beneath the table. Cliff must have hit his mark for she jumped and let out one of her trademark machine gun laughs. Cam still had no recollection of ever meeting the woman before Monday, and it bothered him.

Rod gave him a nudge. "Hey, Earth to Cam." Cam gave his friend a rueful grin, climbed to his feet and collected two more beers from the bar.

"Ruby's got herself a boyfriend already," he said as he sat down again. He took a sip of beer and watched the reaction.

Rod gave a snort. "Shit, that's fast work. Do you approve?"

"I don't approve of her going out behind my back. He's a roughneck and he's too old for her."

"Did you ever think what Elizabeth's parents might've said about you?" Rod asked with a humorous gleam in his eye. "St Bart's was hardly the right side of the tracks."

Cam ignored the remark. "I've checked him out; no record, comes from an Italian family of market gardeners who live south of here. She meets him in the park during his lunch break. He's an apprentice mechanic."

Rod smiled. "You've done your homework."

"I was a detective, remember?"

"Yes, and I wish you still were. Just say the word and I'll have a position for you with Toorrup detectives in the blink of an eye."

Cam stifled a prickle of irritation. In recent months they had gone over this subject more often than he cared to remember. "Look, I'm really grateful for the string-pulling you did to get me here," he said, "but this is all I want. I'm through with high profile jobs that get my name in the papers. I just want to stick it out here, keep Ruby safe and help her pass her exams. When she's done, I'll probably get out of the service altogether, maybe buy a farm."

"You, leave The Job? That'll be the day." Rod looked

thoughtful for a moment, as if carefully debating the wording of his next question. "Have you had any more of those letters?"

"No, none since we moved, thank Christ."

Cam's grip tightened around the beer glass. He'd been arresting officer in a large cannabis haul resulting in charges laid against some senior members of the Razorbacks motorcycle club. Anonymous letters started arriving soon after the arrest, threatening his life if he testified against them. He testified regardless, and a bomb that was meant for him killed his wife and son. The bikies were jailed over the drugs, but there wasn't enough evidence to link them to the bombing. When their bikie sergeant-at-arms died in jail, the letters began again. This time they were about vengeance. This time they were threatening his daughter.

"Have you told Ruby about them?" Rod asked.

"Her nightmares over the fire have only just stopped. I'm not going to subject her to that kind of fear again, even if I do have to wrap her in cotton wool and have her hate me for it." He released his grip on his glass, picked up a beermat and began to turn it around in his fingers. His laugh was bitter. "And you wonder why I won't join your detectives."

"Now you're home, you feel safe?"

Cam's gaze wandered to the bar. "The Razorbacks are an eastern states club; both of us are safer here. Though I'm not getting complacent - some of the clubs communicate."

He looked into the swelling crowd of men and spotted a familiar form pushing his way through the jammed up bodies at the bar. Vince exchanged slurred greetings with the other drinkers and slapped his money down. He was wearing shorts, working boots and a garish Hawaiian shirt about two sizes too small. His hairy white gut protruded through the straining buttons.

"Look what the cat dragged in," Cam said.

Rod leaned back in his chair and followed Cam's gaze. "Who's that?" He lit another cigarette and peered across the flame at the jostling figure.

"My Senior Constable, Vince Petrowski. You must have come across him. His record has more scratches on it than my first copy of *Dark Side of the Moon*."

"Oh, so that's what he looks like." Rod nodded, glad to be able to put a face to the file.

Neither man spoke for a while. They watched Vince barge through the throng, a dripping jug of beer in his meaty paw. He swayed on his feet as he glanced around the room looking for an empty table. Seeing none, he pulled up a chair and sat uninvited at the table occupied by Ruth and Cliff. The couple did not seem to appreciate the intrusion.

Rod raised his eyebrows in query and Cam gave him a brief rundown on Cliff. Rod eyed the mechanic. "I hope Vince doesn't think he's going to pick a fight with him – he looks like he eats nails for breakfast." He nodded towards the big man's feet. "Check out the Ugg boots. Remember how we all used to wear them?"

"You had a mullet too."

Cam lunged towards his friend's bald patch and Rod pulled away, laughing.

Cam had another look at Cliff. He was wearing a sleeveless denim jacket with no shirt and his bulging biceps were smudged with faded tattoos.

"Ruth Tilly's the woman who called the fire in," he told Rod.

"The science teacher?"

Cam nodded. "Vince interviewed her."

"An attractive woman. No wonder Cliff looks so pissed

at Vince." Rod raised an ironic eyebrow. "Maybe he's just going over her statement?"

Cam smiled despite the uneasy feeling that crept over him. Cliff's expression told him Vince was walking through a minefield.

Still keeping one eye on the next table, Cam said, "I'd like to up the Bell case from suspicious death to murder, but I can't be certain until the autopsy." He gave Rod a pointed stare. "I was surprised the Toorrup detectives never showed."

Rod cleared his throat, running a hand across his smooth pate. "I was getting to that. Brass wants you to handle it. Our Toorrup dees are strapped over this bikie thing and we're short-staffed because of the Royal Commission. We can't spare anyone. Besides, you have more experience than the lot of them rolled into one."

"Despite the fact I'm new to the state?"

Rod nodded. Cam paused to think. Bypassing the chain of command would cut through much of the red tape and give him a certain amount of cherished independence.

"What about my team?" he asked.

"You have a team."

Cam laughed. "You mean my Glenroyd mob? Shit, Rod, do you know anything about them? Three rookies with no more than about six years between them. Hell, the girl's only three months out of the Academy."

"You do have Vince."

"Oh sure. I have Vince."

Rod placed his finger on his lip and shushed, tilting his head towards the next table.

Cam lowered his voice a notch. "The lack of experience in the others makes them a liability. Vince's years of experience make him even more of one. I've never known anyone so good at abusing the system."

"Take it or leave it."

"You haven't exactly given me a choice." Cam's scowl turned into a smile. "Yeah, of course I'll take it."

They clinked beer glasses to seal the arrangement.

"I found something at the fire site," Cam said. "A piece of material that turned out to be the elasticised waistband of the guy's shorts. The rest of the clothing was burned away to nothing, but his overhanging belly protected this small strip. When the body was shifted, the waistband was blown by the easterly into the parrot bush. That's where I found it. I could still smell the fuel, which the lab has now confirmed. Someone tried to burn the body, Rod. Lucky for us they didn't do a very good job of it."

Rod gazed thoughtfully into his beer. "Murder? Sounds like you might be right."

Cam continued, "One of the funny things is the conflicting reports of the witnesses about the colour of the smoke. Apparently the fire was reported soon after it started. A fuel fire would still be smoky black at that stage, but two of the witnesses said it was grey, like from an ordinary bushfire. As no one was supposed to know it was a fuel fire, it's as if they were trying to put us off track."

"That or they have bloody lousy memories. I'd rather have material evidence than eye-witness reports any day." Rod paused for a sip of beer. "The body was shifted, you say?"

"Yeah, by Constable Care over there." Cam nodded towards Vince. "Of course he denies it, that's what irks me the most. I have less trouble with screw-ups than denials."

The voices at the next table reached fever pitch. Cam casually climbed to his feet, put his hands on the table and leaned in. He kept his voice low. "I can't prove that Vince moved the body, it's just his word against the woman who found it." He shrugged. "I suppose it doesn't make much difference to the case. The rag would've been discovered at the autopsy anyway."

"But it could have been the end of Vince's career; one last act of incompetence and we could finally have got rid of him. It was just lucky that you found the rag. Without it we could still be viewing this as an accidental death."

"I'm going back to the school tomorrow," Cam said. "Apparently Bell's last job was groundsman there. Now there's an odd couple for you. The husband's a—"

There was a roar of anger and a sudden crash. Cam whirled round to find Cliff and Ruth pinned against the wall by the flipped table, drenched with a mixture of beer and broken glass.

He was over in an instant, and put Vince in an arm-lock while Rod lifted the table off the helpless couple.

The whole pub stared on in shocked silence.

With placating hand gestures Rod addressed the crowd. "It's OK, folks, no big deal. It's all been dealt with—"

Before he could finish, Ruth leapt at Vince. Her fingernails found their mark, digging deeply into his cheeks. As Vince screamed Cam swung him around, using his own body to shield Vince from her fury. But something had been unleashed that she seemed unable to control. Her fingernails continued on their course, biting into Cam's back with brush strokes of fire.

Ruth drew back in shock, breathing heavily through white, dilated nostrils. She stared, horrified at the tears she'd made in Cam's light summer shirt and at the red stains blotting through it.

She passed a hand over her face. "I'm sorry, Cam. I didn't mean to hurt you. It was what he said to Cliff. Then when he flipped the table, I suppose I flipped too."

She fixed Vince with a cold hard stare. He reciprocated with a stream of obscenities. The red stripes down his cheek glistened like war paint.

"Sort this out, will you, Rod? Vince and I are going for a little chat outside," Cam said, pushing Vince towards the door.

When they reached the veranda, Cam allowed his grip to slacken on Vince's arm. Vince shrugged away, attempting a clumsy swing at his senior officer, but Cam caught him by the wrist and twisted his arm behind his back with a force that made Vince gasp.

"You just don't learn, do you, Vince?" Cam slammed the side of Vince's face into the wall, making his fat lips pucker into an obscene kiss. "You haven't got a scooter to ride on, mate," Cam said, leaning in so close he could smell the whisky and beer of Vince's breath. "That was quite a good performance you put on for Superintendent Cummings in there; I'd say suspension pending investigation at the very least."

Vince's face contorted further as he let go a strangled sob. To Cam's surprise, tears started tracking down the bloodied cheek. Cam's hand began to ache and he released his grip, sensing the danger was over. Vince turned and leaned against the wall, then slid to the floor like a melting blob of lard. He took a swipe at the snot that dribbled from his nose. Cam had to turn away for a moment.

In a voice thick with mucus, Vince said, "This job is my life."

"You should have thought about that five complaints ago."

"It was that icy bitch, she provoked me."

"Does Leanne provoke you too, Vince? And what about that bloke who 'tripped' in the cells last year, did he provoke you?"

"You can't prove a thing."

"Not yet. Just as I can't prove your incompetence at the crime scene the other day. I know you moved the body; you compromised the crime scene and then didn't have the balls to own up to it. There's sure to be an enquiry now, and every shonky thing you've done will be exposed. This assault in the pub is the icing on the cake and will give credibility to all the other accusations building up against you."

Vince drew up his knees, flopped his head on to his arms and began to sob.

Seeing Vince broken didn't give Cam any sense of satisfaction. Though he'd be glad to have the man out of the service, his revulsion was tempered by pity as he struggled through the front door of Vince's house to the main bedroom then lowered him on to the mattress on the floor. Cam was about to leave when Vince let out a strangled plea for coffee. Good idea, Cam thought. Maybe over a coffee he'd find out the truth behind the fight. There was something about it that had left him feeling uneasy, as if there was a lot more going on than mere sexual rivalry.

He picked his way out of the bedroom, stepping over the piles of unwashed clothes, holding his breath against the musky smell that clung to his face like a wet flannel.

And he'd thought his place lacked that homey feel.

Vince was divorced with no children, but had somehow managed to appropriate the Senior Sergeant's living accommodation. Cam was glad he hadn't pushed the point and claimed it for himself. The brick and tile house might have been a superior dwelling to his own fibro cottage, but the station cleaning budget would never have stretched far enough to make it fit for human habitation.

Cam went into the kitchen to search for a kettle, a sticky resistance pulling at the soles of his shoes as he walked across the lino. Mounds of dirty dishes coated with tiny black ants snaked around the bench tops; blowflies paddled through pools of goo; splattered sauces decorated the walls like a Pro Hart painting.

He found the cleanest saucepan from the top of a dirty pile and gave it a rinse before putting some water on the stove to boil. The only coffee he could find was in a lidless jar, shared by a shiny black cockroach.

He opened the fridge and recoiled from the stench of rotting meat. When he slammed the door shut, the vibrations tipped over a stack of containers on top of the fridge, including a carton of ant dust. Noxious powder rained down upon him, adding a frosting of white to the sticky lino floor.

"Shit, shit, shit." He grabbed a cloth from the sink and began cleaning up. As he wiped the fridge top, the cloth pushed against a cardboard file and a storm of documents fluttered down to join the mess.

With a curse of frustration, Cam squatted to retrieve what he expected to be a stash of unpaid bills. It was then he noticed the official police stationery. He stopped for a moment, frowned; flicked it over to read the front of the file. It was marked in large red letters: CASE UNSOLVED. The date fell within the timeframe when Vince was acting Sergeant.

Since his arrival Cam had painstakingly gone through every unsolved case in Glenroyd over the last year, but this was the first he knew about any hijacked tanker. What the hell was Vince covering up? Cam let out a tired sigh: more headaches, more paperwork and more incriminating evidence against the man.

Rumbling snores from the bedroom told him Vince was long past the coffee stage. Cam took the water off the stove, tossed it into the sink and threw the pot back on to the pile of dishes on the draining board.

With the file tucked under his arm, he sidestepped the upturned garbage can and walked into the lounge. A milk crate sat in front of an old brown TV. Cam guessed that the bulk of the furniture had been sold to cover Vince's notorious gambling habits, or taken by his fleeing wife.

The only other articles in the room were an ironing board and an iron. Several clean, well-pressed uniforms hung from the doorframe on coat hangers. They seemed incongruous amid the filth and chaos of the house. Cam raked a hand through his hair and glanced at the file in his hand.

"Shit, Vince" he said out loud. "What the hell have you gone and done now?"

12

Cam parked the police ute in the school car park, but remained seated, trying to work out the best approach to Jeffrey and Anne Smithson. He was unsure if Smithson's previously prickly attitude to the police was due to Vince's insensitive handling of the initial interview, or just the man's natural personality shining through. He suspected a combination of both and opted for the kid glove approach; the last thing he needed at this early stage of the investigation was a cry for a lawyer.

He took in the view of the school before him. The brick paved path from the car park led to the administration block, a rectangular two-storey red brick building with white framed Lego-like windows. At right angles on either side ran two identical buildings, one a classroom block, the other the boarding wing. The latter had been closed for many years. Unlike its newly renovated sisters, it was still covered with the ivy that once threatened to strangle all three buildings.

The ute radio crackled. Derek, on duty at the station, was calling Peter to check out some reported stock theft at a sheep property ninety kilometres north of them. That meant Pete would be away for most of the day. Damn: with Vince now suspended, they were more undermanned than ever.

Leanne shifted in the passenger seat. "Shouldn't we just go in and get this over with?"

"I want to check out the back first," Cam said.

87

They crunched across the gravel car park, heading towards the back of the main school buildings. The morning was still and hot, with all the promise of a scorching day ahead. After only a few paces, Cam's uniform shirt was stuck to his back, the scratches stinging. Ruby had been asleep by the time he'd got home last night and he'd been unable to reach them with the disinfectant. This morning he'd left her moaning in bed, stiff and sore from her bike accident, not wishing to upstage her with his own injuries. She'd said she was too sore to go to the stock feeder's this morning, but would try her best to hobble over in the afternoon.

Cam's thoughts turned back to the school. Ancillary buildings were grouped behind the main block, connected to each other by covered walkways. The indoor swimming pool and gym complex opened up to newly paved netball courts, which in turn led to the oval. Cam narrowed his eyes against the glare, just able to make out a restored federation style house shimmering on the far side of the green expanse. He guessed this was the principal's residence. With shady verandas and turned wooden posts, it was an ideal vantage point from which to sit and sip tea while watching the inter-school hockey matches. Beyond the house swept the open farmland of the extensive school property.

Leanne took in the vista with wide eyes and an open mouth. "Wow, I'd love to have gone to a school like this. It used to take me over two hours to bus in to Toorrup High."

"You think it looks grand now, you should have seen it twenty-five years ago. The girls were able to keep horses then. Let me see, over there I think." Cam pointed to a group of dilapidated sheds in the distance. "It doesn't look like they're doing those up, though they seem to be doing a pretty good job elsewhere." He swivelled around in a full circle, whistling air through his teeth as he looked. "These renovations must have cost a bomb."

He switched his gaze back to the school buildings and the mess the builders had left behind. Though this phase of the renovations was complete, someone still had a lot of clearing up to do before the start of the school term. The scaffolding had been dismantled and stacked in a pile. Paint splatters and dollops of concrete patterned the ground and the air hung with the fresh smell of cement.

Three large skips filled with building debris stood near the back wall of the classroom block. He ambled towards them, handing his sunglasses to Leanne. With the help of an overturned bucket he heaved himself up into the closest skip.

"What are you looking for, Sarge?" Leanne shaded her eyes and watched as he carefully balanced around the edge of the skip. "Be careful, there might be glass," she added.

"There is. Lots of it."

There were also rolls of old carpet, bricks, lumps of plaster, empty paint buckets and the rotting remains of someone's lunch. He stepped across to the next skip and crunched across the dry junk until his foot slammed through some plywood, sinking shin deep into refuse. He latched on to a piece of old skirting board sticking up from the pile; it was all that stopped him from falling face down into the muck.

He heard laughter from below.

"I'll remember you when it's time to check the septics, Leanne," he called down. He stooped to sift through some of the surface rubbish, finding pretty much what he'd expect: breathing masks, sheets of old wallpaper, plastic containers.

"What are you looking for exactly?" Leanne said, batting at the flies circling her head.

"I'll know when I find it. You can learn a lot about people from what they throw out."

He stepped on to the third bin and made a similar inspection. A used coffee filter had stuck on to his leg. He pulled it off, looked at it for a moment then threw it back on to the pile.

"Well?" she said as Cam jumped down from the skip.

"Well what?"

"Well, did you learn anything?"

Cam wrinkled his nose and looked down at his soiled uniform. "I think I learned that it's not a good idea to go fossicking through someone's garbage just before an interview." He dusted plaster powder from his pants. "Come on. Let's go see Mr and Mrs Smithson."

Cam addressed the seated couple in Anne Smithson's office. "The body belonged to a man named Herbert Bell. I believe he was once employed as a groundsman at the school."

Anne Smithson's eyes widened, and an ivory hand moved to her mouth as if she were trying to wipe away a crumb without being noticed. Mr Smithson shifted in his chair and cleared his throat.

"That's terrible. We must send our condolences to his family," he said. "How…" His voice came out as a squeak, forcing him to clear his throat again. "How do you think it happened?"

"Until I can prove otherwise, I'm regarding his death as suspicious."

Mrs Smithson took a breath. "Constable Petrowski said it was an accident."

"Such deaths are always considered suspicious until proved otherwise." Cam gave the couple a few seconds to absorb the news and leaned over to Leanne to see her notebook. "Bell worked for you for about six months – is that correct, Mrs Smithson?"

She nodded. "Part time, only a few hours a week."

"I understand you have no official wages record."

Mrs Smithson opened her mouth to speak, but her husband interjected.

"I take care of the monies," he said.

Cam switched his gaze to him. "You paid him cash?"

"Yes, chicken feed, the amount wasn't even declarable."

Cam made placating gestures in response to the man's defensive tone. "That's OK, I'm not here to question you about your taxes, it was just something I needed to double check. Mr Bell was involved in a little social welfare fraud of his own." Cam turned to Mrs Smithson. "When did he last work at the school?"

She raised her eyes to the ceiling for a moment before looking at her husband. "December?" she asked him, shrugging.

He nodded and smoothed his moustache. "Yes, December I think."

Mrs Smithson put on large tortoise-shell framed glasses and flicked through her desk diary. "December the fifteenth to be precise."

Leanne wrote the date in her notebook.

"What were his reasons for leaving, Mrs Smithson?" Cam asked.

Mrs Smithson glanced at her husband. Again he answered for her. "Unfortunately, I had to dismiss him."

"Why?"

"I found him in the potting shed, drunk, and not for the

first time. He became abusive when I started to reprimand him. I had no choice but to dismiss him there and then."

Cam looked at the couple; neither returned his gaze. Mrs Smithson was twisting the pearls at her neck, Mr Smithson tapping his foot. This was getting interesting. After a while Mr Smithson sighed, crossed his legs and rested his hands in his lap. Cam noticed how the knuckles on his right hand were swollen, like a fighter's. He took his notebook from his breast pocket and rested it on his leg. "How did he react when you dismissed him, Mr Smithson?"

Smithson's eyes met his wife's before returning to Cam. "He swore at me."

Cam began to write a nursery rhyme on his notebook. Always be writing something down, he had learned. It gets people agitated. Makes them more likely to say what they'd rather keep to themselves.

"And then what?" he said.

"He turned his back on me and left the shed."

Jack and Jill went up the hill…

"He didn't attack you?"

"No, I would have reported him if he had. Exactly where are you going with this, Sergeant?"

"Mr Bell recently lost some teeth, that's how he was identified," Cam said. "His dentist said he'd an appointment for a denture fitting two weeks ago. Apparently he told the dentist that someone knocked his teeth out in a fight."

Smithson stitched his lips into a thin jagged line and folded his arms. "That's nothing to do with me," he said.

To fetch a pail of water…

Cam's pen hovered above the page. He glanced over at Leanne; her eyebrows were raised, and she leaned forward in her chair to study Mr Smithson as if he was an unusual insect. He'd have to have a word with her about that.

Suspects often gave themselves away with body language, but cops did too. Cam had always likened the questioning of a suspect to an intricate game of poker. You had to know when to hold 'em, know when to show 'em. She was showing too much interest now.

Anne Smithson had turned a lighter shade of pale.

"It would've been quite a punch to get those teeth out. I imagine the person who hit him must have suffered some kind of knuckle damage," Cam continued in his well-practised, neutral tone.

"I know nothing about any fight." Jeffrey's lips pursed. He placed his left hand over his right.

Jack fell down and broke his crown…

Cam leaned over to scratch an itch on his leg, straightened to gaze around the luxurious office. He had never understood the attraction of antiques. Elizabeth's parents had a house full of them and they'd always made him feel uneasy. He was not comfortable with the idea of collecting the possessions of long dead strangers.

"Had you seen or heard from Herbert Bell since he stopped working for you?" he asked.

Husband and wife shook their heads.

"Do you have any idea where he went from here?"

Mrs Smithson explained she'd heard Bell had moved to be caretaker at a neighbouring property. Leanne's pen made scratching noises as she wrote down the address.

Time for an awkward silence, Cam thought, let Jeffrey stew for a bit. The mantle clock ticked on as he took in the degrees and diplomas covering almost every inch of wall space. Between the two of them, the Smithsons seemed to have enough qualifications to staff a university. The largest of these framed documents caught his attention; he narrowed his eyes, attempting to decipher the gothic writing.

The clock bonged out the hour. Its deep vibrations shuddered through the oriental carpet under their feet. Finally Jeffrey said, "Will that be all, Sergeant?"

Cam abruptly switched his gaze from the diplomas back to Smithson. "Where were you on Saturday evening between six pm and midnight?"

Jeffrey stiffened at the unexpected question. "Are you asking me for an alibi?"

"Just answer the question please, sir." Cam's resolve to tread softly began to falter. These two were hiding something and he intended to find out what it was.

"This is preposterous! You surely don't think…"

"It's a routine question, sir. It should be fairly simple to answer."

Anne cleared her throat, meeting Jeffrey's eyes with an unspoken question. He stared at her for a moment then nodded.

Back to her diary, she found the relevant page and began to read softly.

"At 6 pm we had an emergency committee meeting with the Glenroyd progress association. After that we went out to dinner with the Hamptons. On the way home we discovered our neighbours' sheep had wandered on to the road. We tried to call our neighbours on the mobile phone but found we had no range, so we drove over to their house and together rounded the sheep up. When we were finished, they asked us in for a coffee. We didn't get home until almost two."

Up until now it had been Jeffrey jumping in to answer Cam's questions. This response of Anne's sounded like a well-rehearsed reading.

And Jill came tumbling after…

Leanne handed Mrs Smithson a piece of paper and asked for the names and contact numbers of the people they'd associated with that evening.

The clock ticked on while she wrote. Cam's gaze once more roved the room. Finally he said, "I see you were a civil engineer, Mr Smithson. Why did you switch to teaching?"

"I can't see how this has anything to do with the death of Mr Bell," Smithson said.

Anne Smithson, though, seemed to brighten at the change of topic. She ignored the hostility in her husband's voice and said, "Because I asked him to. My husband is a mathematical genius, Sergeant. He was once CEO of Super Tech. I imagine you've heard of the company?"

She wrote down the last name with a flourish of relief and handed the list to Leanne. Cam nodded. Even he had heard of the high-profile engineering company.

"I'd been unable to find a suitable head of the maths department and he agreed to the job. Jeffrey is also a highly skilled construction engineer. It is he who designed and supervised all the renovations." She waved an arm around the lavish office, like a queen in her kingdom. "I would never have been able to do all this without the support of my husband."

Smithson's chest swelled but he only allowed the most humble of smiles to grace his face. Cam wondered about the circumstances behind Smithson quitting his engineering company: shonky trading, a collapsed building? Why would a man throw in a job that probably paid him hundreds of thousands of dollars a year to become a schoolteacher?

"I must compliment you both on the job you have done, though as a future school parent, I only hope the fees aren't going to be reflecting these massive improvements." He smiled, drawing a diagonal line through the writing on his note pad. All Smithson could see was the decisive hand movement. Cam noticed the little man's frown, and the way he touched the knot of his tie.

But Mrs Smithson took the remark with its intended humour. "You don't have to worry about that, Sergeant, just thank the generosity of a wealthy old girl, Jane Featherstone. She died childless and bequeathed a considerable part of her fortune to the school. We plan to name the boarding house after her." She turned to her husband. "It won't be completed for a while though, will it Jeffrey?"

"I hope to get it started by next summer. It'll be stage four of the building project and will mean that we can become a boarding school again. We've had many inquiries from overseas, Asian families mainly. I expect to have doubled the student population within two years."

Cam smiled as he got up to leave. "I'm looking forward to watching it grow," he said.

Cam and Leanne walked back to the car park. "Do you really think that little runt had something to do with Bell's death, Sarge?" Leanne asked

"I don't know if he killed him, but I think he hit him. He didn't get those swollen knuckles from arthritis, that's for sure."

Cam settled into his seat, holding up his right fist to Leanne. Despite the scarring from the burns, it was easy to see how his middle knuckle was twice the size of the others. "Hit someone that hard and your knuckles are never quite the same again."

"Ouch."

"You should have seen the other guy."

"Sure, Sarge." Leanne rolled her eyes, very like Ruby did at one of his dad jokes.

"That little bloke must have been pretty riled to hit out like that, and knock Bell's teeth out to boot," he mused as he started the engine.

"I'll check through the names on this list." Leanne indicated her notebook. "Other than that there's not much we can do until the autopsy."

"Don't you worry, there's plenty to do. You can start by running a background check on Jeffrey Smithson. Go to Super Tech and find out when and why he left."

Leanne let out a low moan.

"Or maybe you'd rather do traffic?"

"Super Tech, I'm on it."

"I want to visit the neighbour Bell was caretaker for. You'd better contact him and arrange a meeting."

Leanne flicked the page of her notebook. "Mr Lou Blayney."

"Yeah, that's him. And Toby Bell said the last time he saw his brother he was living with a woman. There's a chance she might still be around."

"Or else another one."

"Quite." Cam gave Leanne a quick glance. "You can come with me when it's time to break the news. She'd probably handle it better from another female. Softer touch and all that."

"Sarge, that is so sexist," said Leanne, stretching out the *o* in so.

Cam smiled. "It's the truth." He looked at his watch. "Shit. At this rate I'm going to be late for the autopsy in Toorrup. It would've been a good experience for you, but I'm afraid you'll have to stay here."

Leanne smiled. "Bummer," she said.

13

Rod beckoned Cam over to a bench by the wall and they sat down under a garish abstract painting. Cam had been in enough hospitals over the last few years not only to recognise their universal smell and sounds but also the consistent theme of the art works: mashed body parts.

Rod's hound-dog face creased into a smile. "I suppose you've heard the news?" he said.

Cam raised an eyebrow. "No. What?"

"One of the office bearers of Satan's Sons has been admitted to ICU with head injuries."

Cam gave Rod a puzzled look. "Why the smug satisfaction? Doesn't that just mean more trouble?"

"It wasn't even from a fight."

"An MVA, then?"

"Kind of," said Rod, obviously enjoying the guessing game.

"The suspense is killing me."

"OK. This old bloke was riding along the main shopping drag on his brand new custom-made chopper, thinking he was looking pretty cool. He was so busy admiring himself in one of the shop windows he didn't notice that the semi in front of him had stopped at the lights and –" Rod smacked his hands together. "Thwack."

Their laughter was cut short by the appearance of three men in the lobby. Clad in denim and leather, two had shaved heads and bristling beards, obviously having taken great pains to conform to their non-conformity. The third man was shorter, dressed more conservatively than the others and had a luxurious mane of white hair. He saw the seated cops and swaggered over, extending his hand to Rod with a twisted worm of a smile.

"Well, g'day, Superintendent, how're they hangin'?"

Rod kept his hand to himself and remained seated. "Fine until you came in, Matthews," he said. Cam looked from his friend to the man, intrigued by the hostility between them.

Matthews put out his hands, palms up, turning to his companions. "The Superintendent doesn't seem to be in the mood for a chat."

"Nah, and I thought cops were always supposed to be courteous and friendly to the general public. This one treats us like we're common criminals." The speaker grinned and nudged his unkempt mate in the ribs.

"It's just a matter of time, Phlegm," Rod said to the man. "Now get about your business. My cholera inoculation's out of date."

Good one, Rod, Cam thought, trying to suppress a smile.

Phlegm bristled and stepped forward. Cam's hand edged toward his gun; not that he was expecting to use it, more to prevent the wired-up bikie from grabbing it. Matthews gave Phlegm's arm a warning squeeze and directed his companions towards the hospital lifts. Cam caught sight of their colours as they turned and felt a prickling sensation run up the back of his neck.

As the lift doors were closing Matthews called out, "Give my love to Jenny and the boys, Superintendent," and blew Rod a kiss.

Rod remained seated, ignoring him, though his clenched hands were a giveaway. He took a cigarette out of the packet he'd been clutching and flicked it into his mouth. Cam pointed out the No Smoking sign, wagging his finger.

"Shit," Rod said, putting the smokes back in his pocket. He sat back down on the bench and breathed out heavily.

Cam gave his friend a moment to compose himself, then said, "I'm waiting."

Rod passed his hand across his forehead and rubbed his eyes. "The one with the white hair is Eric Matthews. You've probably heard him referred to as Chainsaw."

Cam exhaled through his teeth. "The president of Satan's Sons?"

"Yeah. He's a slippery bastard, getting more powerful by the day. The SS have a monopoly on all aspects of organised crime in the area now that they've all but eliminated their rivals."

"The Dugites. I read about the drive-by."

"Yeah, that was a couple of months ago. Two Dugites killed and I haven't been able to pin anything on Chainsaw or his thugs, though I know they were behind it."

Cam felt a cold patch growing in his chest. "Have they been threatening you and your family?"

Rod shook his head. "It's not the same as in your case, Cam. I've got nothing on them that would stand up in court, so there's nothing to threaten me over. Chainsaw just wants me to know that when that day arrives, I'm in the cross-hairs."

"Then you just make damn sure that you get the necessary protection."

Rod paused and then said softly, "It didn't do Elizabeth and Joe much good, did it?"

Cam said nothing. The threatening letters had never mentioned his family. It was assumed he was the target. It was he who had the armed escort wherever he went, while Elizabeth and Joe were home, alone and vulnerable.

Rod seemed to sense the direction of Cam's thoughts.

"I don't want this little incident to concern you; there's no bikie worries on your patch, yet."

But the backtracking didn't work. Cam could hear the uncertainty in Rod's voice and found himself holding his breath.

Rod continued, "Though this does lead me to my next point. While I was waiting around for you, quite a few guys like that have been coming in to the hospital to check up on their mate in the ICU."

"Any trouble?"

"One of the nurses complained of harassment, but there's been no further trouble since I posted a couple of my guys in the ICU waiting room. But sitting here, waiting for you, I recognised quite a few familiar faces, plus one new face who came waltzing in with a group of bikers like they were bosom buddies." Rod paused. "It was your mate, Cliff Donovan."

Cam let out his breath. "I ran a check on him. The kid Angelo was right. He's never been a club member, not even an associate, though he has been inside. He was convicted for assault during a pub brawl ten years ago and served six months. He's been squeaky clean since then." Cam shrugged his shoulders, trying to dismiss his friend's suspicions. "He sometimes works on their bikes so I guess that's a good enough reason to know them. In fact, there was a bike registered to an Eric Matthews parked outside the workshop the other day. Apparently it was in for a service."

"I'm not saying he's guilty by association. You just need to be aware that one of the outstanding citizens of Glenroyd has bikie connections. Be extra careful."

Cam sighed. "There isn't a place in Australia where someone doesn't have a relative or a mate who's a bikie." He looked at his watch and grimaced. "I'm going to be in the Doc's bad books. Better get to that autopsy."

"Wait a tick. Have you had a chance to talk to Vince about that file you found over at his place?"

"No, but I've re-opened the case and I've assigned Pete Dowel to it."

"Dowel?"

"One of my young constables. A bright lad, though not bright enough to see what was going on under his nose when Vince was acting sergeant. I'm going to pay Vince a visit on my way home this arvo if I have time."

"Do that. Internal Affairs will be coming to see you next week."

Cam nodded and made a move towards the lifts.

"Hang on. There's something else." Rod hesitated as if unsure how to phrase his next sentence. Cam knew what was coming and felt himself tense.

"You don't have to attend the autopsy. I can stand in for you."

Cam chose to focus on an old lady shuffling across the lobby with a walking frame. She was a lot easier on the eye than Rod's suffocating look of sympathy. He had attended many autopsies in his career, but none since the fire. He'd been regarding this one as a test. Would he pass or fail? That was something he had to find out.

"Thanks, Rod, I'll be fine." He clapped his friend on the back. "I'll catch you later." He began to move away but Rod reached for his arm, stopping him mid-stride.

"You don't even know where you're going," Rod said.

"The basement." Cam paused for a beat. "Aren't they always in the basement?"

"Well, yes, but don't you want me to introduce you to Dr McManus?"

Cam punched the down button of the lift. "We met at

the crime scene." He watched the lights flicker as the lift descended.

"Oh yes, of course," Rod nodded. As Cam stepped into the lift, he said,

"Jenny wants to catch up. She's worried about you. Why don't you call in for a drink on your way home tonight?"

Cam raised his hand to acknowledge the invitation, though they both knew he wouldn't show.

14

"Wheel the body in, Igor," McManus said to a man wearing white overalls and gumboots.

Cam gave a start, but made a conscious effort to keep his face blank. The wheels of the gurney rumbled across the tiled floor as the morgue attendant pushed the body to the autopsy table.

McManus caught Cam's eye and gave him a wink. The pathologist was covered from head to toe in surgical greens. The only parts of him that showed were his eyes and a pair of the most magnificent eyebrows Cam had ever seen. They twisted and curled across his brow like two great hairy caterpillars, expressing the thoughts and feelings of their owner more effectively than words ever could. Now they were raised, questioning Cam's reaction to the little joke. Cam attempted a smile, knowing that it would not be reflected in his eyes, sure the caterpillars had not missed the significance of his strained demeanour. He was not only out of practice with morgue humour; he had lost his taste for it too.

McManus took the shoulders and the attendant the legs. With a, "One, two, three, ally oop," the body was transferred on to the table. The attendant wheeled the gurney back into the corridor and the double doors flapped twice.

Then there was silence.

The pathologist cleared his throat. The phlegmy noise bounced off the tiled walls and stainless steel fittings. He clapped his latex-covered hands and rubbed them together with ghoulish enthusiasm.

"Now then, Sergeant. Exactly what is it we are trying to ascertain here?"

"I have evidence to suggest that this body was deliberately burned. Preliminary examination at the crime scene suggests burning post mortem. Deliberate burning could be an indication that the victim was murdered."

"But first we have to rule out natural causes," McManus interrupted. "Maybe he died at home and the grieving loved one decided to eliminate cremation costs?" The caterpillars arched their backs, the brown eyes underneath sparkled.

That was a possibility. Cam thought of the 'grieving loved one,' the brother, Toby. He was probably as good at rorting the system as his brother ever had been. Maybe it was a genetic tendency.

McManus turned to the notes he'd spread out on a nearby table. "Body number 0018/2005. External examination revealed the burned body of an elderly male." He looked up. "How old's this guy supposed to be?"

"Officially fifty-seven, unofficially sixty-seven."

McManus seemed nonplussed. "Oh, one of those." He nodded and returned to the notes. "Well-nourished, weight approximately one hundred and three kilograms, with allowance for fluid loss, height one hundred and eighty centimetres. Extensive charring of skin save for a small strip along left side of the body, presumed to be the side on which he was lying when burned."

Cam nodded.

"Eyeballs missing, presumed from crow pick."

"Crow pick?" Cam interrupted.

"If the rest of him is anything to go on, the eyeballs should have still been in situ. The heat would have solidified the protein so they would have been cooked, like hard-boiled eggs, if you will, but still present." McManus peered at Cam. The caterpillars arched their backs.

Cam remained impassive. This was all part of the test. Be distant. Compartmentalise.

The pathologist continued, "The sockets are still slightly moist. If the eyes were missing before burning, the sockets would have been much more charred. I think you can rule out the notion that our possible killer took them for trophies.

"No sign of external injury or ligature marks, though given the burns at this stage it is hard to ascertain this from a mere external examination." He pointed to the X-rays on the screen. "No recent evidence of broken bones, though the left humerus shows signs of an old fracture."

He walked to the screen and pointed out something on the illuminated bone. It looked just like any of the other bones to Cam, but he nodded all the same.

"Any fibres, Doc?"

"Aha, I was getting to that." McManus was back at the table, shuffling through his notes. He read, "Traces of fibre evident around victim's mid section." He explained what Cam had already guessed. "The gut prevented the waist area from getting too badly burned."

Cam found himself holding his breath.

McManus continued. "The fibres matched the rag found at the scene."

Cam let his breath out, the glow of a minor victory making him smile beneath the mask. "Yes. That's what I suspected. Now I can prove that the body was deliberately burned."

"There's something else here for you, Sergeant, another puzzle for you to solve. I found traces of sheep's wool between several of the toes of the right foot. Now how do you think that would that have got there?"

"Shoes?"

"No evidence of footwear."

Cam rubbed his chin. "Could the body have been wrapped in a wool blanket?" he asked.

"To the naked eye, the wool looked untreated, but it will have to go to the city lab for further analysis. That could take a few days I'm afraid."

"There were sheep at the crime site. They'd recently been shorn but there were clumps of wool lying around and clinging to the bushes."

"I suggest you go back and get some then. You might want to send it to the lab so they can compare it to the fibres I found."

Cam agreed, but he knew what was coming next and felt his body tense. He took a deep breath as McManus walked over to the body. Cam expected him to jerk back the cover like an artist revealing a prize-winning sculpture, and was surprised at the reverential way the pathologist folded back the sheet. He realised then it was only ever he who'd been the butt of the pathologist's jokes.

But McManus's respectful manner did little to soften the blow of the body's revelation. Cam suppressed a gasp. It was so much more horrible out of context. The blackened figure looked like a mummy in its sarcophagus. No longer pugilistic, the arms lay at its side, meaning that someone had had to cut the contracting tendons or break the arms for the X-rays. Cam offered a prayer of thanks that he'd not had to assist in that procedure.

The bony, eyeless dome rested on an unforgiving pillow of steel positioned over an in-built trough at the head of the table. There was a hose to wash away the waste, and near this, still at the head end, a set of scales, very like the ones used by greengrocers. On another table, the tools of the trade were laid out in orderly rows, an incongruous mixture of carpentry and surgeon's instruments.

And the smell.

Cam took a deep breath of Vicks from his mask, seeing for a moment the head of his wife, then that of his son, lying over the trough. He flashed to a plastic box full of ash. The crematorium had only finished what the murderer had started.

He closed his eyes, trying to shut away the image. *You're weak; you're failing,* a voice inside him cried as the hammer of defeat pounded at his temples. Don't give in, another voice chided. His hand moved up his neck to his ear.

"Sergeant, are you OK? You're looking a bit peaky."

Cam drew in a ragged breath and nodded. "Go ahead, let's get this over with."

Despite the coolness of the room he could feel the sweat trickling down his back and under his arms. Mustering all his willpower he forced himself to concentrate on what was going on in front of him.

McManus adjusted a mike, talking in a smooth bass as he worked.

First the Y incision, across the chest from shoulder to shoulder, then down the abdomen to the pubic bone. The scalpel crackled through the outer crust of burned flesh; the incision turned quite pink as it penetrated the inner depths.

"A pretty pathetic attempt at cremation, eh, Sergeant?" the pathologist said.

"Yeah, I think the bushfire brigade was more efficient than our guy had hoped."

McManus reached into the chest cavity, cut through the connecting tissue and removed the heart.

"The heart has retained its shape. It is a deep red colour, on the way to dehydration." McManus spoke into the mike. Then as an aside to Cam he said, "I'm not sure if I can get any blood samples from this but I'll give it a go." He weighed the heart before placing it on the dissecting table and managed to aspirate a small amount of fluid for the lab.

"Does the heart look normal to you, Doc?" asked Cam.

McManus sliced it into a cross section. "Taking dehydration into account, the size and weight appear about normal. Possibly slightly overdeveloped cardiac muscle that could indicate an early congestive cardiac condition, but early days. His arteries are within the range of normal for a man of his age."

"So we can rule out heart attack?"

"Unless histology shows otherwise, it's unlikely to have been the cause of death."

McManus removed the liver, weighed it and put it on the dissecting table. He muttered something unintelligible into his tape recorder. The caterpillars wriggled with interest.

Cam asked him to translate.

"I said, scar tissue indicative of cirrhosis of the liver."

"Would that have killed him?"

"Not yet, but would have if it remained untreated. Coupled with the weakened heart, he would have been dead within a few years. It's well on the way to being nicely pickled though."

He carved off a piece of liver and placed it into a specimen jar.

Next came the lungs. McManus sliced through the connecting tissues, vessels and nerves. Extracted from the pleural cavity, they squelched like gumboots from a mud hole. Cam felt the room began to spin. He grabbed the side of the autopsy table and had to fight the urge to run from the room. He tried to concentrate on his breathing. Get a grip, Fraser, do your job. He was behaving like a rookie. He knew it, and he hated it.

McManus balanced the lungs in both hands and frowned. "These seem unusually heavy."

His words cut into Cam's thoughts like a life-saving foghorn. He watched the pathologist place the lungs on the scales then followed the beckoning finger to the recorded weight.

"I'm sure you are familiar with a normal set of lungs, Sergeant."

Cam grunted an affirmative.

"Now, these are interesting. They are considerably heavier than normal. Proportionally they have a higher fluid content than the other organs, despite being exposed to the same heat intensity. See the lobes?" He pointed with the tip of his scalpel. "These are more dilated than I would expect. Quite swollen, as a matter of fact."

"So what does that mean?"

"Pulmonary oedema – swelling caused by water retention."

The pathologist moved the lungs to the dissecting table. He carefully sliced through one of the lobes then aspirated some fluid.

"Of course there are several physical maladies that could cause a lung reaction such as this, congestive cardiac failure for one; though I suspect it would be too early for symptoms such as this to show. But look here, look at the colour of this fluid."

He held up the specimen vial.

"It's a lot lighter than the other aspirations," Cam observed.

"It's been diluted, that's why. This man breathed in a

lungful of water."

Cam felt his pulse rate quicken. "He drowned then?"

"Certainly looks like it." The pathologist shook his head from side to side. "A horrible way to go." He probed the other lung. "No evidence of smoke or ash. You are correct in your assumption that this man was burned post mortem. Hang on now, what's this?" He bent closer to inspect the mass of spongy tissue, startling Cam with a sudden yell of, "Eureka!"

Cam looked at the thing dangling from McManus's forceps and drew in a sharp breath of recognition.

"Hey," he said, "it's a piece of weed."

"Caught in the right descending bronchus, a common area of entrapment. But is it weed or grass?"

"No, the leaf is too broad for grass. May I?" Cam relieved McManus of the forceps and examined the ribbon of green under a magnifying glass. After a moment's study he said, "It's dam weed, Doc, I'd know it anywhere."

They both looked up and exchanged expressions of triumph.

"There's your cause of death then, Sergeant: fresh water drowning. I'll send it and the other samples off to the lab, but I'd bet my last dollar, that's it. I'd better continue with the rest for the sake of routine. I suppose you want the stomach contents analysed too?"

"His last meal might tell us something."

"Yes. I imagine it'll look a bit like an underdone haggis." He gave Cam a wink, and the caterpillars wriggled.

15

Her hands were shaking so much she was having difficulty doing up the buckles of her overalls. They weren't real overalls as in work clobber of course; her Gramma had bought them for her in Sydney from a trendy little boutique on The Rocks. She'd never worn them before; they made her look too young. Now Ruby was glad she hadn't chucked them out, as they were perfect house-cleaning clothes. She giggled aloud. Jesus, who'd have thought Ruby Fraser would go voluntarily to some nut-ball teacher's house to clean?

She wasn't sure if she was shaking from nerves or excitement and concluded it must be a mixture of both. She liked the weirdo teacher and she was sorry for what she had done. But it wasn't as if she'd gone to the school intending to commit a crime in the first place. She'd only ridden to the school to get away from the dotty old biddy at the stock feeder's, and see what kind of prison her dad was going to lock her in next. Angelo had told her about the hippy English teacher and when she saw the car she couldn't resist the chance to see if there was mull stashed in the glove box. She'd wanted it for Angelo – she didn't even like the stuff much. The only time she'd ever smoked it she'd coughed herself silly and made like an idiot in front of her friends.

She'd only done it to get back at her Dad.

Shit, but she hated this waiting; Cecelia had said she'd be coming at nine and it was already ten past.

Ruby sat on her bed to tie her sneakers, then moved to

the window in the lounge to gaze down the street and listen for Cecelia's car. Her nerves were stretched taut; she had to do something to pass the time or she'd snap. There was a mountain of washing up at the sink and she made a move toward it, but stopped just in time.

She poured herself some milk from the fridge, drank it then left the scummy glass on top of the pile.

At last she heard the car chugging outside. She opened the front door to give Cecelia a cautious wave. The woman beckoned her over and indicated for her to climb in.

"Is your dad at work, Ruby?" Cecelia asked as they took off from the curb with a screech. Ruby nodded, suddenly feeling shy and nervous. She began to play with the buckles of her overalls; it seemed no amount of fiddling would get them untwisted.

She wasn't ready for Cecelia's next question.

"What does he do?"

Ruby's head snapped up from her task.

"Your dad," Cecelia qualified.

Ruby ran her tongue around her lower lip, knowing that whatever lie she told would be as transparent as water to this woman.

Cecelia took her eyes off the road for a moment and smiled. "It's none of my business, I'm sorry."

"That's OK. I don't mind." Ruby took a deep breath. It felt funny to have an adult apologise, especially as she was the one supposed to be doing all the grovelling.

"He works for the government."

She'd have to tell Cecelia sooner or later. She was after all enrolled at the school where Cecelia worked. She'd tell her when she'd done the cleaning, when she wasn't feeling so nervous. It was awful to have a dad as a cop. Even before the fire it had been hard. Friends never wanted to stay for dinner despite the fact he was rarely home. And she'd often noticed how they'd hesitate before telling her things, worried that she'd squeal to him.

But she never squealed.

Sometimes she thought her secrets were the only things she had left.

"The government?" Cecelia repeated with raised eyebrows, probably realising he could be anything from a postman to a bus driver. "Did you tell him anything at all about yesterday?"

"I told him I'd fallen off my bike and a lady took me home."

"What did he say?"

Ruby bent her elbow and regarded the surgical dressing her father had so carefully applied to it. "I don't think he heard me. He was in a hurry to get to the pub."

Cecelia Bowman lived in an old single storey cottage. Hammered into the ground by time, the house stood firm and squat as if weighed down by its expansive umbrella of corrugated tin roof. Colourful hanging baskets dangled on chains from the eaves and swayed in the breeze like rainbow pendulums. Cecelia and Ruby parked in the driveway. A neighbour weeding her front garden looked up and gave them both a wave. Ruby waved back, forgetting for a moment she didn't belong here.

Cecelia's bloodhound, Prudence, sat waiting for her mistress beside a blood red standard rose. Her tail flicked when she saw Cecelia and she bounded towards them as they passed through the gate of the small, fenced garden, almost knocking her mistress over with her enthusiasm. The dog accepted Ruby after a cautious sniff, leaving a thick string of drool on her overalls. But Ruby's squeal of revulsion soon became a laugh when she saw the warmth of Cecelia's smile and the humour in her eyes.

The dog followed them into the cool of the old house. Cecelia told her what needed doing, showed her the cleaning equipment, then disappeared into her study to sew. She was making pouches out of blue and pink baby flannel for the orphan joeys at the wildlife sanctuary, she'd explained. Soon the whirr of the sewing machine was the only indication that Ruby was not alone in the house.

Ruby enjoyed the cleaning more than she thought. It was as if she'd been given a licence to snoop: to find out everything she could about this woman. She started in the kitchen, wiping the surfaces and cleaning the sink.

Bunches of dried herbs dangled from the ceiling and left a fragrant dust of seeds and crushed leaves on the bench tops. She wiped them away first, noticing how they filled the kitchen with their scent, evoking images of delicious foods like roast turkey with stuffing, pizza, pasta and fresh garden salads. One set of shelves was stacked high with recipe books, and on the other neat rows of sparkling jars contained ingredients with unpronounceable names.

The fridge was covered in pieces of paper curling over a colourful assortment of fridge magnets. She removed them so she could give the fridge surface a good wipe. Most were photocopies of children's poems: Jane Davis year 8c, Claire McDonald, 8a, Jackie Godet 8c: all written in loopy childish writing. One of them was dedicated to 'Miss Bowman, best English teacher ever.' There was also a hand-drawn picture of the slobbering bloodhound, Prudence, sitting next to the standard rose. This must mean that some other girl or girls had been to Cecelia's house and met her dog. Small greasy fingerprints dotted the fridge door, adding further evidence to her theory.

Ruby wiped them away as quickly as she wiped away the fleeting notion that she was somehow special to Cecelia.

Prudence followed her wherever she went, her toenails clicking on the polished wood floors. The dog's sad expression never changed, even when Ruby fed her a homemade biscuit from a tin she'd found in the kitchen cupboard. Ruby laughed aloud when the dog wagged the tip of her tail but continued to look miserable. She bent down and pulled at the dog's jowls.

"Come on, rubber face, things can't be that bad. You just have to make the best of it."

Shit: "You have to make the best of it." Wasn't that what her dad was always saying? Shaking her head in disgust, she went to clean the other rooms.

Framed photos covered almost every spare inch of wall space in the hall. Ruby took each one off the wall to give it a thorough clean, spending the longest time on the wild animal photos. She liked the echidna the best. The photo had been taken in the early evening and it was standing on its shadow looking as if it couldn't decide between worms or ants for dinner. She smiled and carefully put the photo back on the wall. She wanted to spend longer looking at the other animal photos, but time was running out and she still had the vacuuming to do.

On the way home they called in at Flo's for a milkshake. Flo's was an old fashioned diner and the only good thing Glenroyd had going for it. It was cool in a retro way, with vinyl records hanging on strings from the ceiling, pictures of old rock 'n roll stars on the walls and a jukebox in the corner that could have been a Star Trek prop. The owner, whose name really was Flo, had hair as tall as a chimney and always smelt of smoke. Ruby could imagine her stooped over the pots in the kitchen, the cigarette in her mouth sprinkling the secret ingredient that people always said was the *je ne sais quoi* of her cooking. She made good milkshakes though, and Cecelia ordered them both a chocolate.

The diner was deserted except for a figure at the corner table. Ruby saw it was Leanne before she could think up an excuse to duck back to the car.

Crap crappity crap. This was not what she needed right now. She'd wanted to tell Cecelia about her father in her own time, one on one, but now she was sprung. Cecelia would think she was hiding things from her; any remaining hope she'd had of this woman liking her was lost.

Leanne gave her away, just as she'd feared.

"Hey, Cecelia," the policewoman called out. "Come and have a bite of this mud cake, it's nearly as good as yours." She saw Ruby and did a double take. "Well, hello, Ruby. Come and sit down." She patted the plastic chair next to hers.

Ruby hadn't known Leanne long, but liked her despite the fact that she worked for the enemy. She forced out a smile and drew up the chair.

Cecelia waved a hand between the two of them in surprise. "So how do you two know each other?"

She probably now thinks I know Leanne professionally, Ruby thought. Caught me in the middle of some kind of heinous crime like tying a firecracker to the tail of a cat. Ruby rested her chin on her hand and sighed. She was beginning to know what it felt like to be a hardened criminal.

Leanne said, "Boss's daughter – you know, Sergeant Fraser. You met him when you found the body."

Cecelia raised her eyebrows and opened her mouth to

speak. Ruby jumped in first. "I was going to tell you, Cecelia."

"I reckon she's embarrassed her dad's a cop," Leanne said with an understanding that surprised Ruby.

Cecelia laughed. "Really, Ruby, it's no big deal." She turned to Leanne. "I came across Ruby after she fell off her bike, took her home. We've been friends since." She waved a finger at Ruby. "Of course, the eyes. You have eyes just like him. I thought they looked familiar."

Ruby winced. She hated her eyes; she'd always wished they'd been like her mother's, large and brown.

Leanne changed the subject, thank God. "Have you tried some of Cecelia's mud cake, Ruby? I tell you, it's to die for." She took a bite of the cake in front of her, wrinkled her nose and whispered out of Flo's earshot, "It's much better than this shit."

Ruby laughed. Now she felt like one of the girls.

"I thought cops only ate doughnuts," Cecelia said.

Leanne's voice was muffled through a mouthful of mud cake. "American cops eat doughnuts, Aussie cops eat mud cake. It's in the International Code of Conduct."

The women seemed to be good friends despite being so different, and soon Leanne was offering an explanation. "I failed English and had to repeat to get into the police service. Cecelia tutored me in exchange for housework, that's when I first sampled her cooking. I tell you, it was almost worth failing for."

Cecelia gave Ruby a sideways look. "I'll do anything to get out of housework."

"Suits me," Ruby said with a secretive smile.

"How are you going with the murder investigation?" Cecelia asked.

"My end's going nowhere fast. Seems everyone in this

town knew of Herbert Bell but no one can tell me anything about him. I just popped in here for a sugar fix before pounding the beat again. We're all hoping the autopsy will show up something. Sarge is there now; I don't envy him that job."

"He doesn't care," Ruby said without thinking. Both the women looked at her as if she'd just declared she didn't believe in God.

Cecelia said, "He probably does, Ruby. It just wouldn't be professional if he showed it."

Ruby shrugged and began piercing the froth of her milkshake with her straw. Leanne broke the awkward silence. "So are you looking forward to your new school, Ruby?"

Shit, here we go again. She turned to Cecelia. "I'm going to your school. I was going to tell you that too, I just didn't, I didn't…"

Cecelia gently squeezed her arm. "Ruby, it doesn't matter. I'm sure you would have told me sooner or later." She raised her hands to her mouth. "Of course, you're the Fraser I'm seeing tomorrow. You and your dad are coming in for interview. Oh shit." She bit her lip and looked at Leanne. "Ruth and I gave him a hard time in the lab the other day. I'm glad I've been warned. I'll need a good think about how to approach this."

Leanne gave a hearty laugh. "Oh yes, I heard all about that – jeez, you and Ruth, drinking in the lab, what a couple of dags." She grinned, running her finger around the plate to scrape up the last of the icing.

Cecelia coloured.

Leanne shrugged. "It's OK. Just act like it never happened."

The older woman nodded but still looked worried.

Ruby giggled and took a sip of milkshake to stop herself from laughing any more. Her dad had told her about coming across the drunken teachers in the science lab, though of course she'd pretended she wasn't listening.

Leanne licked her finger clean and waggled it at the two of them. "So, Sarge doesn't know that you two know each other?" she asked.

Cecelia shook her head. "Do you want him to know, Ruby?"

"Maybe. Some of it," Ruby said, looking down at her glass, the straw still between her lips. Cecelia would know which parts to leave out.

Leanne glanced at her watch and stood to leave. "Duty calls. What are you doing this arvo, Cecelia?"

"I've made some more sleeping bags for the joeys," Cecelia said. "I'm going to drop them off after I've driven Ruby home." She turned to Ruby. "Maybe you'd like to come with me to the wildlife sanctuary sometime?"

Ruby's heart skipped a beat. She beamed back at the older woman.

"I think you've got your answer," Leanne said, laughing.

16

THURSDAY

Cam's previous impression of Anne Smithson had been of a quiet composed woman, more than happy to shelter under the protective wing of her overbearing husband. But away from him now, and in her own comfort zone, she was articulate and talkative, barely drawing breath as she showed him and Ruby around the school.

She seemed to have a warm nature, and showed genuine interest in Ruby's welfare. It was reassuring to know that despite the tension of the last few days, Anne Smithson was treating him like any other new school parent.

The school tour had come to an end and it was time to complete the business end of Ruby's enrolment. Ruby lagged further and further behind as they walked the long corridor to the registrar's office.

Out of earshot, Mrs Smithson took the opportunity to whisper, "I read Ruby's last school report and I want to point out that she will be starting Glenroyd Ladies' College with a clean slate. If it helps, I do have an understanding of what you have both been through."

Cam was touched by the sincerity of her tone. She took a business card from her jacket pocket and handed it to him. "This is the name and phone number of the school counsellor. She's very good." She hesitated. "It often helps to talk about these things."

Cam glanced down at the card then back to the principal. Was she speaking from experience? Did he see hidden pain in the depths of those grey eyes, or was it purely an empathic response to his own?

They stopped at the door marked Registrar and waited for Ruby to catch up. He became aware of a strange pulsing sound coming from behind the closed door: the squawk of an exotic bird, monkeys, waterfalls, and rhythmic drums. Surely these soothing rainforest sounds would have drowned out Mrs Smithson's gentle knock? Cam had the sudden urge to laugh, imagining the New Age schoolmarm behind the door, resplendent in kaftan and beads or maybe a silk turban with a long feather. GLC had changed more than he'd imagined.

Elizabeth, if you could only see us now.

Ruby finally sloped over to join them. Whatever she thought of the music she gave no indication of it. He thought he might make her giggle if he could only catch her eye, but her arms were crossed, her face its usual mask of sullen indifference. She'd been the same for most of the tour until they'd reached the gym and started to search the honour boards for Elizabeth's name. When they'd found it her face had brightened, but only for a moment. Now the mask was back on and Cam didn't feel like laughing any more. He wondered if girls were ever turned down on the strength of these interviews.

Mrs Smithson glanced at her watch, then back to the closed door with a look of veiled annoyance. "She can be a bit unorthodox at times, but she has a wonderful way with the girls," she said by way of an apology.

She knocked louder and the music abruptly stopped.

Cam knew he would be coming across Cecelia Bowman at some time or another at the commencement of the school term, but he hadn't considered that it might be now. What goes around comes around, Ms Bowman, he thought, with a small amount of anticipatory pleasure.

But her demeanour was calm and she met his eyes with a pleasant smile. He soon realised she was not going to give him the satisfaction of showing any embarrassment over the incident in the science lab.

"Mr Fraser, let me introduce you to Cecelia Bowman. She's not our usual registrar but is filling in for Mrs Godfrey who's still on holiday. Miss Bowman is head of English and also our vice principal."

Cecelia smiled again, shaking his hand.

Mrs Smithson continued, "Oh of course, you've met, at the…" And then a strange thing happened. She began to bite at her bottom lip, as if fighting to retain her composure, as if the mere memory of the crime scene was a Pavlovian trigger for some kind of an anxiety attack.

"At the crime scene, yes," said Cam.

Mrs Smithson said, "I really should go now. I'm supposed to be meeting Jeffrey."

Cecelia put a reassuring hand on the small of her back. "It's all right Anne," she said, guiding her a small way down the corridor. "I can take care of the rest."

Mrs Smithson gave Cecelia a weak smile of gratitude before excusing herself. Cam watched her as she walked away, concerned at the sudden change in her demeanour. Even Ruby had lost some of her self-absorption and looked confused. When their eyes met, he gave her a small shrug.

Cecelia invited them in to her bright airy office and sat down with them on chairs arranged in a semi-circle in front of her desk. They discussed subject choices, books and uniforms. Ruby's brief sojourn in the world around her had ended and she resumed her expression of boredom, fixing her gaze upon the view from the window.

Cam tried to involve Ruby in the conversation with

frequent questions and jocular comments. But when he fished for enthusiasm she responded with a shrug; when he tried for a smile she screwed up her exposed toes as if enduring tremendous physical pain.

It was all becoming very wearing.

With an increasing feeling of unease Cam became aware that Cecelia Bowman was regarding him with the same kind of relaxed detachment with which he'd viewed her at the crime scene. Now it was her turn to assess and observe and the feeling made him uncomfortable. The look she was giving him was the kind you gave someone who was endeavouring to complete an impossible task; ten out of ten for effort but better luck next time.

She handed him a pile of forms to fill out, watching as he struggled with the pen. Constricting scar tissue impeded the flexibility of his fingers and the pen kept slipping from his grasp. He gave up, and passed the forms to Ruby. A strange half-smile lingered on his daughter's lips as she wrote.

In the ensuing silence his gaze fell to the tramline creases of his best pants, then the soap scum on his otherwise clean dark blue shirt. Licking his finger he began to worry at a white patch on the sleeve. When he looked up Cecelia was watching him.

"You caught me," he said with a self-conscious smile.

She smiled back, "I have that problem all the time. That's why I wear lighter colours."

She was wearing an elegant pale blue skirt suit, a style that Elizabeth would have loved, though it did not seem as comfortable on Cecelia as it would have been on his wife. The shoulders looked lopsided and the skirt was slightly twisted as if she was happier in jeans and cheesecloth. Maybe even a kaftan. He remembered the music and smiled to himself. Elizabeth had only ever listened to classical.

Finished with the forms, Ruby was looking at the framed animal photographs on the walls. For the first time today he caught the flicker of interest in her eyes.

Cecelia noticed also. "Are you interested in photography, Ruby?" she asked, giving his daughter a look he couldn't fathom.

"I like the animals," Ruby said with her own secretive smile. She got up from her chair to examine one of the pictures, tapping at the glass with a long painted fingernail. "What's that?"

"Funny looking, isn't it?" replied Cecelia, standing up to join her. "It's a very young joey. When I rescued it from its dead mother it was smaller than the palm of my hand, its skin was almost transparent. We kept it in a heated esky in the science lab. Every week I took a photo of it and the science teacher tabled its development with the girls. No one thought it would live, but it did, and I let it go back into the wild last year."

"Cool," Ruby said.

Cecelia glanced at Cam and smiled.

"What about that one?" Ruby pointed to another picture.

"That's a puggle. A baby echidna."

"They lay eggs and suckle their young like platypus," Ruby said to Cam as if dipping into a well of knowledge he could never hope to attain.

"That one there – " Cecelia pointed to the neighbouring photo – "is my pride and joy, photographically speaking."

Cam got up from his chair to join them. He saw an elegant, streamlined creature standing on a rock, silhouetted by moonlight, staring across a silver dam.

"A fox?" he asked, incredulous. "They're usually shot on

sight around here."

"Dad!" said Ruby. She shook her head and raised her eyes at Cecelia to indicate he was beyond hope.

"It may be just a fox to you, Mr Fraser, but it took a whole week to get that photo. I had to build a hide and stake the dam out every evening until I caught him coming down to drink. I think every mozzie in the district came down to join in the bloodfest."

She laughed. He liked the sound of her laughter; it had an infectious quality to which even Ruby had warmed.

Ruby forgave his insensitive remark about the fox, gracing him with a condescending smile. "That's what the National Geographic photographers do," she said. "Sometimes they have to hide out for weeks just to get the right shots."

He raised his eyebrows and nodded to her superior wisdom.

Cecelia addressed them both. "Would you like to come and have a look at the photographic lab? Ruby might like to choose photography as one of her electives."

Ruby's face brightened. Cam felt his spirits lift.

"Before we go, do you have any more administrative questions?" Cecelia asked.

Cam shook his head. Ruby looked at him for a moment, then at Cecelia with a mischievous gleam to her eye. Cam knew the look and prepared to make a snappy retort.

"I'm going to be getting a belly button ring. What's the policy on body piercing here?"

17

The room was dark and stifling. Cecelia flicked on the air conditioning unit and pulled up the heavy black blinds, letting the sunlight stream in. "It doesn't take much to convert this into a dark room big enough to hold twenty working students," she explained. "It's only temporary. Jeffrey's planning on building a permanent photo lab soon."

Cam blinked in the harsh light. At the end of the room was a trough-like sink, above this shelves of photographic chemicals. With contagious enthusiasm Cecelia explained the functions of the various pieces of photographic equipment leaning against the walls or sitting upon the shelves. Soon she and Ruby were poring over proofs and photo albums, talking about light and shadows, shutter speeds and animal hides.

Cam sank with relief into an old armchair and closed his eyes, only half listening to their conversation. The rise and fall of emotions over the last few days had taken their toll; he had been bombarded with so much information his brain could barely process it, and exhaustion was setting in. And now with the murder at the school, his two main areas of concern were overlapping in the middle like a Venn diagram.

The autopsy had shown that Herbert Bell had died from fresh water drowning. Cam had delegated Constable Pete Dowel to coordinate a search of local waterways for evidence of the primary crime scene. Given the number of dams, ponds and creeks in the area, not to mention the river that flowed through town, this was no small task. Even with the help of the local State Emergency Service, they would need a small miracle to find the right body of water. And if they did happen to hit upon it, the chances of finding any useful evidence in the deteriorating outdoor crime scene were slim. But the search still had to be attempted. Cam had suggested they searched in an outward radius from the patch of school bushland where the body was discovered.

He had no doubt there was a connection between the school and the death of Herbert Bell. Whether it was circumstantial or more sinister remained to be seen. Conflict of interest! a voice cried out in his head. Should he really be sending Ruby to this school? Yes, another voice answered. This is what Elizabeth would have wanted. Even her parents had agreed with the idea, and that was no mean feat. He was not often on the same wavelength as his in-laws.

And besides, the Herbert Bell case had nothing to do with Ruby.

He shook his head, trying to dislodge the splinter of paranoia that had settled there. Glancing at his watch he realised it was time to return to the station and tackle the mountain of paperwork Vince's suspension had generated. And there were still uniforms and books to buy.

He extracted his protesting daughter from the mess of proofs she and Cecelia had strewn over one of the work tables, and when Cecelia gave Ruby an open invitation to her house to view some more of her work, she accepted with alacrity. Cam was pleased; maybe such a diversion would take her mind off that Angelo boy.

He reached into his back pocket for his wallet, handed Ruby some notes and told her to go and find the uniform shop. He was expecting a sour look of protest and was surprised when she jumped off the step and began skipping down the path.

"Try and be quick about it, love, I've got to get back to work," he called out. Eyeing her skimpy outfit he added, "And don't forget you're still growing. Make sure you get clothes that'll give you plenty of room."

Ruby pretended she hadn't heard and disappeared around the corner. Cecelia looked at him and smiled. "You've no need to worry about that, Mr Fraser," she said.

"Cam. Please."

"Cam. Mrs Farrel at the uniform shop won't let her get away with anything that's too small."

"That's a relief. Everything she wears seems too small to me."

Cecelia laughed. "It's the fashion, Cam. All the girls dress like that these days, it's not just Ruby."

Cam hesitated, half in and half out of the demountable, unsure whether he should catch up with Ruby or leave her to her own devices. Cecelia solved the dilemma by asking him back inside and putting the kettle on. After making the coffee she cleared some junk off a couple of chairs and they sat down.

"I didn't want to mention this in front of Ruby, but I should have those photos ready for you tonight. I would have done them sooner, but it's been a hectic couple of days." She took a sip of her coffee and leaned back in her chair.

Cam tilted his head and raised an eyebrow.

"You know," she smiled. "The photos I took of the dead body." She took in his puzzled look. "Didn't I tell you? I thought I had. What with one thing and another…"

"You took photos?" Now he'd heard everything.

"You're looking at me as if I'm some kind of ghoul," she said with a laugh. "I worked for a while as a photographic journalist – we're trained to shoot first, ask questions later. Photographers have to be opportunistic, you never know what you might miss if you hesitate." She frowned when he blew out his cheeks. "I thought you'd be pleased."

He slapped his hands on his thighs, lost for words. "I am pleased," he said. "I just wish you'd told me earlier."

"I thought you had police photographers for that. I didn't think mine would make much difference."

"We do, but when they took their photos, the body was not in its original position."

"Of course, that's right; mine show him on his side. Well, at least they'll prove to you that I was telling the truth."

Cam smiled, and not only because this woman seemed to have that effect on him; the photos would be invaluable to the case he was building against Vince. "I didn't doubt you for a moment," he said.

"So – tonight, is that OK?"

"Tonight will be fine." He took a sip of his coffee. It was hot and strong, just how he liked it.

"Would you mind if I asked you a few more questions, Ms Bowman?"

"Not at all, as long as you call me Cecelia. What cap are you putting on, cop or father?"

"Cop." Cam chuckled. "It fits better."

His gaze drifted around the photo lab. Something had caught his eye earlier and he wanted clarification. He stood up and moved towards a glass-doored cabinet, squinting at the photos pegged across a line of string, like clothes on a washing line.

"That's the drying cabinet," Cecelia said.

Cam nodded and gestured to the glass door. "Do you mind if I take a closer look?"

"Be my guest." She got up to join him.

He reached inside the cabinet and removed a photograph depicting the newly renovated area he and Leanne had explored the previous morning.

"Those on the line are the before and during photos. I'm going to take the afters when the mess is cleared away, then have them published in the school magazine," Cecelia said.

The skips were in the same place, though not as full as when he'd been rummaging around in them, and the scaffolding was still standing. Cam put on his reading glasses and tried to make out a pile of indistinct shapes on the ground near the back door. "What's all that?" he said careful not to touch beyond the edge of the wet photo.

She took the photo from him and stepped closer to look at it, bending her head. Her neck was arched and graceful as a willow branch. He didn't mean to breathe in just then, but he did, catching her scent: fresh, like rainwater on rose petals.

"I'm not sure, but I think they're boxes of supplies for the labs. The plastic containers are for chemicals. I have similar chemicals in here." His interest seemed to puzzle her. "Do you want to have a look at them?"

He looked at the photo for a moment longer and shook his head, partly to signify no thank you, partly to shake away a longing he did not wish to remember. She clipped the picture back on to the line in the drying cabinet and they returned to their coffee.

Cam took a sip. "How well did you know Mr Bell?" he asked.

"Hardly at all. Lucky for me our paths didn't cross much."

"You didn't like him, then?"

"I have to know someone well to be able to come to a conclusion like that and I had no desire to even get that far. He was a sleazy old drunk who worked in the school grounds. Why Jeffrey even hired him in the first place beats me. I suppose he was cheap."

"You say sleazy. Can you add to that?"

"It used to worry me how he looked at the girls. Luckily they all got the vibes and kept their distance. He never did them any harm – in fact I think they'll miss him, he was good entertainment value and provided them with a constant source of gossip. They used to call him fruit and veg. You see he wore these really short shorts and when…" She decided to go no further and hid her smile with her hand.

Cam nodded, battling to keep a straight face. "What do you know about the circumstances of his sacking?"

Cecelia put her cup down and looked at Cam for a moment. The smile that had been playing at the corners of her mouth turned into a broad grin.

"I thought you knew all about that. Jeffrey said it was like the Spanish Inquisition in Anne's office yesterday."

"It's always handy having more than one version." Cam hesitated, wondering about her loyalties to Jeffrey Smithson. "Do you think Mr Smithson could have hit Mr Bell?"

"I don't have to think, Cam, I know he did. I was there. Why the puzzled look – I thought you knew that? I don't blame him really. I would have done the same."

"You would have hit him because he was drunk?"

Cecelia let go with a full laugh. "Oh my goodness, is that what Jeffrey told you? Poor Jeffrey, he would have been mortified by all this."

"I'm lost. Enlighten me."

Cecelia took a deep breath. "Jeffrey hit Bell in the potting shed because he was caught stealing Anne's underwear from her washing line. I know this because I'm the one who caught him, red-handed. I reported it to Anne and she got quite upset. Then I told Jeffrey and we confronted Bell in the shed together. Jeffrey was so mad I thought he was going to kill him." Her hands flew to her mouth when she realised what she had said. "Oh my God."

18

"Let's go pick him up Smithson now," Leanne said, leaning a buttock against the side of Cam's desk, as casual as if she were in a school common room.

Cam shook his head. "Slow is fast, remember, Leanne? It's early days yet. We'd never be able to build a case against him with what we have. He's not going anywhere. He hit him, but it doesn't mean he killed him."

"You said Mrs Smithson acted all weird when she introduced you to Cecelia. Maybe that's why. Maybe it suddenly dawned on her that Cecelia might tell you what really happened in that potting shed."

Cam nodded, thinking. "I think you might have something there. We know Smithson hit Bell, but it's the only fact we have. That he murdered Bell is pure speculation."

He took off his glasses and rocked back in his chair. Absently scratching at an itch on his leg, he started to think out loud. "Another fact we have is that Bell was drowned; we know that from the autopsy. After he was drowned his body was moved to the bush and set alight. He was drowned at around 11 pm on the Sunday night, but his body wasn't torched until the next morning."

"Maybe it was dumped in the bush straight after the drowning? The killer had second thoughts about just leaving it like that and returned the next day with a can of petrol to burn it."

Cam nodded. Arching the fingers of his hands together he tapped his fingernails against his teeth. "Alternatively the body could have been stored somewhere overnight.

It could have been brought to the bush the next morning, then set alight. There were wool fibres between the toes, so maybe he was wrapped in a wool blanket."

"But the pathologist thought the fibres looked untreated."

Cam sighed, wondering when the lab results would come through.

Leanne said, "It's hard to imagine Smithson capable of drowning anyone. Motive or not, he would never have been able to hold Bell's head under water on his own – unless Mrs Smithson helped, of course."

Cam raised a dubious eyebrow. "Hardly. Anyway, they can both account for their whereabouts on the night he was killed, and for Sunday's bushfire."

Leanne began to kick her foot against his desk, as if the rhythm helped her thought processes. After a while she said, "I spoke to Super Tech in Adelaide. Apparently when Smithson left he was still their golden boy. He wasn't sacked, just resigned for personal reasons."

"Did he get much money out of the company?"

"He sold his shares, also got a big pay out – a couple of mill in all. Apparently he put a lot of his own money into remodelling the school."

Cam tapped his pen against his teeth. "That's a lot, but still not enough to cover all those renovations. Enough for a good loan though. Stop kicking my desk. You're giving me a headache."

"Sorry, Sarge." She paused to get her thoughts back on track. "Yeah, but some of the money came from that old biddy's endowment. Remember, they were going to name the new boarding house after her?"

"Yes, I remember, Jane Featherstone." Cam said. "It might be worth looking into the affairs of this generous benefactor."

"She used to live in a big old mansion down Tannery Road. She was supposed to be the richest person in the district. Her father made his money in mining after the First World War."

Cam thought about this while Leanne continued. "Anyway, Smithson sold all his shares in the company then moved to WA when his wife got the Principal's position at GLC. He spent a year getting his Dip Ed, though as far as I can tell hasn't done much teaching."

"Yeah, he seems to be more the power behind the throne. What about her?"

"She was deputy head at some posh girls' school in Adelaide. Resigned during long service leave, then got the job at GLC."

"I was speaking to Ms Bowman about her. She says she's a terrific head but has been acting strangely since the underwear theft."

Leanne giggled, and Cam gave her a sharp look. "It's no laughing matter, Leanne. Many serial sex offenders start off as snowdroppers. They get like alcoholics. Why stop at a sip when you can have the whole bottle?"

Leanne hung her head for a full two seconds, but looked up when Pete Dowel knocked and entered the office. Pete had spent his day organising the search for the primary crime scene and was still wearing his mud-splattered black overalls. Cam knew the search had not gone well, even before the scowl the handsome young constable shot Leanne's way. Cam shooed her off his desk as if she were an annoying child.

"Still no luck?" Cam asked.

"Nothing but heatstroke, mozzie bites and wet socks. I had to send one of the SES blokes home, thought he was about to have a heart attack. We were one vehicle short for the rest of the afternoon."

"Send them out again tomorrow."

Pete constricted his expressive mouth, a dimple deepened on each cheek.

"Nothing from SOCO either, Sarge," he said, "but the finance guys in Toorrup wanted me to pass on a message to you. They said Toby Bell recently withdrew ten thousand dollars from one of his accounts."

Cam arched his eyebrows.

"What do you reckon, Sarge?" Pete continued. "He could've paid someone to do his brother in for him."

"But why would Toby kill his brother? What has he got to gain?" said Leanne.

"At this stage of the game, the killer is the only one who knows the whys," Cam said.

"Who knows what's in a man's heart?" said Pete. It sounded like a quote though Cam couldn't place it.

"Show off," Leanne muttered under her breath.

Cam asked Pete, "Have the money boys and girls questioned him about it?"

"No, they want us to do that," Pete said.

"Christ, I feel like I've just about worn a path over to Toorrup over the last few days." Cam flung his glasses to his desk and rubbed the bridge of his nose.

"Well, how 'bout I go and talk to him, then?" Pete said, obviously hoping to get out of tomorrow's continued search.

Cam regarded the young man's sweat streaked face. "OK. Go see him first thing tomorrow morning."

Pete slapped his hands together. "Sure thing, Sarge."

"How did you go with the stolen tanker case?" Cam asked.

"I found out the company name, name of the driver and

where it was going but nothing else. What about you? Any luck with Vince yet?"

"I called by on my way back from the autopsy but he wasn't home. I'll try again tomorrow. Did you find out what the tanker was carrying?"

Pete pulled a face. "Liquid fertiliser, for what it's worth." He met Leanne's eyes and shrugged.

Leanne grinned. "Liquid fertiliser? Jeez, someone must be getting into their veggie patch in a big way."

Pete threw her a scathing look. "Maybe the contents were irrelevant. Maybe it was the parts they were after. There's good money in truck parts. It happened nearly ten weeks ago. It's probably in bits all over the country by now."

Cam agreed, glancing at the clock on his office wall. "I guess it's almost knock off time for you two then?"

"Word, Sarge," Leanne said.

"I beg your pardon?" Cam frowned.

Pete said. "It's Afro-American slang, meaning enthusiastic agreement. She gets it from the internet chat rooms she's always hanging about in."

Cam stared at Pete blankly. These kids were losing him.

"I'm not always hanging about in chat rooms," Leanne said, her hand edging towards her mouth.

"Hey, keep your hair on. Anyone would think I was accusing you of not having a life or anything."

"I have a lot more of a life than you do. At least I don't sit around the house all my days off, reading law books. At least I…"

Cam put his hands up like a traffic cop. "Children, shut the hell up."

Pete pushed a raven's wing of hair out of his eyes, refusing to look at Leanne whose lips had stretched into a thin white line.

"That's better," said Cam. He still hadn't worked out the relationship between these two. Most of the time they behaved like competitive brother and sister, but there had been at least one instance when he'd caught Pete looking at her in a most non-brotherly way. She, though, always seemed oblivious.

"Oh, Sarge," Leanne said, "I traced down Lou Blayney. He's an absentee landlord from the city. He told me where the key to his gate is kept and says we can help ourselves to Bell's caravan whenever we want."

"What did he say about Bell?"

"He said something like how he didn't like to speak ill of the dead, but that he was a good for nothing old so-and-so and he was going to give him the boot when he saw him next."

"What about the woman, Gay?"

"Yes, she was there when he last visited."

"Good, we'll tackle her tomorrow, too. You're on call tonight, remember, Leanne. Off you go then."

19

Cam dug his vegetable patch until the sun had all but dipped below the ridgeline of the western hills, leaving a floss of pink in its wake. The ground had baked hard over summer and he'd had to crack through it with a pickaxe before he could even attempt to shovel it into the mounds for the vegetable beds. He threw down the garden tools only when his hands were puffy with blisters, his shirt soaked with sweat.

A quick shower left him feeling tired but loose, and with just enough time to knock up an omelette for dinner.

"What's with the shirt, Dad?" Ruby asked while he was cooking.

"What's that supposed to mean?" Cam said, glancing down at his checked shirt, looking for a tear or a smudge of grease.

Ruby sniggered. "I mean you must be planning a hot date tonight. You're in your dress flannel."

"Ha ha, very funny." She squealed when he flicked the tea towel at her.

It was the first meal Cam had enjoyed with Ruby since moving to Glenroyd. There was little conversation, but the silence didn't hang with the usual tension, only the lingering smell of frying mushrooms, bacon and onions.

He did the washing up while Ruby sat at the table, head bowed over a photography magazine Cecelia had lent her. Mrs Smithson was right; Cecelia did have a way with young girls. She'd made quite a connection with Ruby already.

Ruby was still reading the magazine when Cam left for his appointment.

Now his headlights punched through the darkness of the dirt road leading to the school. He turned off the radio and rolled down the window to breathe in the sweet dusty scent of the bottlebrush grass and feel the whip of the breeze in his hair.

The spectral shape of a frog-mouthed owl watched from his perch on a wooden fence post, blinked and turned his head almost 360 degrees to follow the car as it came to a stop at the school.

It was dark in the deserted car park, no lights shone from any of the school buildings. Cam stood still for a moment to allow his eyes to adjust. A cloud unveiled the full moon, making the path to the photographic lab shine.

But the sound of shattering glass made him stop mid-stride. Somewhere ahead he heard the thud of soft-soled footsteps. Then he caught the smell on the breeze: scorched wood, carbonised plastic, oxidised metal.

Riveted to the spot, he tried to control the sudden panic that threatened to paralyse his limbs. A sharp breath caught in his throat and his gut tightened; it was what he needed to get himself moving.

The smell grew stronger as he jogged towards the prefab. One of its windows was broken and shining with a flickering light. He stopped dead, his eyes fixed on a group of small dancing flames. A trickle of fear, a slow moving terror, began to wash through him. For a moment he wasn't looking at a burning blackout blind, but at floral curtains billowing from a broken kitchen window. The small flames ignited with a whoosh.

Now he could hear their screams.

He had to get them out.

Oh God, not again. He fought the panic that threatened to overcome his reason. Slowly, deliberately, he reached out and brushed the door handle with his fingertips.

Still cold.

He flung the door open and dropped to his knees. The room was alive with dancing light and flickering shadows. On the far window one of the blackout blinds writhed and flapped in the flames. Near the adjacent window, he made out Cecelia's still form. And then that blind went up too, turning the front of the prefab into a wall of fire.

She began to stir, then moaned and lifted her head.

"Elizabeth!" he cried, "stay down!"

As he crawled towards her, another whoosh set the side wall alight, sending greedy tongues of flame ever closer to the shelves of photographic chemicals. And then the door banged shut and the room filled with choking clouds of smoke.

Cam scrabbled forward, coughing as the noxious fumes seared his lungs and bit into his eyes. On her hands and knees now, Cecelia looked at him through a shroud of smoke.

She must have seen him though her face remained blank, her body still and trance-like. He grabbed her by both shoulders and gave her a shake. She responded with a sharp intake of breath then lurched into a fit of coughing that was drowned in the fire's roar. On hands and knees he guided her towards the closed door, reached for the handle and twisted the knob.

Nothing happened.

Now it was his turn to panic. He wriggled and pushed at the knob with both hands.

It was locked rigid.

He sprang to his feet, took a step back and threw himself

at the door, shoulder first. It still refused to budge; he might just as well have been hurling himself against a brick wall.

"The key, where's the key?" he gasped at her through the smoke.

Cecelia moved her head from side to side, unable to get the words out. He dropped down beside her and cupped her face in his hands, the heat stinging his neck, pushing at his back.

"The key!" he yelled.

"In the lock. Outside," she managed at last, hauling herself to her feet.

As the fear detonated inside him, a sudden burst of clarity released a memory: a robbery case; thieves bashing through the wall of a transportable home because they couldn't break the lock.

With a well-placed kick Cam crunched the toe of his work boot into the fibro panel. When Cecelia realised what he was doing she started to help and soon they'd created a jagged space large enough to crawl through.

They collapsed on to the brick path, filling their lungs with heady draughts of the sweet night air, until she gasped, "The chemicals!"

Throat too dry to reply, Cam pulled Cecelia to her feet and half-dragged, half-carried her through the flowerbeds. They struggled on until their legs gave out and they fell on to an open patch of lawn.

They lay still for a moment, catching their breath. She tried to speak but her words were snatched by a paroxysm of coughing. When the fit passed, he helped her to sit up.

"Are you OK?" he croaked.

She passed a hand across her face and nodded.

"The chemicals you use in the lab; are they flamm—"

The ground shook as an explosion blew out the last of the prefab's windows, spraying glass and smoke into the night sky. Cam threw himself over Cecelia as the sound reverberated inside his chest and pushed against his head with ear-bursting pressure. Debris rocketed into the air and small particles rained on his back. He tensed, any minute expecting the big one that would tear them to pieces.

But only the silence came.

He looked up. Shredded photographic paper drifted down on them like confetti.

Cecelia stirred. He eased himself off her.

"The photographic chemicals aren't, but the fixing agents are."

Her voice was low and hoarse. She attempted to smile but as he looked, the smile faltered and the tears began. She started to shake.

He pulled her towards him and wrapped her in his arms, as much to stop his own shaking as hers. As he buried his face in her singed hair, he took deep breaths, trying to slow the pulse racing in his ears.

He remembered the first time Ruby had visited him in hospital. One look at his bandaged face had made her tear loose from her grandmother and flee. They'd eventually found her in a city park, sobbing so much she had to be sedated. Now it was he who wanted to run. To stop himself, he clung to the woman harder and screwed his eyes shut, fighting to get the air into his lungs.

Slow down. Breathe. Focus. Breathe.

Focus on what just happened. Be rational; think. A fire-bomb in the photographic lab, but why? To destroy something – the photographs of the crime scene, perhaps? Maybe, but why the locked door? How many people knew about Cecelia's photos? Had word of them spread to Vince? Would he kill to protect his job? Vince was a lot of things, but not a killer - or was he? Cam had been policing long enough to know there were no constants in human behaviour. He could still see the image of Vince slumped on the veranda floor of the pub, the immaculate uniforms hanging in the near empty room.

My job is my life.

"Cam? Are you all right?"

He'd been mumbling. Her voice brought him out of himself. He released her from his grip, nodded and took a deep breath.

"Are you burned at all?" he said in a stranger's voice.

"I don't think so. Maybe just my hair." She looked at him with concern. "You?"

"I'm fine." He responded quickly, too quickly. His abrupt reaction startled her.

The sound of voices rose above the gentle crackle of the flames. A switch flicked and the lawn was flooded in bright light. He pressed at his stinging eyes with the heels of his hands. When he could finally focus, he saw three people standing near the smouldering remains of the prefab.

He climbed unsteadily to his feet and stumbled forwards on rubbery legs, shouting and waving at them to get away. Movement from behind told him Cecelia was trying to follow. He turned and put a gentle hand on her shoulder, pushing her back into a sitting position on the lawn.

"Stay where you are. I'm going to get you some help. You need to see a doctor."

She started to protest, but her words were choked with another fit of coughing. She probably had smoke inhalation, concussion at the very least.

He gave her shoulder a squeeze. "It's going to be OK, but

you have to stay here." He hated to have to push her down, but she hadn't the strength to walk and he hadn't the strength to carry her.

Cam made his way over to the onlookers who'd retreated to the edge of a grove of trees. The first person he saw was Jeffrey Smithson, wearing a brown dressing gown and carpet slippers. His face was grey in the spotlight, his eyes hard as pebbles as they took in Cam's dishevelled appearance.

"Good God, man, what the hell happened?" he asked.

Anne clutched at Smithson's arm. She was in a pink nylon dressing gown and had a yellow scarf over her head.

Cam was about to answer when she interrupted in a faltering voice. "We called the bushfire brigade when we heard the explosion." She turned to face the blackened ruins. "Though it doesn't look like there's much left to put out."

Smithson extracted his arm from her grasp and placed it around her shoulder, drawing her close in an expression of tenderness, moving in its sincerity. What was it with this couple? Cam asked himself. What could be the reasons for Smithson's hostility towards Cam and his inquiries, other than guilt over Bell's death? So much of his behaviour seemed driven by an almost paranoid desire to protect his wife - what was he trying to protect her from?

"We're waiting for your explanation, Sergeant. Have you any idea how valuable the equipment was in that lab?" Smithson said.

He spoke as if he was holding Cam personally responsible for the damage. His accusing tone felt like a jab to a raw burn and jolted Cam back to his senses. He rubbed his sooty face with his hands and fought to keep the tremolo from his voice.

"Ms Bowman was working in the lab when a fire bomb was thrown through the window…"

Mrs Smithson gasped and put her hand to her mouth. "Cecelia?"

Another voice said, "Cecelia? She was in there? Where is she? Is she all right?"

Ruth Tilly's staccato questions fired into Cam's head like bullets. He paused, trying to reconcile her presence. Then he remembered that she too lived on the school campus, in a flat above the science lab.

"She's over there." Cam pointed to the perimeter of the lawn.

Mrs Smithson untangled herself from her husband, saying to Ruth, "She'll need water. I'll run to the school and get some." She looked back over her shoulder as she hurried to the school's front entrance. "I'll bring some back for you too, Sergeant."

Cam thanked her, then called out to Ruth who was disappearing in the other direction, into the shadows. "Can you take Cecelia over to the medical centre, Ms Tilly?" There was no acknowledgment, and he raised his voice. "She's not badly hurt, but I think she has concussion."

Jeffrey met Cam's eye and gripped his arm. "Vandals, you think?"

He heard the sound of coughing and Ruth's soothing voice coming from the darkened perimeter of the lawn. "I can't say yet," Cam said, switching his focus back to Jeffrey. "Did you or your wife see or hear anything unusual this evening?"

"We were watching television. Channel 2, a programme about the wildebeest migration across the Serengeti. The first thing we heard was the explosion."

He was on the defensive again. The question only

required a yes or no answer but Cam felt as if he were being presented with another alibi.

A siren wailed in the distance, coming closer. Jeffrey cocked his head to one side, narrowed his eyes. "And what about you, Sergeant? Who invited you here at this time of the night?"

"I was here to pick up some photographs from Ms Bowman. The prefab was on fire when I arrived."

Cam turned his back on Mr Smithson and reached for his phone. First he dialled Toorrup Police Station to report the incident, then he phoned Leanne at home.

Leanne's mother answered. He could hear her yelling for her daughter above the clatter of dishes and the strangled violins of a TV melodrama. It seemed to take forever for Leanne to pick up and he could feel Smithson's eyes boring into his back while he waited. When she finally came to the phone, Cam explained what had happened.

"Are you all right, Sarge? Your voice sounds kind of weird," Leanne said.

"I'm fine. I want you to call Ruby and tell her I'll be late home. Tell her I've been called out on a case or something, but for God's sake don't tell her what's happened here." He'd have to get rid of his shirt and jeans before he saw Ruby, have a shower at the station. Just one whiff of the smoke could set her off. "After you've seen Ruby, go fetch Pete and get over to Vince's."

"Vince? Surely you don't think…"

"Just get on over there, Leanne, I don't know what to think."

He sounded harsh; he knew it. The pause at the other end of the phone told him she thought so too.

"OK," she said, then took a deep breath. "Uh, what exactly should we say to him?"

"Tell him something's happened at the school and we need his advice. Tell him it's delicate, that I'm coming over to explain. Just keep him there and stop him from doing a runner."

Cam replaced his phone just as Mrs Smithson reappeared with a bottle of water. After drinking half of it he poured the remainder over his head, scrubbing at his hair and face, grateful for the cool relief.

Jeffrey moved over to his wife and put his arm around her waist. "How's Cecelia?" Cam heard him ask her.

"I think she'll be all right. Ruth's going to take her to the doctor."

"Thank heavens for that," her husband said.

Cam drank down the last drop of water then wiped his mouth on his shirtsleeve. He gestured to them with the empty bottle. "You can go back home now. There's not much more we can do until morning,"

"I hope that's not meant to be an order, Sergeant. I intend staying here until the last flame is extinguished," Smithson said.

Cam could not stop himself from raising his eyes skyward. "Suit yourself."

Anne Smithson gave her husband's arm a squeeze. "There's nothing we can do here. Let's just leave it to the experts, Jeffrey."

She pressed her mouth into a thin line and indicated with her eyes that it was time to go. He made a huffing sound and smoothed down his moustache. Finally conceding to his wife's common sense, he nodded a curt goodbye to Cam and turned his back.

The couple moved off, arm in arm. As Cam watched their blurred silhouettes pass under the spotlight's beam, some of the mystery, at least, became clear.

20

Leanne negotiated her way down the dark gravel driveway to Pete's rented farm cottage. She could see him silhouetted in the doorway, tucking in his uniform shirt. He waved and walked over to the passenger side, filling the police Commodore with the odours of cigarette smoke and pine scented shower gel.

He grinned as he fastened his seat belt. "You didn't have the siren on, did you, Leanne?"

"Siren? Don't be a dumb-arse, Pete." Leanne had let her neighbour's kid give the siren a quick blast just before she'd left home. She'd figured the wondrous expression on the small boy's face was worth the flak she'd get from Pete if he found out.

"I thought I heard it in the distance."

"This is hardly an emergency."

"That's what I thought. Why does the old man want us to check up on Vince anyway?"

"Because of the fire at the school. He thinks Vince might have done it to get rid of the photos that proved he moved the body at the crime scene."

Pete gave a snort of disbelief. "Vince wouldn't do anything that dumb."

"Best to cover all options, I guess."

"Jeez, you're even beginning to sound like him."

Leanne aimed for a pothole and savoured the snapping sound of his teeth. After orchestrating some more jarring bumps she turned back on to the bitumen.

"I hate the way you call him the old man. It really bugs me."

Pete rubbed his jaw. "Why? Because you have a crush on him? Because me calling him old man reminds you that he's old enough to be your father?"

Leanne screwed up her face and hissed her annoyance at him.

"It's obvious, Leanne. Don't deny it."

"Shut up." In a softer voice she added, "What would you know anyway?"

"Only that you look at him just like the girls at school used to look at me. You follow him around with your tongue on the ground, yes sir, no sir, three bags full sir."

She caught his smirk in her peripheral vision and went in for the kill. "Yeah, *used to* look at you. Doesn't happen much these days, does it? Failure's kind of a dampener to the old love life, eh, Pete?"

She regretted the words as soon as they'd left her mouth. Pete had been a star WAFL player and was really going places until he did his cruciate in. He'd been chewing himself up over it for the last two years, and here she was, rubbing in the salt. God, she was a bitch sometimes.

"Sorry Pete, I didn't mean that." She took her eyes from the road and risked a quick glance at him. "You're not a failure, you just had some bad luck, that's all." Her face broke into a grin. "You're such a cocky bastard; someone has to put you down every now and then."

"I don't know what I'd do without you, Leanne." He smiled back. "Anyway, I know something about your hero that I'll bet you don't know. I'll tell you if you're nice to me."

Leanne risked him another glance. "Go on, tell me. I'll be nice."

"I was having a drink in Toorrup the other week, catching up with a mate who'd spent some time over east. He'd heard of our Sergeant Fraser, seems he was a detective in Sydney."

"Yeah, I heard that too. His wife and kid were killed instead of him, yada yada yada, that's old news."

"Maybe, but when he sprung the bikie gang, he was undercover. They don't usually like cops with families to go under cover. Sometimes they have to go under for months."

"So, what are you getting at?"

"He was undercover because he volunteered, that's why. He begged for the job apparently."

"Shit." After some thought she added, "Kind of puts things in perspective doesn't it?"

"You mean stop whinging and get on with things?"

"I didn't say that," she said softly. "I just believe that when one door closes, another opens. I mean now you can't play footy any more, you've taken up all that reading and studying and you're doing really well - you'll probably be commissioner one day. You'd get a lot more out of that than kicking a bag of air around an oval."

"You're a brick, Leanne." He sounded like he meant it.

Leanne pulled up outside Vince's street. As they got out of the car, a dog barked from a garden several houses down; otherwise the neighbourhood was quiet. Vince's old Falcon was parked on the road outside his house. Leanne leaned a hand on the bonnet as she passed by.

"Cold?" Pete asked.

"Yeah."

They walked the concrete slabs to Vince's front door. The fly screen was closed but the door open. Silver flickers and muted sounds of the TV came from the living room.

Pete rapped on the flimsy frame of the fly screen. "Hey, Vince," he called, "It's Pete and Leanne. We need to have a talk with you."

There was no answer, only the computerised roar of a TV audience.

"Maybe he's in the shower," said Leanne, stepping back from the porch to view the front of the house. "There's a light on in the bedroom." The curtains were drawn. She tapped on the window.

"He might be asleep. I don't fancy the idea of waking him up," she said.

"Don't worry, I'll protect you."

"Wow, I feel so safe now."

Pete pushed the flyscreen and it closed behind them with a crack. He reached for the light switch and called out again but there was still no answer. Any minute now Leanne expected a drunken Vince to come charging out at them, draped in a towel, or worse, nothing.

They glanced around the empty living room then walked towards the closed bedroom door. Leanne gave it a gentle tap and gingerly turned the knob. She saw a bare mattress and some discarded clothes on the floor. Pete stretched over her and pushed the door fully open, then walked with a John Wayne swagger to the only other thing in the room, a small freestanding wardrobe. He pointed to the closed wardrobe door and placed a finger to his lips.

Leanne giggled, whispering, "He'd hardly be in there, moron."

He scowled. "We've got to be thorough," he said as if he wanted to hear her laugh again. He made his hand like a gun and pointed to the wardrobe. "We know you're in there, Vince. Come out with your hands up."

With a melodramatic flourish he flung the door wide, and the hinges made a splintering sound. He looked at Leanne and pulled a face. Her hand went to her mouth when he tried without success to jam the lopsided cupboard door back.

"Vince is going to kill you for that, Pete."

He shrugged. "He's not to know we were even here. He's probably just walked to the pub to drown his sorrows. We'll have one more look around, go there next."

They searched the remainder of the house and the tiny backyard: no sign of Vince. Pete took out his phone to report back.

"Wait on a minute, Pete. We haven't checked the garage," Leanne said, moving towards a door off the lounge room. Pete gave an impatient sigh and followed.

The smell hit her as soon as she opened the door. She took a step back.

"Yuck. He must have some burst pipes, either that or his septics…"

Pete gripped Leanne by her shoulders and swung her away from the open door.

"It's not the pipes," he said softly, reaching for the light switch. He drew in a sharp breath. "Oh sweet Jesus."

21

The fire unit arrived, lights flashing and siren wailing. The sight and sound bored into Cam's aching head like a dental drill. He wiped the sweat from his eyes and watched with alarm as the four-wheel drive mounted the curb and charged across the lush lawn, churning up turf like a deranged lawnmower until it came to a halt several metres from where Cam was standing.

The cavalry had arrived.

Cliff turned off the noise. He and Angelo jumped from the vehicle before Cam could close the distance between them.

"Wait on a minute, guys," Cam said, indicating for them to slow down. "No need to go charging off like a bull at a gate."

Cliff stopped and turned. "I don't need some city cop telling me how to do my job." The spotlight shone at an angle across his face, casting one side in shadow.

Cam shrugged. "You're the boss."

Cliff leaned into the fire vehicle and snatched his yellow helmet from the dash. He was wearing his heavy fireman's boots; his Uggs lay on the floor on the passenger side next to a water bottle and a six-pack of beer.

"Be prepared," Cam said, not hiding his sarcasm. Angelo turned away and smiled.

Cam tried to tell Cliff what had happened, trotting to keep up with the big man's giant steps. But as they approached the smouldering ruins, he was forced to hold back as renewed contact with the poisonous fumes irritated his already sensitive lungs. As he doubled over into a fit of coughing he felt a hand on his shoulder.

"Sergeant Fraser, are you OK?" Angelo asked.

"Yes, I'm fine now." He felt as if he'd just coughed up a lung. "I think that's the last of it."

He straightened, wiped his mouth with the back of his hand, then pointed to the bear-like figure at the ruins. "I was trying to tell Cliff to be careful. There could still be explosive substances in there. Even a small flame could set them off." He shrugged, letting out a painful breath. "Well, he's supposed to be a fireman, I guess he knows what he's doing."

"He gets excited sometimes. When he's wired up like this he thinks he can take on the world. It's just about impossible to tell him anything." The boy's hand unconsciously moved to his face where his fingers probed his bruised eye.

"We'd better go and make sure he doesn't do anything stupid then," Cam said.

They picked their way over the pieces of smouldering chipboard, floorboards, glass and mangled metal. The floor of the prefab was still more or less intact except for the area to the far left where the chemicals had been stored and where the explosion had originated. Here, it was no more than a jagged crater with branches of twisted steel joists rising from its epicentre. Pieces of floorboards, still shimmering orange with the heat, radiated from the hole like the glowing petals of a flower.

Cam didn't venture closer, though Cliff and Angelo in their protective gear were bolder. They kicked at the debris, assessing the danger: carefully, Cam hoped. The remaining flames seemed benign enough, but it wouldn't take much of a breeze for them to rekindle and threaten the other school buildings.

Cam walked back to the fire unit with Cliff, who radioed base to say no backup was required. The big man's initial excitement had eased now he realised it was only a mop-up job. The scowl on his face suggested all he wanted to do now was get the job done and go home to bed.

Overcome with a sudden weariness himself, Cam shuffled over to a nearby tree and sank to the ground. The moon was full, the stars no more than pale pinpricks. He leaned back against the tree, feeling the damp of a light evening dew seep through the seat of his jeans. The gentle fingers of a breeze ruffled his hair and provided a welcome cool to his face, helping him fight the desire to close his eyes. He followed the actions of the fire team as they carried out the same well-practised ritual they'd performed at Sunday's bushfire.

As Cliff unwound the hose, he yelled to Angelo to turn the pump on. His orange overalls were unbuttoned to the waist and his muscles rippled under the artificial light. His yellow helmet glowed, the visor reflecting a star of light under which his black beard bristled. He adjusted the nozzle of the hose and yelled again at Angelo, who was still looking at the ruins. He made no move towards the pump, but shouted something back at Cliff.

Cliff threw the hose down and stalked towards his spiky-haired apprentice. Cam hauled himself to his feet and followed. The dynamics of the fire team had become interesting.

He watched the big man approach Angelo.

"Are you deaf or something? What the hell is your problem, boy? You trying to be a smart-arse again?" Cliff bawled.

"Cliff, it's different this time, this is really dangerous,"

Angelo said.

Angelo spotted Cam walking up behind his boss. Their eyes briefly met. When he turned back to Cliff his voice was less hesitant.

"There's all sorts of dangerous stuff in that mess," Angelo said. "Electrical cables, too. We've got to turn the mains off before we spray or we'll be fried."

Cliff ripped off his helmet, threw it to the ground and stepped closer. Cam moved to stand by the young man's side.

"I guess you don't get too many residential fires way out here. Probably never even had one. It's an easy enough thing to forget," Cam said.

"I didn't forget," Cliff spoke through gritted teeth, not taking his eyes off Angelo.

"I see, this was just a test, eh? Putting the apprentice through his paces. Good thinking," Cam said.

Cliff switched his glare to Cam for a moment, then back to Angelo. Cam could see the big man struggling to save face. "Where are the fucking mains then, smart arse?" Cliff bawled.

"I don't know, Cliff. You know the school better than I do," Angelo said.

"Try the front porch," Cam tilted his head to the formal entrance, flashing Cliff a smile straight from the Toby Bell School Of Charm.

Cliff scowled and headed toward the school building.

The smile immediately left Cam's face. "Shit," he said out of the side of his mouth. "Is he always like this?"

Angelo gave a cautious smile. "No, not always. He's been losing it a bit lately, but. Pressures of work, you know?"

"What was that about you getting into trouble before?"

Angelo watched Cliff stomp up the school's front steps

and shrugged.

"Did he get angry at you at Sunday's bushfire too?"

"Yeah. Off his chops at me."

"Why?"

Cliff yelled at Angelo to turn on the pump. Cam followed Angelo back to the fire unit and Angelo flicked the switch, lurching the pump to life. When he aimed the spray at the ruins they were enveloped in foul-smelling steam.

Cam gagged down another coughing fit.

Angelo shouted above the noise. "That fire in the bush wasn't too fierce." The water from the hose hissed like a nest of snakes as it hit the hot metal. "And it only covered a small area, so we thought we could handle it. Cliff said not to use the hose on one part, he said it would be more efficient to make a firebreak and let the flames burn out on their own. We'd also save water that way. The fire truck only carries six hundred litres. We cleared a good size break, then Cliff went down the line to check something. The wind came up and the flames grew higher, so I grabbed the hose and put them out. He went off his rocker at me."

"And he hit you then?"

Angelo said nothing; his expression said it all.

"It sounds like you did the right thing. You used your initiative." Cam lowered his voice when the hulking figure of Cliff reappeared. There was no doubt in his mind that he was looking at a man quite capable of murder. "Tomorrow at lunchtime come to the station. We'll drive out to the school grounds and you can show me where that patch of flames was."

The young man made no sign of acknowledgment. Cliff yanked the hose from his hands and continued the spraying. Cam wondered if he'd show up.

His mind switched from the Bell murder back to the

bombed photo lab. It was easy enough to guess what had happened: a Molotov cocktail through the window, then the exploding chemicals. But why? Who?

Firemen were often the arson squad's worst nightmare. A crime involving fire was hard enough to investigate. A diligent fireman put the icing on the cake, destroying what little evidence there was left with water, foam, heavy boots and damaging equipment. By the time the Volunteer Bush Fire Brigade had finished, there'd be little evidence left here to tell him anything. Cam let out a breath and scrubbed at his face.

Then his mobile rang. It was Leanne.

22

Pete and Leanne were waiting for him on the front steps of Vince's house. The young man stood up as Cam walked towards him, and flicked a cigarette butt into the bushes by the side of the house. He realised his mistake when he saw the set of the Senior Sergeant's jaw and the cold hard gleam of his eyes.

Cam pointed to the bush. "Pick it up."

Pete retrieved the butt and stuffed it in his pocket. "Sorry, Sarge, I wasn't thinking. It's shocking in there."

The neighbour's reticulation fizzed to life; there was a cool draught and the air became heavy with minerals.

Cam heard a sniff and saw Leanne standing on the steps. Under the porch light he could see the glistening redness of her eyes.

"You all right, Leanne?"

She nodded and turned away, pulling something grey and crumbling from her pocket and dabbing at her nose with it.

Vince's old Falcon was parked alongside the curb. Cam attempted to look through the grimy passenger window.

"The bonnet was cold when we got here," Pete said.

"Torch," Cam said, putting out his hand.

Pete unclipped the torch from his belt and Cam shone it around the vehicle's interior. It was unlocked, the keys still dangling from the ignition. An Elvis Presley marionette hung from the rear vision mirror, empty choc milk cartons and hamburger wraps littered the floor.

Pete's hand moved to the handle.

"Don't touch it yet. I want it dusted first," Cam said.

"Er, yes of course." Pete glanced over to Leanne. Their eyes met, she shrugged, then buried her nose in the crumbling tissue again.

Cam handed her his clean handkerchief, pushed past Pete and walked into the house. He came to an abrupt halt outside the main bedroom. Not expecting the sudden stop, Pete lurched into him from behind. The younger man sprang back, pushing the hair from his eyes with a nervous flick of his hand.

"Calm down, Pete, you're as jumpy as a louse on dipping day."

Cam turned on the light and scanned the bedroom. It all looked pretty much the same as when he'd dragged Vince home from the pub. The mattress was still on the floor almost hidden under a tangle of sheets. A Hawaiian shirt had been added to the pile of festering clothes. But there was something different, and it took a few moments of chin rubbing to see what it was.

The cupboard door was hanging at a tilt.

"Did you touch anything in here?" Cam said, pointing to the room in general.

"We searched the whole house before we found the body, so yes, I suppose we did touch some things. We had no idea, we–"

"The cupboard door. That damage is new. What do you think?" He jabbed his hand at the broken. "Signs of a violent struggle perhaps?"

Pete hesitated before answering, "No, I did it when I was looking for him."

Cam's stare could have frozen water. "You thought he was hiding in the cupboard?"

"We were fooling around. Before we knew there was

anything wrong." Pete's voice was so soft Cam could hardly hear him.

"We?" Cam looked over to Leanne. He had never known her so quiet.

Pete straightened up and looked Cam in the eye. "It was me, Sarge. Leanne didn't do anything."

"First the smoke and then this. The next blue's going in your report – have you got that, Constable?"

Pete clenched his jaw.

Cam's footsteps pounded from the bedroom to the lounge and stopped outside the closed door leading to the garage. He glanced at the young officers behind him, breathing deeply, preparing himself for the first blast of the odour he could already detect creeping through the cracks in the door.

They'd left on the faulty fluorescent light, which flickered and clicked like the spooling film of a silent movie. A woman's bicycle, maybe Vince's ex-wife's, leaned against the back wall. Several old suitcases were stacked next to it, the kind you could imagine Bogart and Bacall clutching at a desolate railway station. The cement floor was stained with patches of oil, the walls lined with stacks of plastic flower pots, piles of brittle women's magazines, a wheelbarrow, crates of empties, an old tyre. The detritus of a life.

Parallel steel beams supported the pitched garage roof. A rope tied between the fishing rods and prawn nets dangled as limp as the Elvis in Vince's car.

A forty-four gallon drum lay on its side underneath the rope, and near it the body, covered by a stained white tarp. Cam squatted and drew back the tarp. He shivered and his stomach lurched as he looked upon the distorted purple face of his Senior Constable.

He turned his face away and forced himself to breathe through his mouth, beckoning to Pete and Leanne. They approached reluctantly.

"Have you ever come across a hanging before?"

Leanne shook her head and looked at Pete. His gaze was locked on the roller door at the end of the garage.

"I have, only one. It wasn't like this though. It's different when you know the person," he said in a small voice, his anger at Cam now as distant as his stare.

"Did you cut him down?"

Pete stammered, "I thought he was still alive. He was still warm."

"That's OK," Cam said. "Though you shouldn't have covered him with the tarp." He kept the accusing tone away from his voice; the kids had been through enough for one night. Pete's shoulders sagged with relief. "Did you try CPR?" Cam added.

"No. As soon as we got him down we realised it was too late," Leanne said.

Cam pulled the tarp completely off the body. Vince had put on his dress uniform; the silver buttons and polished shoes twinkled like party lights under the flickering fluorescent. Cam turned his face away, click; then back, click. He had to close his eyes for a moment.

"Go into the lounge room, grab the standard lamp and plug it in here," he said to Leanne, pointing to a power point in the garage wall. "I can't see a damned thing. And Pete, open up the roller door and let some fresh air in."

The job was more tolerable with the new light and the fresher air. Cam's eyes travelled from the tip of Vince's highly polished shoes, up the sharp creases of his trousers to the top of his head. He loosened the noose. Though padded with a towel, the inverted V-shaped bruise on the side of the neck was clearly visible. He shone the torch on the neck and pointed out the telltale sign to the young constables. His latex-covered fingers moved across the uniform jacket and came to rest on a piece of paper protruding from the top pocket. He removed the paper and read the note out loud. It was Vince's writing; he'd recognise those chicken scratches anywhere.

"*I'm sorry.*" Cam paused and looked at the shaken youngsters. "*Vince.*" He let his breath out with a sigh. "That's all." He shrugged and flipped the paper just to make sure.

He turned to Pete and rubbed his grainy eyes. "You two go on home. I'll deal with SOCO and the pathologist," he said.

"We don't mind staying, Sarge. You're done in, what with the fire and everything," Leanne said.

He gave her a glance to indicate that he appreciated her concern. "No, I'll stay here. Off you go. And on your way home, call in on Ruby and tell her I won't be home till morning. She's probably still up watching the late movie."

Pete nodded. "No probs, Sarge."

As they turned to leave, Cam called out, "And make sure she's locked the house up properly."

23

From the front porch Cam could hear the softened voices of the SOCO officers as they placed Vince's bagged clothes in the back of their vehicle.

One of them commented that it was the third police suicide in three months, how the Police Royal Commission was causing a big drop in morale. The other man's answer was low and muffled. Cam wondered if either man knew Vince; suicides were always grim but even worse when they involved a fellow officer. He sat down and leaned his head against the brick wall, allowing the cool mist from the neighbour's sprinkler to waft against his skin.

After a few moments he stood up and rejoined the SOCO team. He pointed out Vince's car, and they dusted it for prints inside and out with no luck; visually, all the prints looked the same. They would be run through the database, but Cam could predict that their owner would be Vince.

The SOCO boys moved into the house and Cam held back, still looking at the car. The position of the driver's seat was bothering him. He opened up the driver's side door and sat in the seat, placing his hands upon the wheel, his eyes away from the dangling Elvis. He had to stretch his feet right out to reach the pedals, only then feeling them through the toe of his boots. Vince and he were about the same height. There was no way that he would have been comfortable with the seat this far back, even if it was only a matter of reversing the car out of the garage and parking it on the street.

Cam was pondering this as he walked back to the garage. He found Freddie McManus, the forensic pathologist, holding a thermometer under a standard lamp, squinting in the poor light, caterpillar eyebrows furrowed with concentration. McManus had not cracked a black joke since his arrival.

"Can you give me a time of death yet, Doc?" Cam asked.

"I'm still working on it."

Cam nodded and wiped the back of his arm across his forehead. "It's a hot night."

"Quite," the pathologist replied. "He's a big boy, would take a while to cool down."

"My officers found him at about nine. He was still warm then," Cam said.

McManus wiped the thermometer and put it back in his bag, then squatted at the body again. Pushing Vince on to his side, he pulled up his jacket and shirt. Cam shone his torch on the area, noticing the purplish skin where the blood had collected.

The pathologist pressed his gloved finger into a patch on Vince's back. The skin blanched and returned to the purple colour when the pressure was released. McManus allowed the body to roll back on to its original position and moved to Vince's head. He cupped the jaw in one hand and gently manipulated the joint from side to side.

"Lividity's not fixed yet, rigour's only just starting," he said. He placed the head back on to the concrete floor. "Your man's been dead somewhere between three and five hours, Sergeant."

Cam looked at his watch and scrabbled through his own set of mental calculations. So Vince had died at seven at the earliest, nine at the latest. If Vince hanged himself at seven, there was no way he could have bombed the photo lab.

Cam had arrived at the school at eight, just as the bomb was thrown. If Vince had thrown the bomb then, he may just have had time to rush home, change and hang himself minutes before the arrival of Pete and Leanne. The body was still warm when they found him at nine. Then again, Cam realised, on a night like this, it probably would still have been warm if he had hung himself at seven.

Death before eight and Vince was innocent, after eight and he might still be guilty.

The pathologist gave Cam a questioning look. "Any the wiser then?"

Cam's hand rasped against his jaw. "When you do the autopsy, Doc, will you be running the usual blood toxicity tests?"

"I always test for drugs and alcohol."

"Good."

McManus regarded Cam over the top of his glasses. "Something tells me you're are not convinced this is a straight suicide."

"I tend to be a fence-sitter 'til I see all the evidence."

"That's the way to be."

"It infuriates my junior officers." Cam gave a tired smile and pointed to the overturned drum. "Is that how you'd do it then? Climb on a drum with a noose around your neck and just jump off?"

McManus stared at the drum for a moment. "Hell no," he said. "If I wanted to do the job properly I'd want a bigger drop than that, big enough for the hangman's knot to snap against the neck and break it. With a drop like this, of about three feet, a person would slowly suffocate." McManus shivered. "A horrible way to go."

"You'd think a police officer with Vince's experience would have learnt that."

The pathologist shrugged, stooped over his bag and began to pack away his equipment. "Not for me to say."

A thought struck Cam. "Wouldn't his service revolver have been quicker and cleaner? Why didn't he use that?"

Cam spent the remainder of the night with the Scene of Crime officers. When they'd finished collecting the evidence at Vince's house, they drove to the school to sift through the wreckage of the photographic lab. Preliminary findings indicated the cause of the fire and subsequent explosion was, as Cam had suspected, a Molotov cocktail through one of the front windows. They found the doorknob under a nearby bush and took it back to the lab for fingerprint analysis, though Cam doubted it would yield anything incriminating. Vince, if it had been Vince, was too much the experienced officer to leave prints behind.

The stick-tall and balding SOCO sergeant reminded Cam of Jacques Cousteau, but when he opened his mouth to speak, sweaty bush hats and iron ore replaced the image of glistening wet suits and salt spray. Cam tried to focus on the man's slow, soporific tones, but science had never been his strong point, and fatigue was dimming his mind. The man droned on and on about fire patterns, accelerants and chemical reactions.

"Did you get the fax?"

Cam jerked himself awake, "What fax?"

The man gave a belly laugh. "You should be home in bed, mate. I faxed you this evening. You wanted to know about the glass we found at last week's bushfire, remember?"

Of course, this was the same SOCO guy who'd collected the evidence from the bushfire scene. Cam tried to shake the cobwebs out of his brain. Maybe Cecelia wasn't the only one with concussion.

"I wasn't at the station this evening. What did you find?"

"We recovered glass from two Jim Beam bottles; one was broken, one complete. Both were covered with the prints of your vic, Herbert Bell."

Cam nodded. "Anything else?"

"We found remnants of twisted tin. A jam tin to be precise. It had no detectable prints, but we did find traces of gunpowder on it." The man could see he now had Cam's full attention and gave a self-satisfied smile. "And it gets better."

"Go on."

"Some of the glass shards were from a magnifying glass."

Cam's heart skipped a beat as the implication hit him. "A magnifying glass bomb?"

The man clapped Cam on the shoulder. "I thought that'd wake you up. Not a very big one, but enough to set the bush alight."

A magnifying glass bomb, a simple but most effective timing device. Cam's voice rose with excitement. "A small amount of gunpowder at the bottom of a tin topped with a magnifying glass. The sun's rays shine down on to the powder and when the temperature reaches ignition point– boom!"

"Not even much of a boom – more of a pop actually," the SOCO officer said.

Cam thought back to Vince's interview with Ruth Tilly. "The witness who reported the fire said the smoke was dirty white."

"Well, they were wrong if they saw the fire when it'd only just started. The gunpowder, plus the fuel the body was soaked in, would have made the smoke oily black, certainly until the accelerant was all burned up. What time was the fire reported anyway?"

"11 am. The witness thought it'd only just started," Cam said.

"What was the weather like then?"

"Hot, heading towards thirty-eight degrees at a guess. It was cooler the next day because of the wind."

The man's fingers danced over the buttons of his calculator. Cam peered over his shoulder but the numbers meant nothing to him.

"I'll keep it simple."

"I'd appreciate that."

"Taking into account the environmental conditions, the angle of the sun, and the ignition temperature of the gunpowder, it would have taken several hours for the bomb to heat up enough to explode. I'd say it would've started cooking with the very earliest of the sun's rays."

Cam frowned and rubbed his chin. "So we don't need to be looking for someone skulking around the bushes that morning, because the bomb was probably dumped with the body sometime the previous night."

"That's right, mate. No one started your 11 am fire. The fire started itself."

24

EARLY FRIDAY MORNING

Cecelia Bowman gripped the edge of the toilet bowl and heaved her guts dry. It seemed the only thing preventing her from falling into the murky depths was Ruth's cool hand upon her forehead.

"I'm all right now, I'm fine," she said, sinking on to the tiles of the bathroom floor.

"OK, darl, up you get now and rinse your mouth out."

Ruth helped Cecelia over to the bathroom sink. Cecelia's hands shook as she squeezed the toothpaste on to the toothbrush, cleaning her teeth as tenderly as if they were hanging on threads of silk.

"Better now?" asked Ruth. Cecelia nodded although she could still taste the burned chemicals in her mouth and feel the caustic sear in her lungs whenever she took a breath.

Ruth held a warm flannel to her face. "The doctor said you're suffering from smoke inhalation. All the cilia in your airways have been singed off, just like those of a veteran smoker."

"I'm never going to smoke again."

"You'll definitely give up now." Ruth threw the flannel into the sink and took her gently by the arm, down the passageway to her bedroom.

She should have been prepared for the impact when she heard the scrabble of feet from behind. But her reflexes were dulled and she was unable to sidestep the mammoth paws as they slapped against her back, knocking her from

Ruth's clasp on to the wooden floor.

With what little strength she had, she pushed the slobbering beast away while Ruth got a grip on her collar. The effort caused a fit of coughing. She caught her breath and gasped, "Prudence seems to think she's hungry."

"I fed her when you were in the bath. All I could find were lentil patties. She didn't seem to mind," Ruth said.

"The dog meat's in the freezer."

"Oh, I thought you were one of those obsessive vegetarian types who doesn't give her dog meat."

"Give me some credit, Ruth," Cecelia said as Ruth helped her off the floor.

She flopped on to her bed. The dog climbed up next to her, putting her head on the spare pillow and falling asleep instantly. Cecelia sank back, envious of the dog's carefree slumber, wondering if a peaceful sleep would ever be hers again.

Ruth bustled around the room. With her halo of blonde curls, she looked angelic in the soft light. Watching her, Cecelia wondered how she could ever show Ruth how much she appreciated and valued her friendship. Ruth had always seemed so self-sufficient. She never seemed to get into scrapes, never needed any kind of help or moral boost.

And it wasn't as if Ruth's life lacked tragedy.

"Ruth?" Cecelia said leaning back further into her pillows, her mood continuing along its contemplative path. "Do you still think of your husband?"

Ruth was straightening the patchwork quilt on the end of Cecelia's bed. She stopped what she was doing and looked at her friend, a frown creasing her forehead.

"Sometimes."

"Sorry, I didn't mean to pry. I suppose I'm just feeling a

bit maudlin. There's nothing like a near-death experience to get the old brain cells cranking: life, death, the secrets of the universe, etcetera."

Ruth straightened herself up, letting out a long sigh. "To dwell on death is futile. It's life that counts."

Cecelia closed her eyes and took a breath. "I still think about little Tom."

"Of course you do."

"He wasn't conceived under ideal circumstances. I suppose he was never meant to be."

"You need to get to sleep. Thoughts like that will only keep you awake. I don't want a depressive on my hands." She paused for a moment's thought. "I'm going with Cliff to a bike show in the city on Saturday. We're going to stay the night with one of Cliff's mates, but we'll be back early Sunday morning - why don't you come along?"

Cecelia shook her head. The topic had been changed, just as it always was when she tried to scratch beneath the surface with Ruth.

"I'm not sure I'll be up to it by then. The doctor said I had to take it easy, remember?"

"That's OK. I just thought it might help." Ruth flicked a finger into the air. "I'd better get you a bucket, just in case. I'll be back in a sec."

Cecelia blew out a breath. At least she'd got a valid excuse to miss the bike show. Cliff was one of the few people Cecelia had met to whom she'd taken an instant dislike; he emanated violence the way a pot-bellied stove gave off heat. On several occasions Ruth had sported mysterious bruises for which she had no explanation other than liking it rough. It was at times like these that Cecelia would catch a glimpse of the vulnerability as fragile as the tip of an icicle, buried deep within her friend.

Ruth reappeared. "How are you now? I'll bet that bed feels good," she said.

"Just about everything aches, even my hair."

"You were very lucky." She drew the curtains, and put a glass of water on the bedside table and a bucket by the bed. She stood over Cecelia, looking at her with anxious blue eyes. "Would you like me to stay? I will if you'd feel more comfortable."

Cecelia didn't trust herself to speak. The concern in her friend's face was enough to start the tears welling.

Finally she sniffed. "There's a spare mattress under the bed. You can grab some bedding from the linen cupboard."

"OK. Go to sleep, Cecelia. When you wake up you'll feel much better. Things are always worse in the middle of the night."

Cecelia clutched her pillow to her chest and Ruth rubbed her back in slow circles until she relaxed. Then, overcome by her own weariness, Ruth succumbed to the mattress on the floor.

But sleep didn't come to Cecelia. She knew it wouldn't. She lay awake listening to the rock-crushing snores of her bloodhound and Ruth's soft breathing from the floor by her bed. Every time she closed her eyes, she was back in the prefab, the flames growing closer, building up like the screams inside her head. Her heart pounded in her head with a sickening rhythm. She took some deep breaths to slow it down, noticing how the rhythm seemed to have synchronised itself to the ticking of the alarm clock and the noises of the night. From the river a banjo frog called to its mate with a slow resonant twang. The old gum in the back garden creaked to the whisper of the breeze.

She listened to the tapping of the moths as they threw themselves against the flyscreen, trying to get to the soft glow behind the curtains. By morning they would be no more than small piles of powdery nothingness on the windowsill.

And then her thoughts drifted to the man with kind eyes, who, in a moment of panic, had mistaken her for his dead wife.

25

The early morning sun filtered through the bedroom curtains making the inside of his eyelids warm and red despite the cold emptiness he felt everywhere else. Cam exhaled and stretched out on the bed with his hands tucked under his head, trying to make some sense out of the previous night.

Vince was dead. He'd destroyed the photo lab and come close to murdering two people in an attempt to protect his career. Overcome with remorse he had then taken his own life. No, this was all too neat, too tidy. Suicides are rarely so transparent. Vince had never obliged anyone in life; why then would he be so obliging in death?

The facts pricked at Cam's mind like a grass seed in a dog's pelt: the car seat, the suicide method, the time-frame, the motive, even the note did not ring true. He stared up at the purring ceiling fan as it shifted stale air around the room, willing it to blow the fuzz from his brain. But he received no blinding revelations, just a noise from the kitchen to disturb his thoughts.

Ruby.

"Hey, I was going to make you McDaddy's," Cam said as he stumbled into the kitchen, rubbing his sore eyes and stifling a yawn

She'd already filled a mixing bowl with cereal and was putting on the finishing touches of strawberries and cream. He marvelled, not for the first time, at how slim she managed to stay.

"That's OK, Dad. I'm not really hungry."

She moved into the lounge room, put the telly on and plonked herself down in front of it. His eyes wandered around the room. Well, they no longer lived in a warehouse, but homey was not an accurate description either. Ruby's possessions were spread almost over every square inch of the house. A trail of discarded clothes and shoes led to the bathroom where lotions, potions, powders and gels covered the vanity unit. CDs and videos were stacked in precarious piles along the hearth in the lounge. Cords of electrical gadgets Cam couldn't identify criss-crossed the carpet like the tangled net of an animal trap. He grimaced, knowing only too well who the first hapless victim would be.

"So what plans have you got for today: the stock feeder's?" He leaned across the breakfast bar and poured the remaining handful of cornflakes into a bowl for himself.

Ruby did not look up. Between shovel loads of cereal, she was untangling the wires of her Sony Playstation.

"Cecelia, I mean Ms Bowman, said I could go over to her place and she'd show me more of her photos. I thought I'd give her a ring, maybe go over this morning." She caught his worried frown. "Yeah, yeah, I'll ring you if I go out," she said, her voice flat.

Cam started to cough and splutter.

"Are you OK, Dad? You look like shit."

He nodded and wiped his mouth with a tea towel. Should he tell her about the fire? She'd find out soon enough. He had to say something.

"Ms Bowman's photo lab burned down last night. That's why I was late home. We think vandals did it. Luckily no one was in it at the time. I think Ms Bowman will be pretty busy going over things today. There'll be all sorts of insurance stuff to organise."

He bunched up the tea towel and threw it in the direction of the laundry, scanning her face as he did so, looking for a crack, a grimace or a tear. In the past, even the word fire had set her off.

But she responded like any normal, self-absorbed teenager. "Bummer. I hope I can still do photography at school." She let out melodramatic sigh. "I guess I'll just have to go to the stock feeder's, then."

"You can also put your name on your new uniforms and cover your books."

No response; perhaps he was asking too much.

He'd showered at the station earlier, so his preparations to leave only involved changing into his uniform, grabbing his keys and giving Ruby the usual goodbye speech that resulted in the usual eye roll. Mrs Wilmot would be starting at their house next week. Maybe then he'd be able to leave the house without the usual feeling of dread.

He parked the ute in his reserved space behind the station, immediately sensing that something was different. The cars: there were too many of them. Shit, there was a Channel Nine news van, a couple of unfamiliar newer models and a small crowd of people on the front steps.

Someone hoisted a camera.

"There he is!"

Microphones were brandished in the air like cudgels. The crowd moved towards him with the enthusiasm of a Highland horde. He made a dash for the back entrance, only to find it locked.

Damn Derek to hell. He turned to face the mob. A flash exploded in his face. He saw white ghosts on a dark void.

"…the third police suicide in three months…"

"…Royal Commission…"

"…stresses of the job…"

"…police corruption…"

"Can you give us the cop's name?"

"No comment." Cam pushed his way through the mass of bodies. Just as he reached the front entrance a man said, "Are you the same Sergeant Fraser whose family were killed by a bikie bomb in Sydney?"

He whirled around and faced the crowd. They fell silent, a pack of dogs waiting apprehensively to see who would get the first morsel.

He drew a deep breath. "The name of the constable involved will be withheld pending notification of next of kin. Details of the tragedy cannot be revealed at this stage of the investigation."

"But it was a suicide, right?"

"Please contact police media in Toorrup if you have any other questions. Thank you."

Cam stormed through the front entrance, locked the door on the clicking camera shutters and strode over to Derek at communications. The constable looked up from his crossword puzzle, regarding Cam for a moment through dishwater eyes.

From his lifeless eyes to the ever-present cup of tepid weak tea by his side, there was nothing distinguishing about the man. His personality was grey. Vince had been a veritable Bob Hope compared to this man.

"I heard you had a rough night. Too bad about Vince." Derek rubbed his beaky nose, his gaze falling back down to the paper in front of him. Cam felt like screwing the paper up into a ball and shoving it down the constable's throat.

"Thanks for your help out there," he said.

Derek nodded without looking up. Cam wondered how Derek would react if the station were burning down. Probably finish the crossword first. He was either the coolest customer that Cam had ever met or the dimmest. Cam hadn't worked him out yet.

"As much charisma as a cup of warm piss," he muttered to himself like an old man. Then in a louder voice he said, "You relieve Leanne on traffic this arvo, OK?"

"Right-oh, Sarge."

Cam fixed himself a coffee, then went into his office and closed the door. Prising open the Venetian blinds, he noticed with relief that the press had packed up and gone. He settled down to tackle last night's incident reports, make some phone calls and organise the interviews. He was halfway through his second report when the phone rang.

"Hey, Sarge." It was Pete. "I've just finished having a chat with Toby Bell. He was not impressed at being dragged out of bed at 7 am, I'm telling you."

"So, did you confront him with the account drawings?"

"Yeah, I did. He just about shat himself. I think he was more scared of his wife hearing about what he's been up to than anything I had to say."

The office door opened and Derek appeared. "Mr Smithson's here. He wants to see you."

Shit; a confrontation with that man was the last thing Cam needed right now.

"Tell him he'll have to wait." Cam swivelled around on his chair so his back was to Derek, and continued his telephone conversation with Pete.

"So what was his explanation?" he asked.

"He withdrew the money in a lump sum and gave it to a Ms Tiffany Davis," Pete said.

Cam smiled for the first time that day. "Ah, the niece. Of course."

"That's one name for it, I guess. Anyway, Sarge, I followed

it through and traced it to a deposit on an apartment. It's all bona fide, he's just putting her up in style."

"You've done well, Pete. Good work. That makes up for last night."

"We even then?" Cam could hear the cocky smile breaking through the young constable's voice, picture the deepening dimples of his cheeks.

"Almost. Get back here ASAP."

Cam replaced the receiver and turned back to Derek.

"Sarge, he insists on seeing you now."

Cam sighed and rubbed his eyes. "Show him in, then."

Derek showed Mr Smithson in, closing the door behind him. Cam gestured to the spare office chair but didn't get up. Mr Smithson continued to stand. His face was pale; there were beads of sweat on his forehead. He opened his hands to speak, but thought better of it and reached into his pocket for a handkerchief instead.

"Mr Smithson, are you feeling all right?" Cam asked, taking in his visitor's pasty complexion and the slump of his thin shoulders.

"I... I want to know what you're doing about the fire."

Cam searched the man's face, trying to fathom the true reason for his visit. "I'm waiting to hear back from forensics, though I'm not pinning much on the physical evidence. I still have some other leads to follow up." Cam put his elbows on his desk and steepled his hands. He stared at Smithson for a good ten seconds before continuing: "Is that all you wanted to speak to me about, Jeffrey?"

Smithson unfurled his handkerchief as if it were a flag of truce and began to dab at his face. Cam got up from his desk and poked his head out of his office door, calling to Derek to bring in a pot of tea. He pulled out the spare chair and indicated for Smithson to sit down.

Smithson stared blankly at Cam for a moment then took off his jacket, sinking into the chair with his head bowed as if all the energy had been sucked from his system.

"When you're ready, mate. I'm not going anywhere." Cam sat back down behind his desk.

Smithson took a breath. "When we got back home last night, my wife and I had a talk. She persuaded me to come and see you to…" He waved a limp hand in the air.

"Put the record straight?"

"Quite." He nodded and looked into his lap for a few seconds. "I hit him. You know that? I hit him but I didn't kill him."

Cam nodded. "Go on."

"Did Ms Bowman give you the details?"

"Some, but I'd like to hear your side of the story."

"She caught Herbert Bell stealing Anne's underthings from the washing line. I was consumed with rage when she told me. When we found him in the shed, I felt like I wanted to kill him. Cecelia had to hold me back, but not before I got a solid punch off into his face." He looked down at the hand on his lap and rubbed at his swollen knuckles, as if still feeling the sting. The glazed look in his eye told Cam he was far away, back in the potting shed.

Derek knocked then entered the office with a tea tray. Smithson started, took a deep breath and pulled himself back to the present.

Cam poured tea. Smithson seemed mesmerised by the hot amber liquid, staring at it as if it might provide him with some kind of a release. Eventually one corner of his mouth curved into a slight smile. "I felt a lot better after that."

Cam pushed a cup of tea towards Smithson and took a

sip of his own before saying, "I'd consider anger to be a normal reaction to the situation you've just described." He took a breath. "But I consider hitting him to be an over-reaction."

Smithson opened his mouth to speak, but couldn't find the words. Cam continued. "From our first meeting, I got the feeling you were trying to protect your wife from something. My best guess is she's been the victim of some kind of violent crime. That might also explain your assault on Bell." He took another sip of tea, not taking his eyes off Smithson. "Am I right?"

The older man sighed, nodding.

"I'm sorry you didn't think of telling me about this earlier." Cam tempered his stern tone with compassion. "Your lies and hostility to my inquiries have hindered the investigation and cast both yourself and your wife in a suspicious light."

Smithson passed a hand across his face, focusing on the teapot. He took a breath and spoke in a flat tone, as if the smallest of inflections might provide a weakness through which his barely contained emotions would escape.

"We lived in Adelaide. I used to work long hours. We almost lived separate lives, both involved with our own careers. I came home late one night and immediately knew that something was wrong. She always left lights on for me, but this time the house was completely dark and the front door was unlocked. I went up to the bedroom and…"

He made a small sound, almost like a hiccup. Cam was sure he would lose it now but Smithson took a breath and managed to keep himself together. "She was tied up on the bed. She'd been raped and left lying there. She'd been alone in the dark for hours. The physical scars healed, but…" he sighed, and shrugged, glancing at Cam before shifting his gaze back to the tea tray.

"She took the long service leave she was owed and we began to re-evaluate our lives. I never wanted to be in a job that took me away from her again. I resigned from my company, did a Dip Ed, then we applied for the position at Glenroyd. It all seemed so perfect. Just the challenge she needed to help her to forget the trauma. We threw ourselves into turning the school around. You've seen how much we've achieved in such a short time."

Some of the old pomposity had returned to his voice, but Cam forgave him for it.

"But then the underwear theft seemed to open up the old wounds. I suppose it was the sexual connotations…"

"Was the rapist ever caught?"

Smithson shook his head. "No. We've had no closure."

Cam cleared his throat. "You know, Jeffrey, it's as much in your wife's interest as it is in ours that we find the perpetrators of these violent crimes at the school." Cam paused, studied Smithson for a moment then said, "Do you see where I'm going with this?"

Jeffrey looked at him and licked his thin lips. "I've been stupid. I've not co-operated, I've lied to you."

Cam acknowledged this with a nod. "You may not have had closure for the rape case, but working with us now, helping us solve these violent crimes, will at least give you both peace of mind in this instance."

Smithson took a deep breath, closed his eyes as if trying to ward off physical pain. "What do you want to know, Sergeant?"

The many unanswered questions: the murder of Herbert Bell, the fire, Vince's death – maybe Smithson couldn't provide answers to those, but there was something else.

Cam tapped at his teeth with his pen.

"Tell me about the estate of the late Miss Jane Featherstone."

Smithson looked perplexed. He shrugged his bony shoulders. "She was an old girl of Glenroyd, passed away about eighteen months ago at St Luke's retirement home in Toorrup. She had no family and left all her money to the school. That's really all there is to it."

"How much?"

"Just under a million dollars. It covered the science lab and some of the new classrooms."

"And who was the executor of the will? I'd like to see a copy."

"I haven't seen a copy myself, Sergeant, it was a private will. The executor transferred the money to our account. It was all so easy, so uncomplicated, a gift. I signed for it, I declared it to the tax department, I did nothing wrong."

His voice rose. He was on the defensive again, almost back to his old self. Cam made placating hand gestures then took a sip of tea, giving the man the chance to calm down.

"Who was the executor?" Cam asked.

"A teacher at the school, an old girl herself and the granddaughter of Miss Featherstone's best friend. You've met her: Ruth Tilly, the head of our science department."

26

Cam continued with the paperwork and the phone calls, occasionally pausing to tap his pen against his teeth or squeeze the palm exerciser as if hoping to extract answers from it. The last violent crime committed in Glenroyd was an incident of road rage over six months ago. A year before that a pub brawl resulted in a serious head injury. Now, three violent acts since his arrival – a coincidence? Cam didn't believe in coincidences. His instinct told him they were related, but how, why and by whom?

At one stage Derek knocked and entered, leaving a fax on his desk. It was from Scotland Yard and contained information he'd requested earlier. He became so engrossed in his reading he forgot his meeting with Angelo and started with surprise when Derek showed the boy into the office.

"Hey," said Cam getting up from his desk. "Glad you showed up."

"Cliff doesn't know I'm here. He's gone out for lunch. I walked so he won't see my car gone."

Angelo walked over to the Venetian blind and prised the shades. Cam almost suggested he wear a false nose and glasses next time, but managed to stop himself in time. Angelo didn't seem such a bad kid, but the kiss he'd witnessed irked him and what Angelo might get up to with his daughter in the future worried him even more. He had a feeling of animosity towards this kid he knew he would have to get over. At times like this he missed Elizabeth more than ever.

"That's fine," Cam said. "What he doesn't know won't hurt him."

He locked the fax in his desk drawer then drove Angelo to the scene of Sunday's bushfire.

It came as no surprise to discover the body had been found in the same area Cliff had abused Angelo for spraying. Cam had yet to interview Bell's de facto over his disappearance, but the more he thought about it the more the names Cliff Donovan and Ruth Tilly occupied his mind. But what was missing? What was the simple clue that tied them to these crimes? Their names continued to float around in his head with no anchors but wary circumspection and gut instinct.

"How long have Cliff and Ruth been going out?" he asked Angelo during the drive back.

"A few months, maybe."

"So what's she like, then?"

Angelo selected one of the shrugs from his wide vocabulary. "She's OK." He reached into his top pocket for a cigarette.

Cam shook his head. "No smoking in here, son." His sentence dangled in the silence as he appraised his passenger. "You're acting nervous – you nervous, Angelo?"

Angelo rubbed at his mouth, craving that smoke. "If Cliff knows I've been talking to you, I'm history."

Cam risked another glance. "Have you stopped to think that might be because he's got something to hide?"

Angelo said nothing. The white fence posts on the side of the road flashed passed in a blur.

"If your boss was doing something illegal, would you tell me about it?"

Angelo pointed to a truck stop ahead. "You can drop me

off here. I'll walk back."

Cam continued driving. "You know I'm conducting a murder investigation, don't you?"

"Cliff wouldn't murder anyone." Angelo's eyes darted to the speedo then to the door of the ute. He seemed desperate enough to make a jump for it. Cam didn't want to push him that far.

"OK, fair enough, but what about handling stolen property? A tanker truck was stolen in Glenroyd about ten weeks ago. I'm guessing it ended up in a chop shop somewhere, maybe a chop shop near where it was stolen – any ideas?"

"Vince talked to Cliff about that. I wouldn't know. Listen—"

"Talk much, did they?"

"They were mates, OK?"

Cam was getting under the boy's skin, just as he'd hoped.

"Cliff used to come around, but then they had some kind of a blue. They were yelling in the workshop. I heard them. I thought they were going to kill each other. He stopped coming around after that."

"What were they yelling about?"

"I dunno really." Angelo turned his head away.

"Something about the tanker maybe?"

Angelo looked at the passing scenery and stitched his lips together.

"How long ago did they have that blue?" Cam continued.

"A few weeks I guess."

Angelo fidgeted in his seat. "Listen Mr, er, Sergeant Fraser. I've done what I can, I've shown you where I was doing the spraying, where Cliff did his rag at me, I really can't help any more. I can only tell you what I know, right?

Whatever else Cliff is up to is his business. I stay out of it. I don't like Cliff much and I guess you know that, but still, I don't go dobbing people in just for the sake of it either. You asked me about the fire, I told you. That's all I know."

Cam pulled over to the side of the road and let him out. He sat in the car and watched Angelo kicking a beer can along the dirt verge until a cloud of red dust swallowed him up.

So what did the kid know that he wasn't telling?

27

Cam arrived at Cecelia's house at about two that afternoon, his steps ringing hollow on the wooden veranda. He felt a flutter of apprehension. After what they had been through last night, the stiff formalities of a police interview seemed somehow inappropriate.

He wondered if she would feel the same.

The door opened before he had the chance to knock and Ruth Tilly stood before him. If he'd been a serial sex offender he might have received a more benevolent look. Her eyes narrowed and the top of her lip twitched into a slight curl. He repressed a flinch when her arterial red fingernails rested against the scarred skin of his forearm.

Leaning towards him she whispered, "She's really not yet ready to be interviewed, Cam. The doctor wanted her to stay in bed."

"It's important, Ruth." He became aware of the brackish odour of the river stagnating near the back boundary of Cecelia's house.

"Go easy on her then," Ruth said, in a low husky voice. "She's had a bad night." She took in his pale face and the bags of fatigue under his eyes. "Come to think of it, you don't look much better yourself."

The pressure of her fingers increased. Cam decided he could do without her concern and allowed his arm to drop. There was a shadow of movement from behind and Cecelia appeared from the interior of the dark house.

Ruth turned to her. "I suppose I'd better be going now. Cam's come to ask you some questions." The whites of her eyes flashed as she rolled them upwards.

Cecelia hugged the taller woman and thanked her for staying. Cam watched and marvelled. Physically, the women were diametric opposites. Like opposing colours on a paint chart, each seemed to highlight the other's attributes. One was tall and curvaceous with wavy blonde hair and the other was small and dark haired, like a wood nymph. One left him cold, the other provoked feelings he thought he'd forgotten.

Cecelia gave her departing friend one last wave, then turned back to Cam. He wondered if she was feeling awkward, as he was. He took off his cap and gestured with it to her front door. "May I come in? I need to ask you some questions?"

She ushered him into the cool dark hallway and through to the lounge. He took in what he could of the house as he walked, noticing the jarrah floorboards and rough plaster walls covered with framed photographs. The unusual mixture of furniture in the lounge, far from a hotch-potch, was a palette of complementary colours and bold design. The red fabric of the overstuffed armchair highlighted the colours in the tartan couch that in turn seemed to have no problem with the geometric design of the rug upon which it rested. The wooden furniture was of all types: pine, jarrah and oak, almost every surface covered with teetering piles of books and bizarre knick-knacks: misshapen blobs of clay and papier-mache ornaments. Gifts from pupils perhaps?

Cecelia smiled. "If the look on your face is anything to go by, this is not what you expected."

Cam swept his arms around the room. "Where's the purple satin and the candles? The crystals and the tarot cards?"

Cecelia laughed, "You obviously think I'm some kind of new age crazy."

"Magic happens," he said, quoting the familiar bumper sticker.

She raised a finger. "Ah, the music from the office," she said as if that explained everything. "Actually, that was Mrs Godfrey's. I only turned it on out of curiosity. I prefer something with a bit more of a beat."

There was a scrabbling sound across the floorboards. He turned to see a slobbering, doggy dynamo sliding towards him at great speed, riding the hall runner like a surfboard.

"Prudence!" Cecelia chastised as the big dog slid to a stop, hefting its paws on to Cam's chest. "Get down!"

Any awkwardness Cam might have felt earlier was laughed off as he battled with the playful brute. Cecelia eventually got the dog under control and pushed her out of the front door. Cam was still grinning when she sat him down next to a wooden coffee table, piled high with yellow National Geographic magazines arranged in the shape of an Aztec pyramid.

She threw him a damp cloth from the kitchen and he started to mop the foaming streaks of dog slobber from his uniform. He worked down his trouser leg and paused at a bleach stain he hadn't noticed before, looking up when he heard the chinking of ice cubes. She responded to his unintentional frown with an apology.

"Sorry about that, it will come out in the wash," she said.

He shook his head. "It's not the dog slobber that's worrying me. I'm a country boy, this is mother's milk to me."

"When shit on the shoe was just a fact of life."

"Ah yes, those were the days." He looked down at the stain on his trousers again, stretching out the faded fabric so she could see the light peppering of holes.

She quirked an eyebrow at the offending stain. "Someone obviously failed washing 101."

"I failed home economics too," he said, but he'd lost interest in their banter. The stain on his trousers had triggered a memory that at the time was so insignificant he'd stored it at the very back of his mind: a skip of builder's rubbish, containers, a coffee filter. He realised that the irritating rash on his leg had been bothering him since then. He could see now how it corresponded exactly with the cloth-eating stain on his trousers.

Cecelia leaned towards him and rattled the ice cubes in the glass again.

"Sorry," he said with a smile, "I was miles away."

She handed him a glass of lemonade. He noticed her small hands and long fingers. They were the kind you expected artists to have.

"It's homemade. I hope it's sweet enough."

He took a sip and smacked his lips. "Delicious," he said, and it was. He watched her as she settled into the couch opposite, drawing her shapely bare legs under herself. She was only wearing an oversized T-shirt but there was no self-consciousness or embarrassment in the movement. His gaze travelled up her slender neck to her face noticing the shadows, like thumb prints, under her eyes.

"Ruth said you had a rough night," he said.

She lost her playful façade and looked away, somewhere beyond the view from the window, past the hanging baskets that swayed on the back veranda, past the garden that was the colour of mown hay and out to the tepid pools of the drying river.

She nodded her head and turned back to him. "Will I ever be able to forget it?"

"No," he answered quietly. "You won't. But the nightmares will stop. Eventually."

She chewed on the inside of her cheek for a moment, then said, "Do you think someone tried to kill us?"

He had a sudden urge to share his doubts, his fears, his suspicions and speculations; but what he wanted and what the responsibilities of the job demanded were, as usual, at odds. He took a sip of lemonade and put the glass on the table.

"I don't think anyone was trying to kill you, Cecelia, but I have to ask anyway, for the record. Do you know of anyone who might have wished you harm?"

Cecelia took a deep breath. "You can't expect to pass through life without upsetting anyone," she said, "but I can't think of anyone I've antagonised enough to want to kill me."

"How do you get along with the Smithsons?"

"When Anne and I aren't battling over school policies or my propensity for being late to staff meetings, we get on well."

"She seems quite a nervous type."

"Wouldn't you be if you were married to Jeffrey?" He smiled. Cecelia continued, "No, actually. She's not that bad. You have to be tough to be a school principal. She's just been a bit off since the underwear theft, that's all."

"And what about Jeffrey?"

She shrugged and a sleeve slipped from her shoulder. Cam looked away and busied himself picking at a callus on his hand.

"Ruth seems to think he's jealous of me. I'm deputy principal and he's not. He's only had about a year's teaching experience and even he can see that the School Board would never accept him."

"But he is the power behind the throne."

"Oh absolutely, but I doubt he resents me enough to try and kill me."

"What about Vince Petrowski?"

She pulled thoughtfully at her bottom lip. "I've had some run-ins with him. He seems to think he's God's gift to women, that we should all be swooning at his feet. He got quite aggro with me the last time. It was before you arrived, when he was acting sergeant. He charged me with dangerous driving then offered me a way out of it. I told him where he could stick his way out and he became abusive."

Cam nodded. It wasn't hard to imagine the kind of way out a man like Vince would have offered.

"But not violent?"

"No, just foul-mouthed. He sent me a written apology a few days later, which I accepted. I guess he knew you were on your way and was worried I might report him."

Cam blew out his breath. "You won't be having to worry about Vince again, Cecelia."

"I heard he'd been suspended."

He looked at her for a moment before answering. The ceiling fan rotated above them, making a soft flapping sound. "No, not because of the suspension. He committed suicide last night." He hesitated. "Or so it seems. The matter has still to be investigated further."

She covered her mouth with her hand. The flapping of the fan now seemed unbearably loud in the heavy silence. She unfolded herself from the couch and walked to the wall to turn it off. When she turned to face him, her arms were folded across her stomach.

"I never liked him, you know that, but suicide? It makes me wonder what he must have been going through. I feel—"

"Guilty?"

She nodded. "Do you?"

"No, I don't. The story of Vince was never destined to have a happy ending. Suicide is a coward's way out."

She worried at her bottom lip with her teeth. Eventually she looked him in the eye and said, "You surprise me Cam. I never took you to be a hard man."

He shrugged. "In this job you have to be."

He rose to his feet and guided her back to the couch. His hand rested on the small of her back, lingering there longer than necessary. He withdrew when he realised what he was doing. The fire was last night's history; now they were in the present. He was a cop and she was a witness and that's all there was to it.

"I'm sorry to have to upset you with all this, but I still have some more questions," he said.

She settled back down and drew her knees up.

"Can you think of any enemies you might have? A distraught boyfriend perhaps?"

She gave a start and shook her head. "I'm sorry, I was still thinking about Vince. Do you think he burned the building to destroy the photos I was developing for you?"

"It can't be discounted." He tried again. "Are you involved with anyone, Cecelia?"

"No, I've been unattached since my divorce."

"Ex-husband?"

"A poisoned hatpin might be Garry's style, but certainly not a bomb."

Cam raised his eyebrows. He was pleased to see that some of her humour had returned.

"I'm only joking. Our divorce was messy, but the marriage

ended over two years ago. I haven't seen him since. Last I heard he was busy setting up house with his new boyfriend, they were about to open a wine bar in the city."

Her gaze dropped to her toes and a flush blossomed up her neck. She leaned against the armrest of the couch and rested her chin in her hand, half covering her mouth.

"I'd like you to think back to the fire. When I found you, it seemed as if you'd been knocked out. Can you remember anything?"

Cecelia rubbed the lump on the back of her head and focused inward. Cam waited for her to speak.

"I was standing on a stool, reaching up to get some glue from the shelf," she said. "Then I remember a sudden crash and I fell. I guess I must have hit my head. The next thing I remember is the smoke and you crawling towards me."

"Did you tell anyone that you were going to be working at the photo lab that night?"

She shook her head.

He raised his eyes to the ceiling, steepling his fingers. "I didn't notice your car anywhere near."

"I parked it round the front. I had some things I wanted to leave for the secretary. It was easier to carry them in from there."

"Where would you usually park?"

"There's a small car park near the photo lab. I usually park there." Her eyes widened. "You think the person who did this didn't know I was there?"

Cam shook his head. "I don't think you were the target, Cecelia."

"You think they were after you?"

He shrugged and raked his hand through his hair, then reached for his lemonade and swallowed down a large mouthful, trying to get rid of the sudden taste of bile and soot. Now he was certain he could eliminate Cecelia as the target, he had no doubt who the victim was meant to be.

She broke the silence and gave him a puzzled look, "Who would want to kill you?"

Vince, to save his career? Still a possibility.

The killer of Herbert Bell? More likely if he sensed Cam was getting close.

The Razorbacks? The thought made the skin on the back of his neck prickle.

"I'm a cop. Cops always have enemies," he said.

He looked back down at the stain on his trousers, scratched at the itch and said, "The photos in the drying cabinet, the ones of the renovations, do you have any copies?"

"I was going to give them to the secretary to print up for the school magazine." She caught her breath. "No, wait a minute. I do have a couple of copies here at home. I put them in an envelope to post off to my mother. Hang on, I'll get them."

In a couple of minutes she returned and handed Cam an envelope containing the photos. He thanked her and buttoned them in his top pocket.

It was time to pick up Leanne from the station and visit the Blayney property.

But at that moment a tickle in his chest turned into a spasm and before he knew it, he was in the throes of a violent coughing fit. He stumbled into the hall and coughed himself dry. Wiping his mouth with his handkerchief and gasping for breath, he turned, finding her standing behind him.

"Did you get checked out by the doctor?" she asked, with a frown of concern. "They gave me oxygen at the medical centre. It made quite a difference. You should have gone too."

He shook his head and took a deep breath.

"You should have, you have smoke inhalation. It's when the cilia…" She paused and noticed again the scars mottling his arm and the side of his neck. "I suppose I don't have to tell you about that."

"No, you don't."

Sun streamed in from the leadlight above the door, filling the hall with coloured patterns. She reached for his hand and gave it a squeeze. Cam arched his brow, holding her stare. His eyes drifted to her soft smile and her parted lips. He could imagine the kiss, how it would taste. He drew back.

She let go of his hand. He reached for the hat he'd left on the hall table and turned back to her.

Her smile washed over him, like absolution. "You got me out, Cam," she said.

28

It was late afternoon, but even under the shade of the large jarrah the day still sweltered. Gay Cronin's grey hair fell across her face in strings and her T-shirt was dark with sweat. Splattered with yellow paint, her legs looked like co-joined fence strainers jammed into an unforgiving pair of lycra shorts. When she sank back into the faded deckchair, the nylon bulges shimmied in the filtered sunlight.

A country song bounced from a tinny tape recorder by her side. Leanne turned it off, the better for Gay to absorb the sombre news. After a few seconds of silence the old woman opened her mouth and began to wail, revealing a disconcerting cave of bad teeth.

"Herb, my Herbie, what am I going to do without you? Where am I going to go?"

Leanne put her arm around her shoulders. "There, there, Gay. You just let it out. Have a good cry then maybe you'll feel a bit better."

She turned to Cam hovering in the background. "How about you put the kettle on, Sarge? Gay, do you mind if the sergeant goes into your caravan and makes us a cuppa?"

Gay wiped at her face with her T-shirt and nodded her head, knocking her leather bush hat to the ground. She picked it up and began to twist the rim around with her fingers. After sucking in a breath from the airless atmosphere, she let out a wobbly sigh. When she sniffed, a phlegmy sound rasped at the back of her throat.

"Grab some tissues while you're at it, Sarge," Leanne suggested.

Grateful to escape, Cam walked over to the caravan. A freshly poured concrete slab upon which someone had scrawled the words *Herb loves Gay 4 ever* fronted it.

He pushed open the door. Hot and airless, it had the unique old caravan smell of flypaper and mould, though it was a lot more orderly than he'd expected. The double bed in the end alcove was made with fresh clean linen, a vase of flowers sat on the pullout table, clean dishes dried on a rack near the miniature sink.

When he opened the kitchen drawer for a teaspoon, he noticed all the utensils were engraved with Herb's initials, HCB. The plates were named in permanent marker, so was the radio by the sink and the tiny television near the bed; every possession, it seemed, was marked by its owner. It takes one to know one, Cam thought with a cynical smile.

While waiting for the kettle to boil, he wandered back outside. A red cloud kelpie, as old as time, looked up from the marron claw it was munching and stared at him through misty eyes. It wagged its tail when Cam bent to give it a pat, its coat as rich and red as earth, glossy with health. People who looked after their animals well can't be all bad, he thought, until he saw the evil-jawed rabbit and fox traps hanging from hooks off the caravan wall.

Drop nets and scoop nets leaned against the back of the van. A strong fishy smell alerted him to a pile of marron remains nearby, on the fringe of a small wood. A marron poacher: funny how that was no surprise; the succulent freshwater lobster was going for about twenty-five dollars a kilo in the markets at the moment.

Stacks of neatly piled beer bottles reinforced the exterior rear caravan wall. Clean and without labels, they looked as if they were ready for a major home brew bottling operation. His assumption proved correct: the bottles lining the other wall were already full.

The car was parked around the other side of the caravan. She'd carefully covered the windows with newspaper and had been slapping on the yellow exterior flat when they'd pulled up earlier. Then he'd wanted to laugh; now he looked at the industry of her day and felt depressed. He gingerly touched the new paintwork. It was almost dry and spotted with the bodies of trapped flies.

She seemed to have taken an instant dislike to him, because of his authority or his sex, he wasn't sure. When he handed her a mug of tea, she thanked him with a sharp nod. Leanne occupied the only other chair so he squatted on his haunches next to the old woman. He scooped up a gumnut, breathed in its medicinal scent, waiting for one of them to say something.

Leanne was the first to speak. "Sarge, Gay says she last saw Herb here on Saturday evening."

Cam looked from the gumnut to Leanne then to Gay, expecting some elaboration. When none was forthcoming, he said, "Gay, it's really important for us to trace Herb's final movements so we can find out what happened to him. Did Leanne mention that the evidence so far suggests he was murdered?"

The woman's bottom lip trembled despite Cam's gentle tone. Leanne put a hand upon her arm and scowled at Cam, as if grief was some sort of secret women's business. If they were to progress at the speed Leanne was instigating, he thought, they'd be here all night.

"Did you bring the tissues?" Leanne asked him.

He slapped his hands on his thighs and went back to the caravan, allowing several minutes to elapse before returning with a long ribbon of toilet paper.

"Gay was saying Herb always wanted to have his ashes

scattered off the Abrolhos Islands," Leanne said, taking the toilet paper from Cam and handing it to the grieving woman.

"He liked fishing, did he?" Cam asked.

Gay nodded, trumpeting into the paper.

"I see he also liked the odd marron or two."

She looked up from her nose blowing long enough to shoot him a poisonous look.

"That's not what's bothering me, Mrs Cronin," Cam said. "I don't give a hoot about his poaching, or his social security fraud, or any of his other sins, unless they can help us solve the mystery of his death." Cam took a breath, trying to hide his impatience. "We need your help, Mrs Cronin - I'm presuming you want the character who did this caught, don't you?"

Sparks ignited in her muddy eyes. "Too right I want him caught, and when you catch him, I'm gonna scratch out his eyes and cut off his balls for what he done to me."

Cam didn't doubt it for a minute. "Our evidence suggests Herb drowned in a dam. Did he go marroning Saturday night?"

She looked at the deepening sky, giving the matter thought. She ignored him and turned to Leanne. "Yeah, he left about eight and never come back."

"You didn't report him missing, Mrs Cronin. May I ask why?" Cam said.

"We had a tiff, that's why. I thought he'd just gone walk-about. He does that sometimes. He'll go on a bender and not come home for days."

"Apart from your blue, then, had he been acting strangely? Did he seem scared or worried about anything or anyone?" Leanne asked.

"Nah, no more than normal. He was always figuring

someone was out to get him, and that's hardly surprising, seeing as how everyone was. He seemed to piss people off wherever he went." She made a wheezy noise that sounded almost like a laugh.

Cam attempted a smile. "Do you have any idea which dam he might have gone to?"

"There's a few. Any he could walk to that had the marron. Sometimes he went to the creeks looking for koonacks."

Leanne said, "There must be about four dams within walking distance from this place, Sarge, not to mention the little creeks and ponds."

"Shit," Cam said under his breath. He got to his feet and walked away from the women, treading carefully to avoid the gumnuts strewn across the ground like ball bearings. He gazed out across the hills with his hands on his hips. It was that magic moment, just before dusk when the light was the colour of melted butter, the gum trees under the spell of an almost supernatural stillness. The humpback silhouettes of grazing kangaroos stood out among the dotted sheep on the hillside. Birds squeaked, chattered and squawked as if making one last effort to drive off the silence of the encroaching night.

The caravan site was on ground equal in height to the tallest of the surrounding hills, allowing an unhindered view across miles of rolling farmland. Small clusters of dusty gums rose from the wheat stubble. Bare paddocks of dry earth, sliced by eroded gullies, or terraced by perfectly contoured sheep paths, curved down the muscled hills to valleys forming natural water-holding cups. The fading sun reflected off two dams he could see, making them shine like sequins in the setting sun. Just how many more were down there, hidden from the naked eye?

Leanne picked her way across the gumnuts to stand at his side.

"Does she have an alibi?" he asked, still gazing at the view.

"She said she was alone that night, just her and the telly."

"That's not going to do her much good."

"She knew what was on, but," Leanne said, brushing away a persistent fly.

"That's easy: TV guide."

"Yeah, but she watched the same programmes as me. We discussed the shows. She knew all the cliff-hangers, who was caught in bed with who, who stole the jewels, everything."

"I see," Cam said, arching his brow.

"Well, there's nothing else to do," Leanne said defensively. "Besides, do you really think that poor old bat would be able to make it all the way down the hill, do her old man in, then stagger all the way back up again? She'd have a heart attack. It's not like they have a four-wheel drive either. That old bomb's all they've got and it has less chance of making the climb than she does."

"Why was she painting it? What's she covering up?"

"Jeez, Sarge," Leanne said, slapping her palms on to her thighs. "Maybe she thought it just seemed like a good idea at the time? People don't have to have motives for everything, you know."

The lilting cadences of Slim Dusty reached them through the menthol-scented air. Gay Cronin took a swig from a long neck and gave him a wave, his sins now diluted by alcohol. She warbled out the chorus with Slim, the hills sucking down her voice and throwing it back as an empty echo.

Leanne's face clouded with a look he thought he understood.

"There but for the grace of God," she said, shaking her head. She took off her peaked cap and smoothed back her thin hair, drawing in a deep breath as if it might restore some of her usual bounce. "Cripes. How the hell are we going to find the right dam? The Blayney property must be at least two thousand acres. As far as I know the State Emergency Service hasn't even touched it yet."

Cam paused for thought, rubbed his chin and stared through a cone of gnats swarming in a shaft of fading sunlight.

"I think I have an idea."

29

SATURDAY

Early the next morning after a good night's sleep, Cam, Cecelia and Leanne were back at the caravan site, poring over the map spread across the bonnet of the police ute. A gentle snoring emanated from the caravan; they'd been careful not to disturb Mrs Cronin who was still sleeping off last night's bender.

"So what do you reckon, Cecelia?" Cam said. "Can she do it?"

Cecelia patted the slobbering Prudence who strained at the leash, trying to reach the geriatric kelpie. The bloodhound seemed to have the concentration of a fruit fly and Cam was beginning to doubt the wisdom of his idea.

"We've been in a lot rougher country with the State Emergency Service. The problem as I see it is not so much the country as the freshness of the scent," Cecelia said.

"But I thought bloodhounds were supposed to be the Rolls Royce of tracker dogs? They can find a body underwater, follow someone in a car, track scents that are weeks old."

She'd said this earlier and Cam was quoting her word for word. Deep in thought, she missed his sarcasm.

"Yes." She hesitated. "Some can, but the scent is old. Prudence has found people before, but never after this long. One thing in our favour though, is the early morning dew. Damp always heightens the scent."

"They've forecast thunderstorms for later," Leanne said looking up. Cam followed her gaze. The sky was the colour of old tin, the atmosphere so muggy he could almost see it. He pulled at his clinging shirt, trying to invite a phantom breeze.

"Rain will destroy evidence. We've got to find that primary crime scene ASAP," he said.

"And heavy rain will wipe out any remaining scent," Cecelia added.

"Let's get to it, then. You're the boss, Cecelia, what do you want us to do?"

"It's important to keep distraction to a minimum. You follow me, never get ahead and talk only when you have to."

Cam nodded and turned to Leanne. "You follow behind us in the ute, OK?"

Leanne's relief showed through her grin. "And what about you, Sarge? Do you think you can keep up? My CPR's a bit rusty."

"Enough of your cheek. Get in the ute and stand by." He turned to Cecelia. "You ready?"

Cecelia nodded, indicating for Cam to stand behind the dog. She sat Prudence down and adjusted the harness. Putting Herb's old bush hat under the dog's nose she said, "Seek, Prudence, seek!" And the dog was off, like a greyhound from the barrier.

He bent over with his hands on his knees, breathing deeply. When he looked up again Cecelia and the dog were even further ahead, running towards a mob of sheep moving away from them like a flowing body of water.

Cam marvelled at Cecelia's ability to keep on going, though he expected the dog straining wildly on its leash gave her little choice.

Suddenly Prudence charged towards a clump of weeds

on the edge of a small pond. This is it, he thought with excitement, sprinting to catch up. The dog dived into the water, dragging Cecelia behind her.

With an indignant quack and a slap of wings, a pair of wood ducks took flight.

"Shit!" Cam exclaimed, sinking on to the gravelly dirt, giving Cecelia a pointed glare. "I thought you said…"

"Cam, bring the hat over," she said. "That was just a minor distraction."

Cam had forgotten he was still carrying Herb's old bush hat. He could see Leanne smirking from the ute, window up, enjoying the air conditioning. After another sniff of the hat, the dog began to turn in tight circles.

"She seems to think he was here," Cecelia said. "Maybe he stopped at this pond first?"

"Yeah, maybe," Cam said without much faith. Prudence dragged her owner around the edge of the pond, jumping and swerving to stay untangled from the lead. Then, with a noise like a foghorn, she took off again. Now they were charging down the hill, heading for the next hollow at a full run. Cam had trouble keeping up. Kamikaze locusts sprang up from the prickly stubble, flicking against his legs and face. They came to a barbed wire fence with no gate in sight. The dog seemed to think Herb had crawled through it. Gasping for breath, Cam caught up and trod down the lower strand for Cecelia and Prudence. Cecelia turned, taking the lead from him. He ran his arm across his forehead, letting out a breath.

She gave him a cheeky grin. "C'mon Cam, you know you're loving this." Then she was dragged off once more by the baying hound.

He felt his breath catch. He let go of the wire and listened to it hum in the stillness. She was right: he was enjoying himself. Out here it was almost possible to forget fire, murder, grief and guilt. As he watched the girl and dog running down the next hillside, he thought, maybe if things had been different...

"And how am I supposed to get through, Sarge? You going to lift the fence up for me too?" Leanne said, leaning out of the window of the ute.

"This fence has to end somewhere. Follow it down until you find the gate," Cam said over his shoulder, setting off at a run to catch up with Cecelia.

"This is it, Cam, I know it. Prudence knows it too," Cecelia said, sinking on to the large dam wall. She pulled a bottle of water from her belt, took some gulps and handed it to Cam who drank it down gratefully. They had plenty of water in the ute but Leanne hadn't shown up yet.

Cam patted the dog. She'd obeyed Cecelia's command to sit, but still whined and whimpered with excitement. Cecelia kept a hand on her collar, holding her back. "I'll give her a small breather, then we'll walk the edge of the dam," she said.

Cam nodded, looking across the silky expanse of water. A slip in the dam wall had caused an indentation in the middle, turning it from oval to kidney shaped, with a fringe of tall reeds in the hollow.

Leanne pulled up in the ute, parking at a safe distance from the dam wall. She climbed out, leaving the door open. The radio static slashed through the thick still of the air.

She looked as cool as an ice pack in an esky and her smug expression made Cam scowl. "Time to do some work, constable," he said.

Cecelia climbed to her feet, once more sticking Herb's

hat under the dog's nose. Cam and Leanne followed them along the baked dirt of the dam wall until they came to the patch of reeds where the dog bayed and pulled Cecelia into the muddy water.

"Watch out for snakes," Leanne said, hesitating at the water's edge. She looked at Cam, already knee-deep, shrugged and waded in after him.

He whirled at her shout, to find her pointing at a blue object nestled among the reeds. He grabbed a stick and prised out a set of goggles with HCB written upon them in permanent marker. Another flash of blue and he retrieved a pair of similarly initialled flippers.

"Grab some evidence bags, Leanne," he said, slogging back through the reeds with his catch to join Cecelia on the dam wall.

"You look like the cat that got the cream," she said.

Cam smiled, fighting a sudden urge to reach out to her.

Leanne reappeared to bag the flippers and mask. "What now, Sarge?" she asked.

He gazed out at the smooth expanse of water. "We sit and think."

The silence stretched. The dog's head moved; its droopy jowls quivered as it followed the flight of a startled heron.

Finally, Leanne said, "I've never known anyone to go marroning with flippers and goggles. Where's his nets?"

"Maybe he wasn't marroning." Cam pointed to the middle of the dam. "You've got better eyes than me. See the break in the water's surface – what do you reckon it is?"

She squinted. "Can't tell for sure."

Cam climbed to his feet. "Well, there's only one way to find out."

"Sarge, you're not going—" Leanne turned to Cecelia,

giving her friend an incredulous shrug. "Jeez, I think he is. Boy oh boy. Now we're getting a strip show."

He tossed his utility belt to the ground, then his shirt.

"You want the glory?" he asked her.

"No way!"

Cecelia smiled into her hand.

"Maybe we should test your theory that bloodhounds can smell under water?" Cam deadpanned.

"No. I think I'll leave this to the experts," Cecelia said.

Cam picked his way across the gravelly clay to the water's edge. From the top of a dead gum, a kookaburra started to laugh. He waded in; the water between his toes felt like warm tomato soup. When he launched himself away from the shallows, it became a glorious blanket of cool.

The women on the dam wall watched as Cam swam effortlessly towards the submerged object, tiny darting fish flashing silver in his wake.

He reached his destination, let out a yell and gave them the thumbs up.

Cecelia drew a sharp breath. "There must be something there!" she said, scrambling to her feet.

Leanne shaded her eyes with her hand and looked on.

"Have you any idea what it could be?" Cecelia asked.

Leanne shrugged. "Who knows?"

They saw him circle the object, then duck below the dam's surface.

After some thought, Leanne said, "It's funny how quickly you get used to them."

Cecelia tore her gaze from the water. "What?"

"The scars; you know, on his neck and arm. When he took his shirt off I noticed he had some down his side, too."

"Oh," Cecelia said, quickly turning back to the dam, "I didn't notice."

Leanne stood up and flicked a small flat stone across the water's skin. One, two, three skips and it sank.

"Sure you didn't."

Cam's head bobbed up as he took a breath then dived down again. After a few more such explorations, he struck back to shore with an adrenalin-charged crawl.

As he stumbled through the grey goo at the dam's edge, he seemed to be panting with excitement more than exertion.

"It's an old car," he said to Leanne, "resting on an under-water rock pile, its roof just tickling the surface of the water. The recent hot spell has caused the dam level to drop. A few weeks ago it would've been fully submerged."

"Did you get a look inside?" Leanne asked.

"It was pretty murky down there. Goggles would have aided visibility."

"What? The goggles we found?"

"This is definitely our primary crime scene, Leanne. Bell obviously saw something when he was here on one of his poaching expeditions. He decided to do some of his own investigating, bringing goggles so he could check it out properly, but he was caught at it. I poked my hand through the missing windows and groped around. Both door panels have been prised away. I'm guessing something, drugs or money, was hidden in the doors. We'll have to get the car out."

Cecelia handed Cam his dry shirt and he wiped his face with it. She was bursting with questions, but held herself back, suddenly feeling very much the outsider.

Cam sat down and tried to dry his feet, fighting off the

flies. He fumbled with his shoes and socks and said, "Run back to the ute, Leanne, organise a tow truck ASAP."

Leanne started back across the dam wall.

"Oh, and…" He gave Cecelia a quick glance. "Not Cliff Donovan, OK? Get someone from Toorrup if you can."

Leanne acknowledged his instructions with a wave.

Cam turned back. He seemed awkward now. "Uh, this is police business. I would appreciate it if…"

"I kept this to myself?"

He nodded. "Not even your mate Ruth, OK?"

She put her hand on his wet arm, feeling the goose bumps prick under her fingertips. "Of course not."

He met her gaze before breaking away to button his damp shirt.

Cecelia cleared her throat. "So, what's Ruby doing today?"

"I can tell you what I hope she's doing. Whether she is, is another matter."

"Look, I've not got much on. How about I pick her up so she can spend the day with me? You're obviously going to be flat out for quite a while."

He was in the middle of a grateful acceptance when they heard a shout and saw Leanne running towards them at a mad pelt. She pulled up puffing and red in the face.

"Did you get the tow truck?" Cam asked.

"Yeah, but it's not that. Derek just radioed." She took a breath. "There's been an accident in town."

Cam paled. Cecelia's heart lurched for him.

"Car versus pedestrian in the back lane behind Foodland. Hit and run. Pete's at the scene now and wants you there," Leanne said.

"Who, who's the victim?" Cam stammered.

"The old lady who was going to housekeep for you: Mrs Wilmot."

30

"That's Johnny Walker," Pete said through semi-closed lips, the disapproval evident in his eyes.

"You're shittin' me," Cam said.

"Dinkum, Sarge. He's best mates with Jack Daniels."

Cam closed his eyes for a moment. "Go on, tell me what happened."

"Johnny's mum was doing her shopping and he was killing time riding his BMX up and down the back lane. He was doing circuits from the street into the lane when he found himself behind an old white ute, burning rubber, he said. He couldn't see what was in front because of the narrowness of the lane and the dust, but at one stage the ute sped up even more and he heard a thump. Next thing he knew he was having to swerve around a body in the road. Mrs Wilmot."

"What else did you get?"

"Not much. Kid said it was an older model white ute…"

"Like every other vehicle in Glenroyd." Cam rubbed his eye with the heel of his hand.

"And he didn't get the licence plates, but he did say it was a male driver."

"And no one saw the ute leave the lane?"

"Nope."

Cam sighed and looked at the still figure on the dirt.

"The woman with her is Mrs Ira Mason. She's a retired nurse," Pete said.

"How long ago did you call the ambulance?"

"Over twenty minutes ago."

"Jesus. Call again."

Pete started heading for the Commodore. "They're all volunteers," he called over his shoulder, as if feeling the need to explain the tardiness of his townsmen.

Cam moved over to Mrs Wilmot, lying rigid among the potholes. Mrs Mason had covered her with a picnic blanket. A string bag lay on the ground nearby, its contents spilling on to the dirt: a can of baked beans, broken eggs. An oozing carton of milk was already souring the air.

He looked down at her crumpled form. "How bad?"

"Not good," Mrs Mason whispered. "Comminuted fractures to both femurs." She clicked her tongue. "Poor old soul. They often never get over injuries like this."

She pulled the blanket back, without him asking her to. There was surprisingly little blood, though both legs above the knee were a mass of snarled flesh, jutting bone and marbled fat. Cam bit down on his bottom lip. Mrs Mason waved away the circling flies and replaced the blanket.

He squatted and smoothed the powder puff of white hair from Mrs Wilmot's clammy forehead, then brushed the gravel from her cheeks. Bruises were already forming under her eyes.

"She must have hit her head, too." Mrs Mason said, reading his thoughts.

The old woman moaned and her eyes opened into slits.

"Cam. I'm so glad you took the time for a visit." He had to bend his head to hear. "You're very dirty. You take that uniform off now, it needs a good soaking or it'll stain. And don't forget the chooks. They have to be locked up by sunset or the fox'll get 'em. They're good layers. I don't want 'em disturbed by anything. You will look after 'em, won't you, Cam?" She reached out for his hand and gave it a weak squeeze, pleading through eyes he could hardly

217

bear to look at.

"I'll take good care of them. You've nothing to worry about. You try and keep quiet now, Mrs W, the ambulance will be here soon."

His sentence was punctured by the jarring sound of the siren. Some of the onlookers let out sarcastic cheers.

Greg and Mark Wilmot pushed their way through the crowd, rushing over to their mother at about the same time as the ambulance officers reached her. Cam climbed to his feet and stood aside.

First aid was administered. Each son took a hand as she was wheeled to the ambulance. Mark climbed in to join her for the ride.

"I'll take over from here, Pete," Cam said. "You take the kid and his mother back to the station and get the statement."

Cam turned to Greg Wilmot; the man was pale and shaken. He remembered playing footy against him. He'd been a big boy then, but time seemed to have shrunk him.

"She always walked home down the back lane," Greg said. "She said it was much safer than dodging the cars on the High Street." He took a gulp of air. Cam laid his hand on his shoulder. "Who'd want to do that to a harmless old grandmother?" Greg spoke to the back lane in general. Leanne was sending the onlookers home, shooing them away as if they were a swarm of flies.

"That's what I'm going to find out. Have you any ideas?" Cam asked.

Greg shook his head, scrubbing at his face with his hands. The air hung about them like a fog, rancid from the overflowing bins at the back of the shop.

Greg sucked in a breath. "She was going to work for you, wasn't she?"

"Yes, she was."

"She was really looking forward to it."

Cam swallowed. "We were looking forward to having her."

The excitement of the morning's hunt was numbed by the tragedy back in town. Cam and Leanne, lost in their own thoughts, watched the tow truck haul the wreck from the dam. Thunder rolled from the east as thick grey cloud obscured the sun. Soon dollops of rain were pocking the water's glassy surface.

"Well, there goes our crime scene. I guess we'll never know exactly where he was killed," Leanne said, gripping her elbows against the sudden drop in temperature.

"The car might be able to tell us something, though," Cam said, heading towards the leaking wreck. He'd asked the driver to stay in his truck while he and Leanne made their cursory inspection.

The vehicle was nothing but an empty husk.

"No body." Leanne sounded disappointed.

"No plates, no tyres, no engine, no seats, and the water will have washed off any prints," Cam said, trying the driver's door. It was jammed; he stuck his head through the glassless window and leaned down, running his gloved hand along the inside of the gaping panel, finding nothing. The passenger door panel had been ripped off completely, exposing another empty cavity.

He said, "Each door could have held ten kilos or more."

Leanne drew in a sharp breath. The soft line between her eyebrows deepened.

"Remember the coffee filter that stuck to my pants in the skip? They're often used to filter chemicals during amphetamine production. No wonder the colour of my pants was bleached out."

"Let's go back to the skips, then."

"They're gone. I checked."

She slapped at her thighs in frustration. "Well, there's obviously something going on at the school. Let's go and rattle some chains."

"There's no point until we have something to charge them with."

"But the school has to be involved. The Smithsons are definitely up to something."

"Not necessarily. The druggies may have just used the skips as their dumping ground."

Cam walked towards the back of the wreck and peered through the empty rear window. The water was still draining, but as it swirled out through the holes, something became visible on the emptying floor: something that did not belong to the wrecked car. He pulled himself through the back window to investigate, calling to Leanne for an evidence bag.

Rain hammered on the tin roof of the workshop. The breeze from the open door was chill through their wet uniforms. Cliff glanced from one cop to the other, his eyes locking on to Leanne's clinging shirt.

He smirked. "And what can I do for you two?"

Leanne folded her arms and gritted her teeth.

"Just thought we'd pop in for a friendly chat, Cliff," Cam said, feeling anything but friendly. He scanned the workshop. "Angelo around?"

"Day off. You can catch him tomorrow."

"He works Sundays?"

"Yeah, it's a favour to his folks. They need the money."

"That's very big-hearted of you, Cliff."

"I'm a big-hearted guy." His stare switched from Leanne's breasts to Cam's face. He took his time wiping his hands with an oily rag. Cam searched his eyes for a glimmer of guilt, but all he caught was the spark of a challenge. "More questions about the fire I suppose?"

"Got it in one," Cam said.

"I don't see what the fuss is all about. I told you what happened; I've done nothing wrong."

Cliff tossed the rag on to the nearest workbench and shoved his hands in his overall pockets.

"What happened between you and Angelo that day, Cliff?" Cam asked.

The big man shed his nonchalant air, took two strides towards Cam and leaned into his face. Leanne's hand moved to her pepper spray. Cam shot her a look of warning, sensing that Cliff's anger was directed more at Angelo than at them.

"What's the little shit been saying?" Cliff said, fists balled at his side. "After everything I've done for him. What's he bleating about now?"

Cam stepped away, wiping a fleck of Cliff's saliva from his eye. "He hasn't said anything. It's just something I figured out after watching you two at the prefab fire. You have a bad temper, Cliff. I'm guessing you hit him at the bushfire. Why?"

"Is he charging me with assault or something?"

"No. But I want to know what happened."

Cliff hesitated, making a grinding sound with his teeth. "He wasn't doing his job properly, wasn't spraying where it was needed, so I knocked him into line. That's the only way these apprentices learn. If it was left to him, the whole school property would have been destroyed by now and you'd have lost your precious body to boot."

This was completely the opposite of what Angelo had told Cam.

"How did you know the body's location?"

"My girlfriend, Ruth. She saw where it was when you lot interviewed the teachers. If it wasn't for me you wouldn't have a body to fuss over right now."

Cam risked a glance at Leanne. Earlier he'd told her Angelo's version of events and was pleased to see her expression gave nothing away. With his hands in his pockets, he started to amble around the workshop. "You don't mind if I have a bit of a sticky, do you, Cliff?"

Cliff grunted. "I don't see that I have much of a choice."

"You can always insist on a search warrant."

It wasn't much of a risk to take. The years had taught Cam that villains were invariably co-operative in matters pertaining to search and seizure, often waiving their right to a warrant because they were arrogant or stupid enough to think they could outwit the police. He was pleased to see Cliff was both.

"Do you own a white ute, Cliff?"

"No, I don't. Search my house too if you want. You won't find one."

"Where were you at around ten this morning?"

"At Flo's, having smoko."

Cam glanced at Leanne. She nodded, indicating she'd follow it up.

"So what am I supposed to have done now?"

"There was an accident in town this morning. A hit and run. A fella in a white ute was seen leaving the scene."

"And because I've been inside, you thought you might just try and pin it on me?"

"You or one of the other thousand males in the area."

Cam turned his back on Cliff and wandered further into the workshop. He knew where he was heading, but took his time getting there, examining the tools and machines as he went. Cliff followed behind with all the grace of a moving mountain. Finally Cam came to the pegboard for the smaller tools. The stencilled shapes on it showed what belonged where. He pointed to an empty space. "Where's your jemmy, mate?"

Cliff shrugged. "I dunno. Lost or nicked I think."

"Describe it to me and we'll keep an eye open for it."

Leanne wrote Cliff's description down in her notebook. A true tradesman, Cliff could describe his tools like a mother her children. They would compare the jemmy they'd found in the sunken wreck with the tool described by Cliff. If they matched it would be kept as evidence against him. It wasn't much but at least it was a start.

Cam strolled out into the yard. Leanne followed. Cliff stayed in the workshop to read the paper, back to his cops-don't-bother-me-I-haven't-done-anything-wrong attitude.

The rain had stopped and the sharp smell of wet bitumen drifted on the air from the road. Spiders' webs hung like jewelled silk across the rusted pieces of old machinery. Water dripped off the shed roof from the end of a corroded down pipe, forming an oily pool on the baked ground.

Cam and Leanne skirted the puddles, heading for the fire unit. It was parked in its usual place, next to the tow truck, within easy access of the double back gates. Cam opened up the passenger door. The Ugg boots were on the floor, as before. Their significance took a moment to sink in.

"You beauty!" he said, slapping his hand against the roof of the fire truck, spraying them both with water.

Leanne wiped her face with the sleeve of her shirt.

"Sarge?" she frowned.

"The Ugg boots. Remember the sheepskin fibres found between Bell's toes?"

Leanne gawped for a moment, then punched the air. "Yessss!" She glanced at the workshop door and whispered, "The body was put on the seat of the fire truck with the feet resting against the Ugg boots. The wool fibres weren't burned because they were stuck between the toes."

"It also explains how the only tyre tracks belonged to the fire truck, the only footprints belonged to the fireman…"

The workshop door slammed and Cliff appeared, blinking in the sunlight. Hands on hips, he had a wolfish smile on his face.

"Do you mind if I take these boots for a while to help with the investigation?" Cam asked him.

"So long as I get them back soon, I need them when my bunions play up." Cliff chuckled as he walked over to the fire truck. "Besides, who am I to kick up a fuss when I'm talking to a celebrity such as yourself?"

Cam glanced at Leanne to see if she had any idea what he was talking about. She shrugged.

Cliff leaned against the fire truck, obviously enjoying their confusion. Then he laughed, thumping the truck's bonnet with glee before disappearing into his shed. He returned a few seconds later with the newspaper. After wiping the bonnet with a rag, he spread it out, turning the pages until he found what he was looking for.

"Here we go, page four. That picture's a beauty, Sarge. Talk about looking like a stunned mullet."

And Cam did, caught in all the aftershock of the camera's unforgiving flash. Underneath the article about the rise in police suicides was written: *Senior Sergeant Cameron Fraser, formerly with the NCA in Sydney, leads the investigation into the Senior Constable's apparent suicide.*

Cliff rubbed his Brillo pad of a beard, jabbing a finger at Cam.

"So you're the one the bikies were after over east, eh? I thought your name rang a bell. Well, that's mighty interesting now, isn't it, Sarge? I wonder how many other guys out there will find it interesting – you now living in Glenroyd I mean."

Cam sprang forward, stopping himself just in time.

Cliff tilted his head and pointed to his jaw. "Go on then, Sarge, hit me."

Cam balled up his fists. For a moment Leanne's hand on his arm was the only thing holding him back. He ended up stabbing at Cliff's chest with his finger. "Don't think I don't know what happened to Vince," he said, through clenched teeth. "Soon it'll be two counts of murder."

With a flick of his head to Leanne, he headed back to the parked ute.

31

They sat on the back veranda. Ruby chatted to her father about her day, explaining the trip to the wildlife sanctuary in painstaking detail. How they'd fed the orphan joeys from bottles with special milk of a certain temperature to prevent diarrhoea. How the tiny joeys were called pinkies because they had no hair so they had to be kept in insulated eskies, like humidicribs. Then there was the walk by the river with Prudence and the bath they'd given her because she'd rolled in something foul. The pancake making, the photography equipment…

Cecelia watched Cam as Ruby talked, finding it increasingly hard to hide the irritation she felt with his detached grunts and faraway gaze. Damn the man! His daughter was finally talking to him, showing an interest in something, and here he was, so preoccupied with his own thoughts he wasn't listening to a word she was saying. Thank God Ruby was too involved with the narration of her adventures to notice how distracted her father was.

He swallowed some beer and absently watched his daughter slide from her chair to the floor to tickle Prue's stomach. The dog obligingly flopped open a back leg.

"Dad, can I have some money? I want to get some doggie treats for Prue. She's been such a good girl today."

Cam blinked. "Not now, love, it's too late."

"But the Deli stays open till eight." Girl and dog climbed to their feet expectantly.

"No."

"Dad, for God's sake…"

"Ruby, you'll find some doggie treats on the top shelf of the pantry cupboard," Cecelia interrupted.

Ruby gulped her last swallow of Coke, slammed the empty glass on the table. "See what I mean, Cecelia, he thinks he's…"

"While you're in the kitchen, do you think you could make a start on that pancake mess we made? After the feast comes the reckoning."

Their day together had made Cecelia more aware than ever of Ruby's almost vulnerable need to please her. She felt a pang of guilt for taking advantage of it now.

Ruby gave her a brief smile and blew the hair from her eyes. "Oh, I suppose so," she said, dragging out the words.

After shooting her father a death stare, she called the dog and they disappeared into the kitchen.

"Thanks," Cam said, letting out a pent up breath. "I've booked her flight. I'm sending her back to Sydney on Monday. She'll have to miss the start of the school term. There's a chance I'll have to cancel her enrolment altogether and find a boarding school."

Cecelia stared at him for a moment. This was not what she'd expected. "I don't understand."

"You don't need to understand." Short and sharp, his sentence stabbed at her like a pike.

She flinched. He turned his head away.

Cecelia struggled to keep her voice on the level. "Have you told her?"

His pause suggested he was well aware of the difficult task he had ahead. She drummed her fingers on the table, waiting for his answer.

"I'll tell her in the morning."

He fell silent. The sound of croaking frogs reached her

from the river. Their pools were drying; time was running out for them.

"She's not going to be very happy about it," she said when it became obvious he would say no more. "She was telling me she's finally begun to like it here. She's met a nice boy..." She frowned at Cam's snort. "And she's looking forward to starting school at Glenroyd."

"I haven't made this decision lightly, Cecelia. There's a lot going on that you don't know."

"Try telling me."

His answer was to move to the veranda railing, to lean out and catch the gardenia-scented breeze. Prudence clacked through the veranda screen, licking the food from her chops and collapsing at Cecelia's feet. Satisfying day, contented dog, attractive man. The evening should have been perfect.

Nothing was turning out as she'd hoped. The moment she'd opened the door she'd felt the tension emanating from him like a protective force field. It made her revise her earlier intention of asking him to stay for dinner.

"You'd make a good neighbour," she said to his back. He looked over his shoulder at her. The boyish glow of the morning was long gone, his face pale, the skin around his eyes tight.

"Good fences make good neighbours."

He frowned.

"It's from a poem. You've got fences around you, Cam, that even your daughter can't seem to get through."

When he tensed, she could almost see the gaps closing. Then he did the only thing a man like him could do under the circumstances: he switched the topic to work.

He reached into his top pocket for a photo and magnifying glass and rejoined her at the table under the veranda light with its halo of buzzing insects, as if the last few minutes had never happened.

"There's one hell of a lot of chemicals here for one school lab," he said, tapping at the photograph.

Cecelia wouldn't look at the photograph and kept her eyes riveted on him. "You can't expect to get off this lightly, Cameron Fraser."

As she attempted to penetrate his neutral mask, she knew her own face would be reflecting every emotion coursing through her body. She'd never been good at hiding her own feelings; they were a part of who she was and to deny them would be like denying a part of herself. Her disastrous marriage, the stillbirth not long after she'd thrown her husband out – sometimes she felt as if the whole world knew of her troubles. But she believed most wounds mended best in the light. It was frustrating to deal with someone who was trying to heal himself, and his daughter, in the dark.

"We need to talk about Ruby, Cam."

He exhaled. "Please, Cecelia, this is important. Answer my questions, then you can do all the analysing of Ruby and me that you like."

He wasn't giving her a choice. She clenched her jaw and glared back. Getting nowhere, her eyes eventually dropped back to the photo. She shrugged. "Not all of them were for the science lab. Some were cleaning products, some were for the photo lab."

"Did you ever see them delivered?"

"No, but several times Ruth mentioned she had to stay back late for a delivery."

A muscle in his jaw jumped. He handed her the magnifying glass, pointing to something on the photo.

"Have a look at that box and tell me what the writing says."

She peered at the photo closely, sounding out the indistinct letters. "Coffee filters?"

Cam nodded. "Your friend must really like her coffee," he said, not bothering to hide the sarcasm.

Her eyes narrowed. "What do you mean?"

He took a deep breath. "Cecelia. How well do you know Ruth?"

She shot him a look to let him know he was travelling through dangerous territory. Unintentionally, her voice rose. "What do you mean by that? She's my best friend. I've known her since my divorce; she's been very good to me. What are you getting at?"

He persisted, ignoring her tone. "Are you aware that she lived in London for a while, that she was married?"

She could no longer hold his gaze, a fact as irritating to her as the quaver she heard in her reply. "Yes, he was a chemistry professor at one of the universities there. He died."

"Do you know how?"

She had the feeling he already knew the answer. Why the hell did he ask, then?

"No," she said. "She doesn't like talking about it."

"He died in a house fire. A Molotov cocktail through the window. Scotland Yard attributed it to arson. They thought a disgruntled student might have done it, though the perpetrator was never caught."

His implication made her feel hollow and sick, almost as if he was accusing her. "Are you trying to suggest that it was Ruth who set fire to the photo lab?"

Cam shrugged.

"How can you implicate her in this mess? How dare you suggest she tried to kill us!"

"I'm not implicating anyone at the moment, just touching

all the bases. This is how I do my job." Cam returned her burning look with eyes as cool as a frozen pond. "And there's something else," he added.

Cecelia stood and whirled her back on him. He took a step towards her at the same time as they heard Ruby's approaching footsteps. She couldn't have Ruby witness this scene.

"I think you should go," Cecelia said, under her breath.

"All cleared up," Ruby said, smiling as she rejoined them. The smile fell away as she looked from one adult to the other.

"Ruby, we're going now. Gather your gear and meet me in the car." Cam said.

Ruby whined out a protest. When Cecelia held up her hand, it stopped.

"Thanks for having me, Cecelia," Ruby said in a monotone, before turning on her heel and sloping back into the house.

"I'm conducting a murder investigation," Cam said to Cecelia, keeping his voice low. "I expect your full cooperation. You mentioned before that Vince sent you a letter apologising for his inappropriate behaviour at a traffic incident. I'll take the letter now if it's handy, otherwise you can drop it off to me at the station tomorrow morning."

"I'm not sure where it is."

"Find it. It's important."

Ever the officious policeman, she thought. "And I suppose if I don't you'll throw me in jail?"

He blew out his cheeks. "Cecelia, please."

"And I thought we were friends. You're speaking to me as if you think I know something, that I'm hiding something. As if I was one of your witnesses."

"You are a witness," he said, and took his daughter home.

32

Cecelia closed her eyes and leaned with her back against her front door until she heard the car leave. She let out her breath and reasoned with herself. Perhaps she should humour him, see if she could find the damn letter. Maybe once that chore was over, she would be able get some work done, forget the events of the last two days, the anger and doubt he'd sown in her mind. The school term was starting next Wednesday; there were lessons to plan, form lists to organise, timetables to confirm.

She was about to start searching her bedroom when the phone rang. She picked up the extension; it was Anne ringing to make sure she was all right. Apparently Jeffrey had spoken to Sergeant Fraser earlier and they'd come to the conclusion that vandals had started the fire in the photo lab. Anne seemed to think this a satisfactory explanation, obviously knowing nothing about the locked door, and Cecelia wasn't going to tell her otherwise.

Anne mentioned that she and Jeffrey would be spending their last few days of holiday in their city apartment. It would be up to Cecelia to liaise further with the police should the necessity arise. Great.

When she hung up, Cecelia took her correspondence box from her top dresser drawer and sat on the bed with it. She hadn't noticed the letter yesterday when she'd retrieved the photos for Cam and figured it must have got jammed against the side. But when she slid her fingers around the box's edge, there was no sign of it. Back at the dresser drawer she rifled through undies, gauze pouches of potpourri and discarded soaps, again coming up with nothing.

She sank back on to her bed and rested her chin in her hand, trying to remember the last time she'd seen it. She knew she'd shown it to Ruth after the interview with Cam, when they were recovering from the effects of Ruth's moonshine upstairs in her flat. She tried to visualise the scene. In her mind she saw herself putting the letter back in her bag, but the image was cloudy, probably due to the tipsy haze through which she'd viewed most of that afternoon.

Cecelia padded down the hall to where her handbag rested on the table near the door. She started working her way through it, opening clips, searching compartments. Her fingers stiffened as frustration grew. Soon she'd had enough of this methodical search and opened every compartment, tipping the bag upside down. She found crumpled papers, old receipts, unpaid bills and long lost documents: anything and everything but Vince's letter.

Shit, she must have left it in Ruth's flat after all. She put a hand out to the phone, then stopped, remembering Ruth was out for the night with Cliff. Her keys lay on the table among the handbag clutter. Last year Ruth had given her a spare key to water her plants when she was away. When she returned she'd told Cecelia to keep the key and use her flat whenever she liked, as a bolthole from the Smithsons. Cecelia slipped on a pair of sneakers and headed for the front door.

Ruth's flat was as stark as Cecelia's house was cluttered. It took no more than a glance to see that Vince's letter was no longer on the coffee table where she thought she'd left it next to a pile of Ruth's papers. Ruth had recently tidied up;

the small kitchen was immaculate, the pristine carpet striped with vacuum cleaner lines. Perhaps she'd scooped up the letter with some of her own documents and filed them away in her desk? No cardboard box in an undies drawer for Ruth.

A reluctant search for the letter turned into an obsessive quest, as irritation at herself for losing it joined with the compulsion to shove it in Cam's face and wipe away his suspicions of her friend.

In the deepest desk drawer in Ruth's living room she found a pile of papers stacked upon a decorative box. Not finding what she wanted among the papers, she eased the box from the drawer.

It was old and battered; a schoolgirl trend of their time to keep mementos in boxes such as these. Cecelia still had one, stashed away somewhere in the garden shed. Like her own, Ruth's box was decorated with a colourful appliqué design and coated with thick varnish.

She lifted the lid, surprised to discover her no-nonsense friend had hoarded the same kind of sentimental treasures as she had herself: letters from ex-boyfriends, an old school tie, diaries, sports badges, exam results and a large battered scrapbook. She'd written *School Days* on the front above a photo of herself in her old Glenroyd uniform.

Cecelia turned to the first page. To her surprise, another familiar face stared back at her: Cameron Fraser, Year 12, with a love heart pencilled around his picture. No wonder she'd not relished renewed contact with Cam, Cecelia thought, smiling. Perhaps he was a reminder of something she was now ashamed of. The crush might also explain her embarrassing behaviour towards him in the science lab.

She turned the page and found another photo: St Bart's first fifteen footy team. And there, sitting in the centre of the group of boys was the captain, Cameron Fraser.

The next clipping was of a young couple on their wedding day. Cam was clearly recognisable as the young man. His bride's head had been cut out and replaced by Ruth's.

Cecelia snapped the book shut, suddenly feeling cold despite the heat of the third storey flat. She should never have looked in the box; her blind determination to find the letter had violated Ruth's privacy. What did it matter if Ruth had once had a crush on Cameron Fraser?

Everyone is entitled to fantasies. Provided they hurt no one.

As she moved to put the book back in the box, some yellowed newspaper clippings fluttered to the ground by her knees. A headline caught her. Her hand crept to her mouth as she read:

MILLION DOLLAR BIKIE DOPE CROP DESTROYED
Police have destroyed a $1 million Blue Mountains bikie cannabis crop after a tip off from an undercover National Crime Authority officer. The NCA officer had infiltrated the Razorback motorcycle gang while working undercover as a barman at a popular bikie watering hole. The cannabis crop, raided yesterday, was protected with sophisticated booby traps and equipped with an irrigation system. Bikies at the scene of the raid surrendered without resistance and two men have so far been charged.

FIRE KILLS POLICE FAMILY
The wife and a son of a police sergeant due to testify against Razorback gang members, died yesterday when a fire swept through their Randwick home. Police Sergeant

Cameron Fraser found his home on fire when he returned from his older child's netball game, and was badly burned when he tried to rescue his family from the inferno. He was rushed to hospital where his condition is listed as serious. Sergeant Fraser had lead the recent raid on the $1 million Blue Mountains bikie dope plantation and was due to give evidence against two Razorback gang members next month. Police are treating the fire as suspicious and appealing to the general public for information.

Ruth's husband had died in a mysterious house fire.

Cecelia and Cam had almost perished in the burning prefab.

Herb Bell's body had been burned beyond recognition.

Cecelia screwed her hand into a fist and bit into her knuckles until she tasted blood.

33

SUNDAY

The wait for dawn had been interminable, but worth it. Cam stuck his torch in his belt and crouched on his hands and knees on Vince's lounge carpet in the manner of a sniffing dog. He held the tweezers in the growing patch of natural light to examine the fibres he'd extracted.

"A perfect match," he said to himself, feeling his heart leap. No matter how complicated the puzzle, the discovery of the smallest piece was one of the greatest highs he could imagine. Sometimes you just couldn't fight what you were meant to be.

With shaking hands he dropped the samples in a small evidence envelope and buttoned it into his top pocket, giving it a pat for good measure. He took a moment to stretch the kinks out of his back before sitting on the milk crate to make his call.

Rod's voice was croaky with sleep on the other end of the telephone line. "Jesus, Cam, have you any idea what time it is?"

Cam glanced at his watch and saw with surprise it was already 6 am. Time ceased to have much meaning when you'd been up all night.

"Actually, I thought it was earlier." He heard his friend sigh down the line. "After I took Ruby home last night, I called in at the station just as a fax came in. I've spent the night following it through."

"Out with it. It's Sunday morning and I want to go back to sleep."

"I have the proof that Vince was murdered."

The silence was as long as the sigh that preceded it. Finally Rod cleared his throat. "You heard back from the pathologist?"

"Yes, the fax was from him. The toxicology test showed that Vince had chloroform in his system as well as high levels of alcohol."

"Shit."

"I went back to his house last night and sifted through it with a fine toothed comb. I found something SOCO missed. There was a wheelbarrow in the garage with traces of carpet fibre in the treads. It matches the carpet in Vince's lounge room."

Rod thought for a moment, Cam could almost hear the synapses firing down the line. "So Vince was knocked out with the chloroform, changed into his uniform and taken by wheelbarrow into the garage and hanged."

"It seems that way."

"Suspect? Motive?"

"Nothing I can prove yet, but I'm getting closer. Vince and Cliff were mates, but they'd had some kind of a falling out, I'm guessing over the stolen tanker. I think Cliff paid Vince to look the other way when it was stolen. Vince must have decided he needed some extra cash and upped the ante."

"So Cliff wanted the tanker for parts?"

"More than just parts, it was full of fertiliser. The anhydrous ammonia in fertiliser is a major component in the manufacture of illegal amphetamines."

"And that ties in with your theory about drug-making at the school."

Cam caught Jenny's voice in the background, probably grumbling about the early morning call. "Cam, hang on a moment, I'll go to the other room." There was the sound of creaking bedsprings and thumping feet. Rod continued a few seconds later. "So Vince was silenced because of what he knew and what he threatened to tell."

"Exactly."

"How does this tie in with Bell's murder and the attempt on you in the prefab?"

"Bell was knocked off because he knew something valuable was being hidden in the sunken car – he'd probably seen people diving down to it on one of his marron poaching expeditions."

"The drugs from the school?"

"Bell might not have thought drugs; money would be more appealing to a bloke like him."

"So he was killed when he went to see for himself? By Cliff, you think?"

Cam watched the morphing shadows on the carpet and sucked at the earpiece of his glasses while he thought through his answer. He knew in his gut that Cliff was behind this, but would not allow himself to jump to unsubstantiated conclusions just yet.

"Maybe," he said cautiously. "His jemmy was in the car and fibres from Bell's toes look like they come from his Ugg boots. The only footprints at the scene of the bushfire where the body was dumped were from firemen; the only tyre treads from the fire truck. It stands to reason Cliff murdered Bell at the dam when he caught him snooping around, then used the fire truck to move the body and dump it in the bush."

"And what about the fire in the prefab?"

"To destroy photos of the school renovations; they show pictures of chemicals stacked in piles outside the building. They're the most valid proof we have yet of drugs being manufactured at the school. I'm sure Ruth Tilly is involved. She's probably the one making the drugs for Cliff in the science lab. She knew about Cecelia's photos, told Cliff, and he decided to burn down the prefab to get rid of them. The locked door was more opportunistic, a good way of getting rid of a pesky cop. Then of course they realised they could pin the fire on Vince and kill two birds with one stone."

"You never seemed to take Vince's death on face value. You were cagey from the start."

"That pushed-back car seat first got my radar working. Vince was big, but not as big as Cliff. The car seat was like that because Cliff moved the car from the garage to make room for Vince to swing."

There was the sound of a cigarette being lit, then the crackling purse of an inhalation. "Poor old Vince," Rod said, exhaling.

"The suicide note wasn't right, either. It was too short, plus the paper had been cut, not torn from the pad. I think it was a clipping from an apology letter Vince sent Ms Bowman. I've asked Cecelia to look for it, but I don't think she'll find it."

"Well, Cam, everything seems to fit your theory, but you know what you're lacking, don't you?"

Cam tossed his glasses on to the carpet and sighed. "Proof."

"Exactly." Rod paused. "I suppose we could always put the science lab under twenty-four hour surveillance."

"Ancient history. I think they only make the drugs during the holidays, then hide them in the car waiting for Cliff's bikie buddies to collect. Nothing will happen now till next holidays."

"You might have enough to arrest Cliff over Bell, but

evidence he was involved in Vince's death is still a bit light."

"I'm not ready to make any arrests just yet. Who knows what else will fall into my lap if I bide my time? I think the attempt on Mrs Wilmot's life might be tied in to all this, too. I'm going to see her in hospital this morning and I want to speak to Ruth Tilly again, search the lab if I can. I'll get cracking now, you go back to sleep."

"As if," Rod said, putting down the phone.

Cam raised his voice to match Ruby's. "You're going back to Sydney tomorrow and that's the end of it."

"I can't believe you, Dad. This is so not cool. Only last week I was begging you to go back and you wouldn't even listen to me. Now I want to stay and you insist I bloody go."

"It's a question of your safety."

Ruby snatched the unopened cornflake box from the breakfast bar and stabbed at the lid with a sharp fingernail. "Mum and Joe died over three years ago. Just get over it and let me live my life."

He flinched and turned to the mess at the kitchen sink, running the water for the washing up. "Look, love," he said to the rising bubbles, "there are things going on here that you don't understand."

"How do you know I don't understand when you've never even tried to tell me?"

Her voice cracked, but he didn't look up from the task in front of him, he couldn't face her tears now. Swirl, wipe, rinse, stack, swirl, wipe, rinse and stack.

Block out.

Compartmentalise.

He dried his hands on the tea towel, risking her a quick glance.

She'd poured the contents of the cereal packet all over

the floor and was grinding it into the carpet with her feet.

He looked at his watch. "I've got to go to Toorrup. I'll see you when I get back. Get your suitcase packed and don't go out. I'll ask Leanne to look in on you."

He crunched his way across the carpet of cornflakes to the front door. Out of the corner of his eye he saw her reach for the milk.

Cam held Mrs Wilmot's hand as if it was an injured animal; the skin, thin as tissue, showed a network of bulging veins. She squeezed his hand, her puffy eyes opened into slits.

"How are you feeling?" It was the best he could do.

She regarded him for a full ten seconds before answering. "Like I've been run over by a ute."

"I guess I asked for that." He cracked a smile. Her chesty chuckle turned into a nasty cough, making her bruises change colour like the skin of an exotic fish. When he reached for the call button, she held him back with a shake of her head.

"Just give me some water, I'll be all right."

He handed her the glass and she took a sip.

"The cough's from the anaesthetic, they said." His worried expression made her add, "Don't worry, Cam, I'm not about to die on you, though it'll be a while before I can chase you with my wooden spoon."

His gaze travelled to the rectangular tent keeping the weight of the bed linen from her injuries. He'd been told her legs had been pinned together with surgical steel. She'd be lucky if she could walk again, let alone chase him.

She'd been hospitalised for less than twenty-four hours but her room already resembled a florist's. Unfortunately the flowery scent did nothing to mask the hospital smells and associated memories he'd been three years trying to forget.

"I'm a silly old fool for getting myself into this mess, aren't I, Cam?"

Cam shook his head. "It's not your fault, Mrs W, but someone's to blame, and we'll catch him, don't you worry. Can you remember anything at all?"

"The last thing I remember is the supermarket having baked beans on special."

At that moment the door opened with a vacuum whoosh and a small group of women entered, treading with the hesitant steps of unaccustomed churchgoers. Cam looked at their pink and grey uniforms, assuming them to be hospital nurses. He realised this wasn't the case when one of the women walked straight past him, tiptoeing over to Mrs Wilmot.

"We managed to sneak by the ward secretary," she said in a conspiratorial whisper. "I think she thought we must work here." She tittered at her own guile, giving Mrs Wilmot a peck on the cheek. "How are you feeling, love?"

"Like I've been run over by a ute."

Awkward laughter, then sudden silence when they noticed Cam.

"Oh, I'm sorry, officer," a plump woman said. "In our excitement we didn't notice Lulu had a visitor."

He read her nametag: St Luke's nursing home. Now, where had he heard that name before?

Under any other circumstances, he would have insisted the women leave so he could continue with his interview, but the name St Luke's had struck a chord. He decided to let the women be while he processed this latest piece of information. He offered one of them a chair and stepped over to the window. Once he'd faded into the background, the women lost their shyness and descended upon

Mrs Wilmot like a flock of galahs.

Cam's racing mind competed with the noise of the chattering women. Only when he noticed how quiet the room had become did he realise how his unintentional expletive had shocked them all into silence. He was apologising when a nurse with a face like a deformed potato came in and asked them to leave. She impaled Cam with her stare, folded her arms and told him there were to be no exceptions.

He pulled the nurse to one side as the women said their good-byes and trooped out of the room.

"Look, Miss, er, Sister. I'm investigating Mrs Wilmot's accident and something new has just come to light. It's really important that I get to speak to her alone for just a few minutes."

"The poor woman's exhausted. Doctor said visitors should be restricted. The racket from this room was enough to wake half the ward. It's not to be tolerated."

Cam looked at the woman and gave one of the smiles Elizabeth always said could charm a nun out of her habit. "Say, don't I know you from somewhere?" He wagged his finger, glancing down at her nametag. "Sister Cuthbert. Don't tell me you're Sally Cuthbert – Miss Glenroyd Agricultural Show 1976?"

A wave of red coloured the sister's face. "Well, actually that was my cousin; my name's Jean." She smoothed down her apron and looked at her toes. "People say we are very alike, though."

Cam let out his breath; that was a lucky guess. "I went to St Bart's. The Ag show was the highlight of our year, especially the Miss Glenroyd competition."

She arched her eyebrows and searched his face for a familiar feature. There was nothing to recognise, but fond memories softened her expression. "We used to feel so sorry for the boys at St Bart's." Her smile wiped away the wrinkles like a Magic Slate. "I'm not stupid," she laughed, "I know the game you're playing. Go on then, talk to Mrs Wilmot, but no longer than five minutes, understood?"

Cam tipped his hat and gave her another charming beam. When she'd gone, Mrs Wilmot said, "Blimey."

Cam sat down on the edge of her bed. "The end justifies the means. I'll buy her a drink sometime."

"Then I'd better warn her off accepting."

"Listen, Mrs W, I don't have long so I'll get straight to it. You worked at St Luke's nursing home – correct?"

"Yes, for nearly ten years, after I left the tea shop."

"Can you remember a patient called Jane Featherstone?"

"I remember her well. We got on famously. She was a lovely old lady. She reached the grand old age of ninety-six. I'm not sure I'd like to reach that age."

"Apparently she was best friends with Ruth Tilly's grandmother. They were at GLC together."

"That's right. Ruth used to visit her."

"You know she left all her money to GLC, for Ruth to pass on?"

"All her money, Cam?" The laugh made her wince. With a nod he urged her to continue, not wanting her to stop now. "I don't know what you're talking about. She barely had enough money for toothpaste."

Cam frowned. Her face was pale under the bruises; he worried he was pushing her too far, but couldn't bring himself to end the interview, not now he was so close. "I don't understand. I thought she was supposed to be one of the richest people in the area, lived in that big mansion on Tannery Road."

"That's what she wanted people to think. Very few people

knew the truth." Her voice began to fade as exhaustion took over.

"What truth?" He clasped her hand as excitement ballooned in his chest.

She continued to speak, each sentence now punctuated with a heavy breath. "She was one of those old-fashioned types, all breeding and pride. She felt she had to keep up appearances at all costs, even after her brother squandered the family fortune. If you'd looked in the windows of that beautiful house of hers, you'd have seen antiques and priceless paintings. If you looked up good and close though, you'd have seen the antiques were reproductions, the paintings fakes. And upstairs, there was no furniture at all, just mattresses on the floor."

"How do you know this?"

No answer, the slits of her eyes began to narrow. He prompted her to stay awake with another squeeze of her hand.

She gave a start, trying to jerk herself into wakefulness. "She told me, swore me to secrecy. That's how come she asked me to witness the will. She wanted to carry her secret with her to the grave. It was all a matter of honour, you see."

Cam shook his head, worried that the anaesthetic had left the old lady confused. "I heard she left nearly a million dollars to GLC, that she specified in the will it was to go to the science lab, as a bequest through Ruth Tilly, the executor."

"Oh, she left it to the school all right." She took a deep breath. "About enough to buy a rack of test tubes."

With a long exhalation, she fell asleep.

34

She'd never expected it to be like this; it should have been in a lace-covered bed with a gentle breeze ruffling gauzy curtains, and misty, like an old-fashioned movie. This was almost as bad as doing it in the back seat of an old bomb, except maybe an old bomb wouldn't have smelt so bad.

A small sob rose from her chest.

"Ruby, are you all right?" Angelo was still on top of her. He extracted a hand from under her tank top and cupped her face.

"I'm fine." It was a relief to find he'd finally stopped, but she still had trouble breathing, as if all the air had been knocked out of her.

"Did you come?"

"Oh yes," she lied. If that was what coming was all about, *Cosmo* should be sued for false advertising.

As he rolled off her she pulled up her panties and smoothed down her skirt. She felt sticky and unclean and more than a little ashamed. He hadn't even taken off his overalls, just unbuttoned the flies. It must have taken all of five minutes, though it had felt more like five hours. She sat up on the camp bed and watched as he lit a cigarette, the flaring match illuminated his face through the grey light of the room. God, but he was handsome. And she loved him. She wouldn't have done it with him if she didn't love him – would she?

As she got up from the cot, she knocked over the empty can of scotch and bourbon. She watched as it rolled across the oily floor, stopping against the used condom lying there like a dead jellyfish. She met his gaze with a self-conscious giggle.

He nodded towards the empty can and smiled. "You won't need the booze next time," he said.

"I guess I won't. I'll be an old pro by then." Though I feel like one already, she thought. She sank back on to the cot and felt her face cave in on itself. Angelo sat down and put his arm around her shoulders. His other hand still held the cigarette. It created a curtain of smoke between them.

"What's the matter?" he said in a gentle voice. "Are you sorry we did it?"

Between sobs, she said, "No, no, it's not that. I just don't want to go back to Sydney. I love you and I want to stay with you." She saw a sudden ray of hope. "Maybe I could stay with your mum and dad, or maybe you could hide me in a cave and bring me food?"

When Angelo laughed at her comment, she knew her hope was lost.

"You're a cop's daughter, Ruby," he said. "Your dad would have the whole WA Police Service looking for you. Running away won't work. You'll have to just do what he wants and go back. You'll probably only be gone for a few days."

She folded her arms and frowned at him. "Why is it that you always take his side? Is it some kind of a male thing?"

"Don't talk crap, Ruby. It's just common sense."

She was in the process of choosing an appropriate response, either an angry yell or more tears, when they heard the primal thump of a Harley pulling up in the yard. She looked at Angelo with alarm.

"Shit," he said jumping to his feet to pull a corner of the dirty blind away from the small window.

"Angelo," she said, beginning to panic. "I thought you

said Cliff was in Toorrup for the day?"

"It's OK. He hardly ever comes into this back room. We'll just sit tight and wait for him to go, then I'll sneak you out. Besides," he said with a shrug, "there's worse things I could be doing than just jabbing a chick in here. He'd probably laugh it off."

"Just jabbing a chick? Is that all it means to you?"

He clamped his hand over her mouth, cutting off the rest of her retort. "Sh… I didn't mean it like that. Listen to them, will you?" He nodded in the direction of the workshop. "He's got Ruth Tilly with him and he's going off his chops at her."

The tin wall separating the room was peppered with small holes. He beckoned her over for a peep.

"You stupid bitch," the man yelled at Ruth. His red face, Ruby noticed, was a startling contrast to the white mane of his hair.

"Is that Cliff?" she whispered to Angelo.

But Angelo was paying so much attention to the unfolding drama he didn't seem to hear her.

The man backhanded Ruth across her face, and the sound of connecting flesh made Ruby flinch. She grabbed Angelo's hand and he squeezed it, his body tensing as he leaned towards the door. For a moment she thought he was going to rush out and break the fight up, but he held himself back, continuing to watch.

Ruth fell to the ground with a scream. The man looked down at her; Ruby could see the contempt at the corners of his cruel mouth.

"I'm sorry," Ruth wailed, "it's you I love, not him. I'll make it up to you, I promise. I wouldn't have told you any of this if things hadn't changed."

"A cop for Chrissake!" The man shook her from his foot

as if she was a glob of mud.

Ruth sat on the floor looking up at him. A thin trail of blood trickled down her chin from her split lip.

Ruth said, "I know him well, I know his triggers, I know how to get rid of him. No one will be any the wiser."

Ruby watched on, open-mouthed.

Ruth pushed her hair out of her eyes and smiled up at her tormentor. Soon she was pulling herself up and draping herself around him like a mink coat.

The man rubbed her cheek. His voice was softer now. "Well, get rid of him soon, then. You'll have to do better than before. That fire in the prefab was a disaster."

Ruby gasped as the man's words registered. "My dad?" she mouthed to Angelo.

He shook his head and continued to peer through the tin.

Ruth nodded, purring something into the man's ear. The man smiled and pushed her over the bonnet of a blue Ford Escort. Ruby could only see their legs, but she knew what they were doing. She felt sick. With her back to the wall, she covered her hands with her ears.

The tin walls shuddered as the door slammed. Soon they heard the bike start up in the yard. When the roar faded into the distance, Ruby uncurled herself from the floor and Angelo helped her to her feet. Her legs felt like jelly and her heart pounded as loud as the Harley's roar.

She clutched at Angelo's arm. "I have to go and tell Dad. I think he's in danger." But when she turned to the door, he grabbed her and spun her around, holding her tight with a hand on each shoulder.

"You can't do that, Ruby." The urgency in his voice startled her. "They may not even have been talking about him."

"They're up to something, Angelo, and whether it's Dad

they were talking about or not, I still have to let him know."

He shook her hard, making her jaws snap.

"For Chrissake, Ruby! Have you any idea what you're saying? I thought you loved me!" He sounded desperate. Sweat dripped from his upper lip.

Her throat contracted. "I do," she said with a hitch in her voice.

Gently he pushed a strand of hair from her face. "Then don't tell your dad. If you told him he'd find out what you were doing here. You're jailbait, Ruby, you're under age. You want me to go to jail?"

She shook her head.

He trailed his fingers down the side of her face. "How about a smile? When people love each other, they're supposed to be happy. Are you happy, Ruby?"

She nodded and forced out a tight smile.

"Let's seal our secret with a kiss, then."

35

Cam's unheralded appearance at the door of the lab made Ruth look up in surprise. She put down her pen, frowning when he moved over to her at the central island desk.

"Have you heard of knocking?" she said in her school-marm tone.

He put his hands palm down on the desk and leaned in towards her, not answering her question. She didn't flinch or take her eyes from his. Her bottom lip was split and swollen; she licked it as if savouring the taste of her own blood.

"Is this what the police call intimidation tactics?" she said. "If it is, it's not working. All you're doing is giving me the opportunity to examine your scars more closely." She clucked her tongue and peered into his face. "You certainly made a fine mess of yourself, didn't you? How many skin grafts have you had?"

"I've come to search the lab," Cam said, impassively.

Unnerved at last, she took a breath. Her eyes flickered. "Whatever for?"

"I have reason to believe these premises have been used for the manufacture of illegal drugs."

"Drugs! That's absurd!" She slipped off the stool and faced him. Her hands on the desk were clenched; the knuckles stood out like ridges of ivory.

Good sign, Cam thought.

"Your boyfriend, Cliff, hangs out with members of the SS motor cycle club. I believe he's had you making amphetamines in the school lab for them. I'd like to think you're being coerced into doing this. Your co-operation with me now will go a long way in a plea for leniency with the judge."

She laughed. It may well have been her way of covering up her insecurities, but the sound still caused a shiver to run up his back. "I'm sure your theory sparkles with crystal clarity in the attic of your mind," she said, "but I'm afraid it's lost on me. I hope you haven't told too many people about these suspicions of yours: I'd hate to see you end up with egg on your face."

"Touching," he said as he headed towards the kitchenette.

"Wait, I'd like to see a search warrant," she called, a splinter of panic in her voice.

Cam allowed himself a smile. "You should've taken time to update yourself on the new laws before you got involved in this venture. The Criminal Investigation and Fortification Removal Bill 2001: Part 4, clause 45 states that a police officer without a warrant may enter and search premises and places and stop and detain persons. Sub clauses 46 (1) and (2) provide that the police without a further warrant, may stop, detain and search a person or any conveyance if they reasonably suspect the person or conveyance is in possession of anything that may be used to commit an S4 offence…"

"Oh for God's sake just get on with it then."

He'd got under her skin at last; he'd have quoted another three pages if necessary. She returned to work at her desk while he got to work.

Almost an hour later and his search had revealed nothing. Ruth smiled when he slammed the last cupboard door. It wasn't as if he'd expected to find anything major, but he'd hoped at least for a box of coffee filters or some suspect chemicals. Nothing he saw in the lab would serve any purpose other than innocent school science lessons.

He nodded towards the snake in the glass tank. "That's a tiger snake. Highly poisonous."

"How very observant of you."

"May I see your permit?"

"Is this the best you can do?"

Cam put out his hand and clicked his fingers. She sighed and extracted the permit from her desk drawer. After a quick glance, he handed it back.

"Everything appears to be in order, although it says the snake has to be returned to the wildlife sanctuary tomorrow."

Ruth gave an impatient sigh. "I wouldn't be so irresponsible as to keep a poisonous snake in a school science lab, would I? I borrowed it for the holidays to chart some of its behavioural characteristics. Would you like to see my notes?"

"That won't be necessary, but I intend to check up on its return to the sanctuary."

"Be my guest. Pop in again tomorrow and we'll have a drink. We have yet to reminisce."

Cam rammed his hands into his pockets. "I want to see a copy of Miss Jane Featherstone's will. I believe you were an executor."

With a hand on her chin she said, "Let me see if I can find it."

She made a play of looking down her cleavage then reached for the fly of her jeans.

"Cut the crap, Ruth."

She folded her arms. "Well, you don't expect me to have it here do you? It's in a bank vault in Toorrup, you silly billy."

"Bring it to me at the station Monday morning, then."

He'd already requested a copy from the Supreme Court, but would have to wait until Monday for that, too.

"Yessir!" she saluted.

"I also need to see receipts for the chemicals you purchased for the re-stocking of the lab."

"Congratulations, Cam, that is a much more plausible request, though again, you're out of luck. I gave them to Jeffrey the other day; he needed them for the accounts. I believe he and Anne are at home now, why don't you go and pay them a visit?"

Still smarting from his unsatisfactory confrontation with Ruth, Cam decided to leave the ute in the car park and walk to the Smithsons' across the school oval. It would take a few extra minutes, but he needed a walk in the fresh air to calm down. The sky was a perfect blue, the grass lush and emerald green, conditions that usually brought back memories of Aeroguard-flavoured sandwiches, victorious football games and drunken parties. But close as he felt he was getting to the end of the case, he felt no adrenalin rush today, and he proceeded to the Smithsons' house, his steps weighted with caution.

He rapped on the door, straining for sounds from within. When there was no response, he stepped off the veranda and walked around the side of the house; no car in the garage, no washing on the line, the windows all heavily curtained. He tried the back door and found it locked. With a string of expletives and a savage kick, he propelled the Smithsons' empty garbage can down their driveway.

Back at the ute he almost missed the flyer fluttering under the windscreen wipers. Damn this layback country town he thought, slapping his hand down hard on the bonnet, there should be zero tolerance for this kind of thing.

But when he ripped the paper from the wipers, about to ball it in his fist, something made him stop. He knew what it was before he'd even unfolded it.

His heartbeat sped to join a nightmare rhythm of buzzing in his head. He had to fight his tingling fingers for the control needed to open the note. And when he did, all his fears were realised.

His legs felt as if they'd turned to wet newspaper. He had to lean against the ute. He rubbed his face, pressing his fingers into the sensitive scar tissue of his neck. The sharp pain restored his senses enough to focus on the note. It was just like all the others, same paper, same strange mirror image lettering, but the contents were unlike anything he'd ever received; this wasn't just a threat, this was a fact:

We have your daughter. Come to the house indicated on the map if you want to see her again. If you are not there by 2 pm she dies. Come alone or she dies. Bring other cops, she dies.

There was a mud map beneath the writing. He had to travel about ten kilometres down a dirt track to an abandoned farmhouse. He knew the road; the turn-off was just before Glenroyd. It would take a couple of minutes to get there, but he'd no idea how long it would take to get down the rutted track.

He looked at his watch: 1.35.

He took some deep breaths, slow is fast, he reminded himself. As the engine turned over he reached for his mobile phone. Ruby was at home packing; this had to be some kind of horrible hoax.

The phone flashed no service.

He hurled it at the passenger side door and grabbed the radio mike. It came away in his hand; someone had cut the wire. He slammed his hands on the steering wheel and looked at his watch again: 1.37.

After one last look at the note, he got out of the ute and scanned the deserted car park. Ruth's car was gone. There was no one left at the school. He spied a rock lying close to the curb and secured the note under it, then kicked at the dirt and gravel until he had drawn the shape of a large arrow. With all his communication systems down, it was the best he could do.

Cam cut the corner too fast from the bitumen to the dirt road and fishtailed across its width, skidding up clouds of red dust. Slow down, the voice inside him said, but his body wouldn't listen; his foot was an immovable weight on the accelerator.

Soon, the leviathan shape of a hay truck loomed ahead. Large cylindrical bales of hay bulged from its barely visible sides through a smokescreen of dust. He gripped the steering wheel tight, edging close enough to be seen in the driver's side mirrors.

Nineteen minutes left. He'd never get there at this rate. He hesitated before switching the siren on. Would the sound carry all the way to the farmhouse? Would the bikies hear it and presume he'd brought a mob of cops with him? He risked a short blast. The truck driver gave him a cheery wave, but the road was too narrow for him to pull over and he was forced to drive in the spewing wake of the truck for a full minute before it pulled into a farm gateway and he could overtake.

With fifteen minutes to go, he hurtled passed the truck,

sweat stinging his eyes. He took off his cap, wiped his face with it then tossed it on to the floor on the passenger's side.

Which was when he caught the movement in his peripheral vision.

But by then it was too late.

36

My God, has she been raped? was the first thought that sprang to Cecelia's mind when she opened her door to the distraught figure. She took in the tear-stained face and dishevelled clothes, the whooping gasps for air.

"Ruby, what's the matter?" she said, slipping her arm around the girl's shoulders and guiding her into the house. "You go into the bathroom and wash your face. I'll fix us some lemonade."

Ruby shuffled into the bathroom, returning in a few minutes to sit on the lounge. Cecelia watched as she took a sip of lemonade, glad to see some of the colour had returned to her face.

"Has Angelo done something to hurt you?" Cecelia prompted.

Ruby swallowed and shook her head. She latched on to the hem of her red tank top and twisted it in her hand. "No. Yes. Not exactly. He doesn't know I'm here. I promised I wouldn't tell, but I have to. Please, Cecelia…" She looked up from her lap. "You mustn't tell Dad how I found this out, he'd kill Angelo if he knew."

The snake shot from the floor of the passenger's side as if loosed from a bow, sinking its fangs into Cam's forearm and injecting him with streaks of red-hot pain. He screamed, shook his arm and felt the cool of its thick, muscled body brush against his side as it slid back to the floor. Somehow he'd managed to keep the hurtling ute on the road; now he eased his foot off the accelerator and gently applied the brake. He had to think past his fear, be rational. He'd pull to the side of the road, shoot the snake then apply a tourniquet to his arm. He was a big man; the venom would take a while to take effect. There was still a chance he could get to Ruby in time.

But the clutch put up a resistance to the pressure of his foot. He looked down, to see the snake twining around the pedals.

The fangs found their mark upon his calf a second before he could react. Despite the rapid jerk of his legs, it struck again, this time at his thigh, sending molten ribbons of pain into his groin. When the ute petered to a stop on the roadside, Cam tumbled out, acutely aware of the venom throbbing through his veins with each beat of his racing heart.

His left arm seemed to be encased in a sleeve of red-hot lead; even looking at his watch was a struggle.

Ten minutes to go.

Ten minutes to get to Ruby.

He realised he was hyperventilating and tried to slow down his short, sharp gasps with positive thoughts. The hay truck would be along any minute, he told himself. He would flag it down and get the driver to take him to the farmhouse. Meanwhile, he had to attend to the snakebites. Inside the cabin with the snake, the first aid kit was unreachable. He'd have to improvise a couple of tourniquets before attempting any vigorous movement.

He took off his belt and tied it around the top of his arm, tightening it with his teeth. Then, keeping his arm low he eased on to his side to work on his shoelaces. They weren't ideal, but they'd be better than nothing.

The sound of an engine in the distance made him stop. He squinted into the growing cloud of dust, unable to make out what was creating it. One moment there seemed to be two vehicles, the next moment they'd blurred into one – a hay truck, a car, a couple of motorbikes? As he shook his head to clear his blurred vision, the gravel beneath him began to vibrate.

Cecelia put her elbows on the counter and leaned towards Derek, mustering all her willpower to stop herself throttling the obstructive little man.

He said, "I've already told you, Ms Bowman, his radio doesn't seem to be working. Last I heard he was calling in at the school."

Cecelia thumped her fist down on the counter. His teacup rattled and a tide of tea slopped into the saucer. "Then you have to send someone to the school to get him. He's in danger!"

Derek let out a long slow breath. He picked up his cup and began mopping up the drips with a tissue. "Ms Bowman, this is Glenroyd we're talking about, not some outer suburb of Los Angeles. Things like you described just don't happen here." He shrugged. "Besides, there's no one available to follow up on these bizarre claims of yours. Pete's on rostered days off, Leanne's on traffic and I have to stay here at the station."

He looked at Ruby with a smile of forced benevolence and clasped his hands on the counter. "I think that someone's taken this whole situation out of context. I think that someone will be in big trouble with Daddy if we start out on this wild goose chase."

Ruby's eyes bulged. "It's not just me who knows. Cecelia has proof too. Someone's out to get my father you stupid, motherfucking —" Her hand shot out to Derek's teacup, and before Cecelia could stop her, she'd tipped the

261

contents over his balding head.

White-faced under the rivulets of tepid tea, Derek sprang back from the counter in a way that made Cecelia thankful he wasn't wearing a gun.

"Ruby, that's enough," she reprimanded without much conviction. "We're obviously getting nowhere. We'll go to the school ourselves and hopefully catch your father there."

She grabbed Ruby by the hand, leaving Derek slack-jawed and dabbing at his head with a handkerchief, staring at them as if he'd just seen horns sprout from their heads.

They almost collided with Leanne at the station door.

His heart dropped when he recognised Ruth Tilly. Of all the people in Glenroyd, why did it have to be her? And where was the hay truck? Had it turned into the farm and stayed there?

Ruth ran from her car to where he sat leaning against the side of the ute. She surprised him with a look of genuine concern.

"My God, Cam, what happened, have you had some kind of an accident?"

"Snake bite," he said, wondering if he'd lost the ability to make sentences; it was such an effort to get out the words. His mouth was as dry as desert sand and the beginning of a headache taunted the back of his eyes with tight jabs.

Ruth took in his crude tourniquets. "Bandages would be better. I have some in my car, I'll get them. And you should be lying flat." She gently pushed him down. "Have you called for help?"

He shook his head, regretting the movement as spears of pain were unleashed behind his eyes. "Phone and radio stuffed."

Ruth moved towards her car.

"Wait," he cried. "The bikies have Ruby. They're going to kill her if I'm not there by two. The note said she was at the farmhouse at the end of this road. You have to go and tell them what happened, please. It's me they want anyway…"

She hushed him with a finger to her lips. "My phone's long range, it should work. I'll get help, don't you worry about a thing."

Shit, how often had he heard himself say those very words to some beleaguered victim lying by the roadside? As he waited for Ruth to return, he tried to ignore the changes he could feel in his body. He focused his thoughts on Ruby. They'd have to let her go, he told himself. Even bikies wouldn't kill a fifteen-year-old girl, though there were other things they might do. He screwed his eyes tight against the image until a shadow blocked the red. When he opened them again, Ruth was kneeling beside him. She leaned towards his hip, probably to replace the shoelace tourniquet with a bandage.

Then he felt a tugging sensation at his holster and heard the pop of the stud. His eyes widened when he saw what she was doing.

"Help's on its way, Cam," she said with a smile that chilled his blood. "But help for me, not for you. My assistant is as keen to observe the effects of a tiger snake bite as I am, he should be along shortly."

She backed away and sat on a rock, watching him with the clinical coldness of a vivisector. Cam couldn't believe what he was seeing; he had to be hallucinating. She removed a notebook from her pocket, rested it on her knee and wrote something in it; careful to keep the gun in her other hand trained on him. After a while, she spoke.

"I never pass up a research opportunity, Cam. I'm

documenting your symptoms for a paper I'm writing on the *Norechis Ater Occidentallis.* Tiger snakebites can take up to twenty-four hours to kill if not treated. You were bitten three times. They often strike more than once, though of course there would've been little venom in the other bites. It will be interesting to see if your death will occur any sooner." She let out a burst of staccato laughter. "I put the snake in the freezer after you left the lab so it would be sluggish and stay put under the front passenger mat. It must have been good and aggressive when it warmed up. Tell me, how are you feeling – headache? Blurred vision? I believe a victim can also experience severe abdominal pain. Perhaps you won't reach that stage. Maybe you'll just go straight to internal haemorrhage or paralysis."

Cam said nothing. He closed his eyes against the pricking tears of helplessness. When he opened them again, Ruth was leaning over him, very close. Her breath felt like dry ice upon his burning cheek.

His tongue felt stitched to the roof of his mouth; he had to struggle to release it. "Please, Ruth. You have to help Ruby."

"I don't want to make your dying any easier, Cam, but never let it be said I'm inhumane. Ruby was never in any danger. I wrote the note. She's probably in the back room of the workshop screwing her boyfriend or smoking dope as we speak."

Cam murmured a prayer of thanks. The wave of relief washing through him brought with it some lucid thought. "The notes, they were from you, all along?"

"Yes. The bomb was never meant for you. I'd been following you for weeks. I knew your Saturday routine, I knew you'd be at netball and I knew the bikies would be blamed."

He paused, not sure if he could believe his ears. "It was you who killed Elizabeth and Joe, not the bikies?"

She gave him a satisfied smile. "Yes, me all along."

He made a pathetic attempt to flail out, but she pushed him back to the ground with the flat of one hand. His breath came out in gasping sobs. "Why?"

Ruth settled by his side. Her fingers slowly moved across his chest. "Why, Cam? Think hard and you'll know why."

Like a spider, her hand crawled to the opening of his collar. Twisting a tuft of chest hair around a red-tipped finger, she began to tug. "You made a fool out of me, Cam. I wasted years of my life over you."

"I don't understand." He cringed from her, willing himself further into the gravel.

"We loved each other, Cam, but you chose to forget all about it."

Her hand left his chest. Cold fingers brushed his parched lips. Her touch sent shivers through him, worse than any amount of snake venom.

"You seem to have conveniently forgotten about that day at pony club, all those years ago," she said. "My pony got a fright in the arena and bolted off with me into the bush. You jumped on a horse and chased after me, grabbing hold of the reins and stopping us. When we dismounted, you took me in your arms and I knew then that you loved me, I knew then that we were meant to be together."

An image flashed into Cam's mind: a terrified pony, a frightened girl. That was all there was to it. He'd not given the incident another thought since the day it happened.

"I tried to forget about you, Cam, I really did. I even got married."

Cam drew a laboured breath. "You killed him."

"I got my Master's degree, he served his purpose.

You see, I couldn't stop thinking of you, you poor little orphan of the empire. I decided to instigate a little psychological experiment. I was pretty sure when tragedy struck you'd come running back to the only home you've ever had, and I planned on being here, waiting for you when you came. You've always craved security – why else would you join the police? You traded one secure institution for another. You really are a very simple, predictable man, Cam. Unfortunately for you though, you hung on longer than I anticipated, arriving just a bit too late. My passion for you had finally burned itself out. I realised then that your presence would be nothing but a liability."

It was all beginning to make sense. "You got involved with Cliff, the drugs."

She laughed. "Wrong. I got involved with a real man, Cam, someone who does more for me than you ever could."

"He's going to jail for a very long time; the case against him is almost there. They'll still get him, even if they can't get you."

Ruth laughed. "Cliff? That's the whole idea. That's how it's meant to be. Cliff can rot in jail for all I care. I used him just as I used my husband."

Cam's mind became a coloured whirl of pain and confusion. "You set him up? He's a patsy? Then who?"

"My lover, Eric Matthews." She tweaked his nose. "You probably know him better as Chainsaw, the president of the SS motorcycle club."

"Over there!" Ruby said, pointing with the rolled note they'd found at the school. "It's Dad's ute."

"Oh shit," Cecelia said, "it looks like Ruth's there, too. Can you see your dad anywhere?"

Ruby covered up her mouth with her hand. "God, he's lying down, she's bending over him!"

Ruth stood up when she saw Cecelia's car crunch into the siding.

"Now, Ruby, you have to be calm. We have to play this right and you have to think clearly." Cecelia squeezed her hand. Ruby nodded back, trying to be brave. But when she saw her father lying so still, she couldn't help herself. Cecelia's cry of warning came too late. Ruby sprang from the car and raced to her father's side.

Cecelia followed with all the caution of a tightrope walker. Ruth met her eyes and shrugged her shoulders in a what-the-heck manner. Cecelia switched her focus to Cam and stepped closer. His eyes were closed, his breathing tortured, his uniform black with sweat. Tears pooled in Ruby's eyes as she leaned over him to stroke his face.

His eyes fluttered open. "Ruby, be careful," Cecelia heard him whisper. "You have to try and get away, she's a killer…"

Ruby turned to face Ruth. Cecelia sensed what the girl was about to do. She cried out. "Ruby, stay where you are, she has a gun!"

But Cecelia's warning was lost. "What have you done to my father, you fucking bitch?" Ruby yelled, and launched herself at the other woman.

There was a shot. It was the loudest sound Cecelia had ever heard and went on blasting in her head long after the bullet had left the barrel. Ruby went rigid, staring at the swirling dust where the bullet had hit the ground, unable, it seemed, to take her eyes from it.

Cecelia moved to pull the frozen girl into her arms. As the shock wore off Ruby began to shake, to suck in mouthfuls of air.

Cecelia whispered in her ear. "Sssh, take some slow deep

breaths. It's going to be OK – remember?"

Ruby nodded, trying to steady her breathing.

"That was a warning shot," Ruth said. "You won't be so lucky next time." Her voice was firm, as controlled as the hand on the gun.

Cecelia was a lot less composed. "How could you do this, Ruth? I thought we were friends?"

"Your naiveté always appealed to me, Cecelia. Your willingness to see the good in people before the bad." The gun was pointing at her now. "Yes, I always did consider you my friend. I never planned on getting you involved in any of this. It was unfortunate that you happened to be in the prefab when I threw the bomb. When I saw him enter, well, I couldn't believe my luck, so I locked the door. All I'd expected was to destroy a few photos." She shrugged. "I'm an opportunist, Cecelia; you'd have been a necessary casualty, I'm afraid."

Cecelia swallowed. Still clasping Ruby to her, she said, "Are you planning on killing us now?"

"Unfortunately yes, as soon as my assistant arrives. I'll need him to help me clear up. We'll have to think up a way to dispose of your bodies. I'm not going to risk burning again, it's too unreliable." She glanced towards Cam's still form. "I'll leave Cam's body where it is. We'll clear away any evidence and no one will know we were even here. A snake bite, what a terrible tragedy."

"Let the girl have some last words with her father then," Cecelia said.

Ruth thought for a moment, looked at Ruby then indicated to Cam with a flick of the gun. "You go with her, that way I can keep the gun on both of you."

Encouraged by Cecelia, Ruby moved back to her father's side. The tears rolled down her face as she took his hand.

He attempted to speak even though Ruby told him not to. It seemed he had something he needed to say.

"Ruby," he whispered, his face creased with agony. "I hope you know how much I've always loved you. I've never been very good at saying stuff like that. But I hope you've always known that I do. I haven't been a good dad; I get preoccupied with my job. I should never have stayed on as a cop after…"

"Sssh…" Ruby wiped at the tears coursing through the dust on his face. "We have a plan. We're all going to get out of here. And then, when you're better, you can buy me a pony and…" She couldn't say any more. She laid her head on his chest and whispered into his shirt, "I'm sorry too, Dad."

The sound of a car engine drew Cecelia's attention away from Cam and Ruby to a white ute pulling up next to her VW. She put her hand on the girl's shoulder. "Ruby, someone's arrived."

Ruby jerked in a breath, her eyes suddenly wide with hope.

"Angelo!" she screamed.

But he walked over to Ruth, staring straight through the girl, as if she was already a ghost.

"You took your time," Ruth said to him.

Ruby jerked in her breath. Cecelia pulled her close.

"I had trouble finding the place," Angelo said in a conversational tone.

Ruth clucked her tongue. "Never mind, you're here now, you've done well. Eric will be pleased."

Angelo smiled. "I reckon I've more than earned my colours now."

"There's just one more thing."

"What's that?"

"Kill them."

The smile fell from his face. "What?"

"You heard me."

"Ruth, this was never – Jesus, I've done everything else, I've done more than enough!"

"I told Eric you were too young. Now you've proved it."

Angelo's dark eyes flicked around for a moment. Finally he swallowed and put his hand out for the gun.

"Good boy, you won't regret this," Ruth smiled.

Ruby mouthed him a plea then buried her face in Cecelia's shoulder.

Seconds passed. Cecelia waited for her whole life to pass before her eyes.

But all she saw was an empty black void.

Her throat began to twist. She was losing control. She had to stay strong, for Ruby.

And then the gun began to shake in the boy's hand. He couldn't do it. He was looking at Ruby as if she was a pet dog he had to put down but was unable to pull the trigger himself. Ruth's face twisted. As she snatched the gun from Angelo's hand, a shot cracked through the stillness of the bush, uncorking a flock of screeching cockatoos. Cecelia pushed Ruby to the ground. She saw the arch of Ruth's back, the startled look as she fell.

With no time for shock or thought, Cecelia instinctively lunged for the gun before Angelo could get to it first.

"Stay where you are!"

But the gun had about as much effect on Angelo as a stick of liquorice. He ran towards Ruth's fallen body. "Oh God, Jesus!" he screamed, throwing himself over her. Blood flowed like lava from her mouth and pooled on to the gravel.

His hands ran over her bloodied face, his lips met hers

as he tried to blow air into her lifeless mouth.

Cecelia thought she might throw up. She closed her eyes for a moment, trying to erase the sight before her. Then, thudding feet and heavy breathing alerted her to the stumbling form of Leanne crashing through the bushes.

"You cut that bloody fine," Cecelia said, surprised she still had the strength to talk, let alone stand upright.

Leanne gave her a tight smile. "Keep that gun on him." She nodded to the weapon Cecelia still held in her shaking hands.

Leanne re-holstered her own gun, reached for her handcuffs and walked cautiously towards Angelo.

Not sure what to expect from the boy, Cecelia's hand tightened until the ridges of the grip were digging into her hand. But Angelo's bloodstained face was pale with shock; he offered Leanne no resistance. If not for the occasional convulsive sob he could have been an automaton. He allowed Leanne to cuff him to the ute.

Cecelia joined Ruby next to her father. Her throat constricted as she gazed at the girl clutching at his limp hand. Cecelia touched his cheek. He was pale and cold, his lips shiny with blood. She brushed some of the gravel from his neck and felt for his carotid pulse.

"Call the ambulance, Leanne," she said, raising her head to find Leanne already gone.

37

They were having a picnic, all five of them, sitting in the middle of the school oval as a family. A sprinkler, like a giant insect, turned itself on with a splutter and the fine mist floated to their cheeks on a gentle breeze. The girls wore white muslin dresses and laughed when the moisture tickled its way through the thin fabric to their skin. Joe ran in tight circles, catching the drops in his plastic Darth Vader cape. Cam watched and smiled. He was wearing his old school uniform. The shirt was tight and one of his arms ached, but he felt strangely content.

The girls had been picking flowers: wattle yellow, cobalt blue, deep, waxy pink. Elizabeth had picked the biggest bunch, and handed them to Cecelia to add to her own. She smiled, took Joe by the hand and began to walk away. When Cam called out to them, Ruby shook her head.

He struggled to open his eyes; they were wet and sticky. Everything was blurry and indistinct, as if he were looking through water.

He could hear better than he could see.

"Cam, are you awake? Can you hear me?"

He heard a familiar voice, felt a hand squeezing his. He squeezed back. He wanted to reach for Cecelia's face but there was an invisible force pressing down upon him, pushing his limbs into the mattress.

The ring tone of a mobile phone jarred into his senses. Again he heard Cecelia's voice. "Yes he's just woken, but still very groggy. Come in later this afternoon. I'll see you then. Bye, Rod."

It was all coming back to him: Ruth, the snake, Ruby. Ruby.

"Where's Ruby?" he whispered. "Is she all right?"

He could see more clearly now and found himself focusing on Cecelia's soft mouth.

"She got sick of waiting for you to wake up and went downstairs to the gift shop. The doctors unhooked you from the machine a couple of hours ago, gave you an injection of something to wake you up. They had to sedate you; you were fighting the respirator. You've been in a medically induced coma for almost a week." She laughed. "Let's just hope a tiger snake doesn't bite Mrs Bucket's precious poodle. I think they must have used up the anti-venom from all the vets in the district."

"There's nothing wrong with poodles," he heard himself say. He drew a breath and felt some of the weight lift from his limbs. He gingerly re-adjusted his position in the bed. "I'm in hospital? It's over?" He glanced around the single room, the bank of flowers on the table, the Get Well cards trembling on the windowsill like butterflies. The white noise of the hospital buzzed in his head, making it hard to concentrate on what Cecelia was saying.

"The bad part's over. It was touch and go for a while. They lost you for a moment in the ambulance, then you were flown down to the city from Toorrup by Flying Doctor," she said.

Cam became aware of a dull throbbing pain in his bandaged left arm. In contrast to the white of the bandages, his fingers were a grey-blue colour, like water-immersed slugs.

He licked his dry lips. "Ruth?"

Cecelia looked away, biting at her bottom lip. "She's dead."

Cam could feel her pain as sharply as his own. "She killed my family, Cecelia."

She nodded and took a deep breath. Her grip on his good hand tightened.

"Dad! You're awake!" It was his daughter's voice, as airy and vital as the wind. Cecelia moved away and he clasped Ruby to him, felt soft hair on his face. He felt the prick of tears at the back of his eyes, his body shuddered; he lost control.

"You can cry, Dad, it's all right," she whispered raising her hand to stroke his forehead.

"Thank you," was all he could say as the cleansing tears streamed down and he slipped once more into a swirling fog of sleep.

Cam cast a worried glance at his daughter. She was sitting on the end of his bed, biting at her thumbnail. God, hasn't she been through enough, he thought as he listened to Rod.

"Angelo's been transferred to the city nick, no bail," Rod said. He sat on one side of Cam and Cecelia on the other. As the saline drip flushed the drugs from his system, Cam was regaining control of his body. He could move the fingers of his good hand now and caressed his thumb in soft circles on the top of Cecelia's hand.

"He was a nom," Rod continued, "a nominee bikie. Seemed he was co-operating with Ruth and Chainsaw as part of an initiation plan to get his colours. I think there was more to it than that, though. He seemed quite infatuated with her, doing just about anything she asked. She controlled him in pretty much the way Chainsaw controlled her. I tell you, the forensic quacks are having a field day."

Cecelia said, "I always knew Ruth's behaviour could be

over the top, but I had no inkling she was unhinged." Her hand went to her throat. "She always said I was a lousy judge of…" Her voice tapered off.

Cam gave her hand a squeeze.

"Same psychosis as celebrity stalkers have, one of the shrinks told me," said Rod. He chuckled. "Cam was one of the few males who had any kind of contact with the girls of a very isolated school. That was enough to raise him to celebrity status as far as Ruth was concerned."

"But she hated me," Cam said.

"Because you spurned her, by her twisted logic. What's that saying, Cecelia?"

"Heaven has no rage like love to hatred turned, nor hell a fury like a woman scorned," Cecelia said.

Rod continued, "But then she transferred her attentions to Chainsaw and became just as obsessed with him. So when you stepped back into the picture, she had to get rid of you."

Cam saw Cecelia glance at Ruby. His daughter's stiffening posture indicated she did not wish to hear any more.

"I'm just going downstairs for a coffee. Do you want anything, Dad?" Ruby asked.

Cam shook his head. "Off you go then, love."

Cam waited for the door to close behind her. "Is she… is she all right with this?"

"She's getting there." Cecelia hesitated. "I think it's something you need to talk about further down the track."

Cam swallowed, nodded his head.

Rod said, "Angelo and Ruth murdered Bell when they discovered him spying on them at the dam — "

"They used the fire truck to dump the body?" Cam asked.

"That's right."

"She must have stayed in the truck. The footprints were his," Cam mused.

"And she set the prefab alight," Rod continued. "After she'd locked you in, she and Angelo murdered Vince, leaving behind the apology note she'd stolen from Cecelia. After that, she went back to the school and Angelo joined Cliff for the fire call. They timed it perfectly."

"And Vince was involved with Cliff in the tanker theft?" Cam asked.

"Yes. He deliberately bungled the investigation in return for a hefty kickback. Cliff only wanted the tanker for parts. Ruth put him in touch with Chainsaw and he sold the fertiliser to the bikies through her. He swears he didn't know why they wanted it. Ruth was concocting the amphetamines in the school lab for Chainsaw, not Cliff. Cliff was clueless about everything except the tanker. He was never even an official bikie Associate, though I think he was working on it. The relationship Ruth had with him was authorised by Chainsaw to keep Cliff on side. Ruth used him just as she used everyone else."

"Cliff was the only witness who told the truth about the colour of the smoke," Cam mused.

"True. Ruth's report of the fire was a diversionary tactic. Why would she report the fire when she was the one who lit it? They'd obviously have preferred the body to be destroyed by the fire, but when it wasn't, because of Cliff's interference, it was no big deal. They realised they could easily frame Cliff with it - they wanted him out of the way anyway. They planted his jemmy in the submerged car, laying other false clues like the car seat, to make it look like he murdered Vince."

"And it was Angelo who made the attempt on Mrs Wilmot's life?" Cam asked.

"They thought she might tell you about Miss Featherstone's financial predicament."

Cam sighed. "I got all that pretty wrong didn't I? I was sure Cliff was behind all this."

"You got it mostly right, just the wrong bloke," Rod said. "Anyway, Cliff's been very co-operative. He's given us Chainsaw on a plate. We arrested him a couple of days ago on his way to Darwin. The money that allegedly came from Jane Featherstone's will was actually bikie money they'd laundered through the school via Ruth so they could get the science lab done up. If everything had gone as planned they would have doubled their investment within a couple of years. The lab Ruth established was the most sophisticated illegal lab the country has ever had, and because it was under the guise of a school science lab, nothing in it seemed out of place."

"They couldn't have used a whole tank of fertiliser, surely?" Cam asked.

"No, Ruth took what she needed and the rest was distributed to other SS chapters around the country."

Cam's head sank back into the pillow. He closed his eyes. It was hard to take everything in. He could hear Cecelia and Rod talking as if from the other end of a tunnel. When he heard them mention Leanne, his eyes shot open again.

"What was that?" he said.

"I said I've put her in for a commendation for bravery – that was a fantastic shot. It looks like the medal's going to go through. Apparently she was top marksman in her class at the Academy."

Cecelia laughed. "She told me she used to shoot rats in the shed with her dad."

Cam said, "That'll give her a boost. But how's she

handling the…" he waved his hand, unable to find the words.

Rod knew what he was trying to say. "She knows she had to kill Ruth, that she had no choice. I think she was more upset when she heard about Gay Cronin feeding Herb's ashes to the chooks."

"That's rough," Cam said, but it was hard not to smile. "Who's in charge of the station now?"

"Constable Dowel; I think you'll find everything in order when you get back."

Cam let out a deep breath. If I get back, he thought. His eyes strained to read the card on a bunch of white roses next to his bed. *Get well soon, love from Anne and Jeffrey*, it said.

For some reason he misted up again.

Rod took this as his cue and slipped from the room, leaving Cecelia and Cam alone. Cam closed his eyes, felt her cool fingers on his forehead.

"It's all over now," she whispered.

The silence stretched. He almost drifted off.

Finally he opened his eyes again. Grabbing at some loose tendrils of thoughts, he shook his head. "No, it's not."

Cecelia frowned. "What do you mean?"

"It's not over. There's still the matter of a certain dangerous driving charge."

She laughed. "Oh, we can fix that," she said, leaning over to brush her lips against his.

And because the dreams you have on the brink of waking are the ones that tend to last, he kissed her back.

More action-packed crime novels from Crème de la Crime

If It Bleeds   Bernie Crosthwaite

ISBN: 0-9547634-3-2

There's only one rule in the callous world of newspapers: violence excites, death sells – so if it bleeds, it leads.

When hardened press photographer Jude Baxendale is despatched to snap a young woman's bloody body discovered in a local park she reckons it's a grisly but routine job – but she's horrifyingly, perilously wrong. For the murdered girl is her own son's girlfriend, and in a single chilling moment she realises nothing in her life is ever going to be the same again.

Why was Lara killed? Who stabbed and mutilated her? Who hated her enough to dump her body in full public gaze? Jude has to find out. Teaming up with reporter Matt Dryden, she begins to unravel the layers of the girl's complex past. But she soon learns that nothing about Lara was as it seemed…

Soon finding the truth will risk Jude's job, her health, her sanity – and place her squarely in the sights of a killer with a fanatical mission. And some deadly truths are best left uncovered. **Publication date April 2005.**

Also available:

Working Girls   Maureen Carter

ISBN: 0-9547634-0-8

No Peace for the Wicked   Adrian Magson

ISBN: 0-9547634-2-4

A Kind of Puritan   Penny Deacon

ISBN: 0-9547634-1-6

More gripping titles available later this year from Crème de la Crime

---

Personal Protection   Tracey Shellito

ISBN: 0-9547634-5-9

Lapdancers at Blackpool's top erotic nightspot are being targeted, but vandalism, rape and even suspicious death go uninvestigated by the local police. Enter Randall McGonnigal, five foot five of packed muscle – and a bodyguard. For Randall it's personal: she's determined to track down the pervert who attacked Tori, her exotic dancer lover.

As she battles with her own dark side as well as the suspects who emerge from the woodwork, she lays her life on the line to protect the woman she loves – but will it be enough?

Available July 05

Dead Old   Maureen Carter

ISBN: 0-9547634-6-7

Elderly women are being attacked by a gang of vicious thugs in Birmingham. When retired doctor Sophia Carrington is murdered, it's assumed she is the gang's latest victim. But Detective Sergeant Bev Morriss isn't convinced.

She is sure the victim's past holds the key to her violent death: that it's a case of terrifying revenge served cold.

Another gritty mystery for Bev Morris, Carter's hard-nosed female detective.

Available August 05

More gripping titles available later this year from Crème de la Crime

---

No Help for the Dying   Adrian Magson

Runaway kids are dying on the streets of London. Investigative reporter Riley Gavin and ex military cop Frank Palmer want to know why.

They uncover a sub-culture involving a shadowy church, a grieving father and a brutal framework for blackmail, reaching not only into the highest echelons of society, but also into Riley's own past.

The second fast-moving adventure in Magson's popular Gavin/Palmer series.

Available September 05

A Thankless Child   Penny Deacon

ISBN: 0-9547634-8-3

Life gets more dangerous for loner Humility. Her boat is damaged, her niece has run away from the commune, and the man who blames her for his brother's death wants her to investigate a suicide. She's faced with corporate intrigue and girl gangs, and most terrifying of all, she's expected to enjoy the festivities to celebrate the opening of the upmarket new Midway marina complex.

Things can only get worse.

A follow-up to *A Kind of Puritan*, Deacon's acclaimed first genre-busting future crime novel.

Available September 05